PICTURES OF
ANNA

SAM MARTIN

ArrowGate

Published by Arrow Gate Publishing Ltd 2019

16 15 14 13 12 11 10 9 8 7

A CIP catalogue record for this book is available from the British Library.

ISBN 978-1-913142-06-3

EBOOK 978-1-913142-07-0

Arrow Gate Publishing 85, Great Portland Street, London W1W 7LT

Visit **www.arrowgatepublishing.com** to read more about our books and to buy them. You will also find articles, author interviews, writing tips and news of any author events, and you can sign up for our e-newsletters so that you're always first to read about our new releases.

For Jutta, my wife, who recently died of Motor Neuron disease. Pictures of Anna is dedicated to her. Every word on every page is for you Jutta, always and only for you.

Pictures of Anna is inspired by a true story and series of historical events. Some of what you will read happened. Some didn't. It is fiction, not a documentary, and the characters too are fictitious. The names of people and places have been changed — some of them.

ONE

ANNA'S ROOM

Picture this: a small bedroom with three large, wooden packing cases stacked up against one wall. The words '*Ernst Leitz GmbH,*' the name of the old German camera company had been stamped on the side of each case. Someone was moving out. Or moving in. It was the morning of the 23rd of May: a day which would become a significant moment in British history, although few people would know about that just yet, if ever. It was a significant day too in the life of Anna Vieti; it was her wedding day.

It was eerily still in Anna's room. Bright midday sunshine flooded in through the window which for some months now had been framed by coarse, double-lined blackout curtains. It was peaceful. Then suddenly...

BOOM!

The door flew open, and Anna Vieti rushed into the room as if she'd been blown in by a hurricane. Her wedding dress billowed behind in her wake. Stunningly beautiful only minutes before, now there was thunder in her dark gypsy eyes. Her face was streaked black where her makeup had run. With venom, she back-kicked the door shut and ripped off her veil and tiara, sending her long, raven-black hair tumbling free. She flung the headdress down onto the bed and herself down next to it and buried her face in her hands. From somewhere in the house a woman's voice called out to her, 'Anna, Anna?' But Anna heard nothing. Then without a word she got up from the bed, rushed to the dressing table and ran her arm the whole length of its surface, sweeping its contents of perfumes, brushes, makeup, and a single framed photograph onto the ground. As the objects crashed and shattered all around her, she screamed out a pained and angry ''*Nein... NEIN*!!'' Then she reached down, picked the photograph up from the floor and stared hard at it. She became lost in its world.

Picture this: The image is a young man in his mid-twenties and Anna herself, smiling and holding each other close. They are standing on a beach by the water's edge. It's the image of a couple in love. Some distance off, in the background of the image, is a small harbour. The photograph - the centrepiece of an antique brass picture frame with a fancy rococo scroll pattern etched around its edges and a small rose engraved into each corner - was already fading fast from the perfume which had spilt onto it.

Anna would later say that her wedding day was one of the very worst days of her life. She had plenty to choose from, both before and after that day in late May 1940. ''But if I had to make a list, it would certainly be among the worst three or four,'' she later wrote. ''We'd made them so afraid, and we'd filled them with so much angst that they wouldn't allow us to be human anymore.''

But I'm getting ahead of myself here. You'll be meeting me later, further on down the road.

Anna stared into the photograph, into her perfect, peaceful little world, and right into the fading, boyishly handsome features of Guy Schneider. But now everything she saw confused her and the three short weeks since the photograph had been taken seemed like a lifetime ago. *The pictures I have in my head are still crystal clear to me,'* she would one day write, *''like they've been painted onto my mind in the strongest, brightest colours, and fixed forever with the boldest brush strokes, which time has been unable to fade. However much you might want it to...''*

''The strongest, brightest colours.'' That was how Anna thought she remembered it all. In reality, it was all in black and white and no shades of anything in between. Black or white - right or wrong - good or bad. Either one or the other. Nothing else.

THREE WEEKS EARLIER

A dark blue Morris 10 crawled along the sunny High Street in Upper Bexton - a quiet south London suburb a mile away from where Anna had been living with the Williamsons for just over two years. It finally came to a stop in the shadows on the opposite side of the street to 'Guy Schneider, Photographer's shop, situated at the end of a block of shops and small businesses. The man in the driver's seat, Alex Adams, had a pencil-thin moustache which looked as if it might have been drawn onto his top lip. He turned to his bald partner, who looked down at the piece of paper in his hand, then over at the name above the shop across the street, and nodded his head. Adams cut the engine, tipped back the brim of his fancy felt fedora with effortless cool, and took a cigarette out of his tortoise-shell case for his partner Barnes, then one for himself, struck a match for them both, and sat back to wait.

***

At the same time, a mile away from the shadows of Upper Bexton High Street, in a bedroom at the back of the Williamson's small but neat semi, Anna stood on a wooden stool in front of Mrs Williamson and her daughter Jane. Anna was wearing her wedding dress. Jane worked with Anna, they had become good friends, so when Anna was looking for a place to live after she arrived in England, Jane persuaded her parents to let her stay with them. Besides, she reasoned the rent that Anna paid them would come in handy now that Mr Williamson's accident had prevented him from working. He'd had a small roofing business and had fallen forty feet into someone's backyard when some tiles came loose, and now had only one arm and was lame down his entire left side.

"Well?" an anxious Mrs Williamson asked as Anna studied her reflection in the old, cracked mirror which Mrs Williamson had propped up against the wall. "What do you think?"

***

The inside of the Morris 10 was blue with smoke. Adams finished another cigarette and wound down his window to flick out the still smouldering stub. He suddenly froze mid-action and nudged his partner. On the other

10

side of the street, Guy Schneider was exiting his shop. Adams quickly wound his window back up and watched Guy lock the front door behind him. He was dressed exactly as he was in Anna's photograph in a smart, brown tweed suit, polished brown brogues and a red tie. The two men in the Morris watched Guy walk towards his motorbike and sidecar parked in the lane at the side of the shop, put on his helmet, then climb aboard the bike and head off up the High Street. Adams looked over to his partner for the nod, then he started up the Morris' engine and slowly pulled out of the shadows after Guy. At the junction at the end of the street, when Guy turned left, Adams swung his car to the right. For now, they had what they wanted.

THREE

AT THE WILLIAMSON'S

Mrs Williamson was one of those people who always tried to do her best for others but somehow never managed to get it for herself. Sacrifice, or duty, plus an endless and often blind faith were what she'd chosen to get her through this life. She was happy, yet full of anxieties. It was as if she was both at war and peace with herself but she vowed to smile, and the world would smile back at her. That's what she tried to do with Anna now - a smile which didn't even come close to hiding her anxiety as she pinned the hem of Anna's dress up to just the right length, while Jane wrapped things into sheets of newspaper and placed them into one of the *Leitz* packing cases. Anna looked into the mirror and twisted left and then right and then back again and broke out into a happy, excited smile at what she saw reflected at her.

''It's perfect,'' she told Mrs Williamson, whose smile shifted from nervous to relief and looked like she'd just had her death sentence overturned. She glanced over at her daughter with a cheeky smile as she said,

"I was giving up hope it would never be used again. But I suppose... what use is a wedding dress when you're already married to that hospital?"

Jane just pulled a face at her and got on with her packing.

"Take it off, and I'll sew it up," Mrs Williamson told Anna.

Anna climbed down from the stool, careful not to lose any of the pins, and took off the dress. Mrs Williamson reached into her pocket and pulled out a pair of long, ornate, 'chandelier' earrings with a deep Lapis Lazuli blue stone at the centre. She looked at Anna with that eternal well-meaning optimism of hers. ''I thought you might like to wear these.''

Anna looked at the earrings, which were special in a mystic Romany sort of way, but for Anna, there was something else about them. Something 'not quite right'- at least, not for her. She looked back at Mrs Williamson, unsure how to tell her what she knew she had to. It wasn't because Anna didn't possess the linguistic ability to do so. Her accent, which was becoming slighter now with every passing month but still detectable, especially when tired, did little to mask her extensive vocabulary and an uncanny ability to express herself in her adopted language. But that wasn't the issue here.

"They're... they're beautiful." Anna tried her best to let Mrs Williamson down lightly, "but I can't."

Mrs Williamson didn't get it. She tried again, to explain by way of reason. She nodded towards the dress.

''You know, something old...'' Then another nod, this time to the earrings, ''something borrowed and blue. I bought them years ago from someone who called at the door. I thought - you know - with your background...'' She held them up against Anna, just as Anna would and should wear them, ''see how you'll look.''

They really were perfect. Anna was perfect. But she declined, "It's very kind. But I don't really want to look..." Before she could say more, a loud knock on the front door broke their conversation. Anna, happy for the interruption, handed the earrings back to Mrs Williamson.

"That will be Guy."

Mrs Williamson, anxious once again, shouted over to her daughter, ''you keep him at the door.''

They snapped into action - Anna throwing on clothes, Jane off to the door, her mother rushing the sacred wedding dress out of the room, out of Guy's sight – no one heard Anna when she bared her soul to the empty room, ''I just want to be like everyone else here.''

FOUR

SOME PICTURES OF ANNA

Anna and Guy stood arm in arm on the sandy Kent beach, about six feet from the point where the small waves broke and retreated, preparing to pose for their photograph. A hundred yards behind them was the outer wall of a small harbour. The tide was out, and several colourful little fishing boats dotted the beach in front of the harbour. Anna playfully nudged Guy off balance. He nudged her back; get serious! Then they struck their pose and 'click', the image from Anna's bedroom photograph was captured forever, or at least until it began to fade three weeks later. Guy broke from his pose and walked towards the man who had taken the picture, a young man in an RAF uniform who was out walking with his fiancée. Guy thanked him with a smile and set off hand in hand with Anna in the direction of the harbour. As they walked along the sand, Anna broke free to throw a series of lighthearted and exaggerated poses which Guy snapped away at with his camera. Pictures of Anna as she was - vivacious and passionate; vulnerable but sure; innocent yet knowing. The wild, free, beautiful gypsy girl with the cheeky, sexy grin. A whole crazy world away from the sad, angry young woman she would become on her wedding day.

Anna and Guy scrambled up through the deep white sand to the top of a steep dune and looked back down over the sweep of the bay. It was all picture-perfect. It could have been a postcard from heaven. Seagulls soared and glided and squealed above them.

Exhausted, but laughing, Anna threw down the picnic basket that she'd been carrying and fell into Guy's arms in the long coarse grass at the dune's summit.

Until Guy broke away from the embrace, picked up his camera and, with his back towards the sea and facing inland, manoeuvred her into position and took another photograph.

An RAF plane was just coming in to land at the small RAF airbase behind Anna. She began to unpack the basket and at the same time throw a series of comic poses as Guy's camera continued to click away. In the basket was a four-leaf clover which she'd picked up earlier, she held it up for Guy, and he refocused his lens as she gave him a perfect smile for a perfect moment.

"Make a wish," she said, and Guy covered her hand with his so that it was touching the clover, and with their eyes closed, they made their silent wish. Then they sealed it with a long, passionate, you-and-me-against-the-world kiss, as behind them another warplane came in to land.

***

Heavy rain was falling, and lightning fractured the dark, angry sky as Guy's bike and sidecar pulled up at the kerbside outside the shop in the early evening. The local council had painted the kerb white, just as all local councils in the country had been instructed to do, to make it less difficult to make out in the blackout conditions. The trip to the coast had been just as Guy had hoped it would be. Even the storm had waited until they were nearly home. Guy had often gone to the coast as a boy with his mother, who was from Canterbury when he was in England for the summer holidays. Back then they'd take the train and come home only when it was dark, and his shoes were full of sand and his head full of wonderful little boy memories. Now Guy barely waited for his bike to stop before he leapt off and grabbed the basket from Anna, while she pulled herself up and out of the sidecar and made her own mad dash for the side entrance to the shop. Moments later a light went on in the apartment window above the shop.

***

"This is the BBC Home Service" was the start to everyone's evening radio programme, and the daily nine

17

o'clock news bulletin was the focus of many household's entertainments in those dark and uncertain days of 1940, but Guy and Anna didn't want to wait for that, events were too important. Besides, they had an advantage which meant they didn't need to wait that extra hour. Anna sat next to Guy's bulky Bakelite radio set wearing one of Guy's shirts and drying herself with a towel. Her wet clothes lay draped over a chair. She fiddled about with the frequency control, going back and forth over a particular point on the scale, and stopped when she heard a broadcast in German. She bent down and put her ear close to the speaker to catch the faint, fuzzy sound, but it soon faded away again, and 'interference' took over. Guy walked into the room just as the German news report was fading back in again.

"Are they saying anything different to last night's British news?"

Anna hushed him up with a wave of her hand and pressed her ear right up to the speaker. Guy joined her. But after a few seconds, they were forced to give up.

Anna turned away from the radio, depressed and worried. "There's still heavy fighting in Scandinavia. Two British battleships were sunk..." but followed it with an unsure, "I think."

"You *think*? Sounds like you're getting as much out of practice as I am, Fraulein Vieti. Thankfully."

Then he reached over, rolled his fingers over the control button until the music came out of the speakers, and held out his arms in an invitation to Anna to dance. They both managed a hopeful smile as Anna took control and guided him a couple of steps across the living room floor in the direction of the bedroom. But they stopped dead at the sound of shattered glass as the front window imploded and something heavy landed with a thud on the living room carpet. From outside in the street came angry shouts of "Bastards" and "Get the fuck out of our country" and "Nazi cunts."

Guy rushed over to the window and pulled the thick curtain to one side. Down in the street, despite the fading evening light, he could make out a handful of youths disappearing around a corner. He quickly closed the curtains and turned back to Anna. She stood next to him beside the window, transfixed by the brick lying next to her on the floor. It had a piece string wrapped around it, which held in place a handwritten note. Anna picked the brick up and unwrapped the note. It read "Fuck off German shit." She started to shake. Anna let the note fall to the ground and stared down at it, not just stunned but terrified. Is this how it's always meant to be?

Suddenly she was back in a place that she hoped - that she prayed - she had long ago left behind her.

FIVE

TO HAMBURG 1936, AND BACK

Picture this: which is what Anna did in Guy's flat three and a half years later. A shadowy street in dark and chilling times. That time was especially dark and especially frightening for someone like Anna. It was Hamburg on a freezing-cold mid-December evening with thick, soft snowflakes just beginning to fall when Anna and a girlfriend turned a corner in the Altona district, close to where she was living at the time in a small flat which she shared with three colleagues from the hospital.

Up ahead, lying on the icy-cold pavement was a dirty pile of rags with boots laying into it. The pile of rags she recognised as her drunken father, and the boots belonged to three blond gorillas in Hitler Youth uniforms, who had decided to work him over.

Anna started up the street at speed. Her father was bleeding from his mouth and nose. Blood was also pouring from a deep cut to his temple, and pinned to his shabby old winter coat was a dead rat because that's what they called gypsies where Anna lived, Ratten - rats. The three Hitler Youths had caught him crossing the street without paying his 'Rattensteuer', or Gypsy Tax, of one million Reichsmark. Of course, there was no such thing as a Gypsy Tax. That was the point. They told him it was a new Government law, introduced that very same day, which gypsies had to pay to cross from one side of a street to the other and that punishment for non-payment, or even for not knowing about the new tax, was a 'good kicking'. So on behalf of the National Socialists that was what they were doing. Anna's father was in his mid-forties but by now looked a good fifteen years older.

Drink and the times which he lived through had seen to that. Screaming "Papa, Papa" Anna sprinted frantically towards the young Nazis and put herself between them and her father. This was a fight she would willingly take on but one of the attackers - the tallest and strongest of the three - grabbed her and tossed her to one side like a pathetic rag doll. She tumbled over her father and landed in an undignified heap on the ground next to him. Before she could react, a boot had thumped into her. It caught her

21

hard on the shoulder. Then a second boot. She covered her head and her face with her arms and curled up tight into a ball before a third kick - even harder this time - caught her in the ribs. Something cracked and the pain shot right through her entire body. One of the Youths cleared his throat and emptied the vile contents onto Anna's father's face, then followed it with a kick to the head and the heart-felt curse "damned gypsy shit." One of his comrades, the one who landed the last, hardest blow to Anna, was still standing over her. Anna could see and his breath in the freezing night air. She closed her eyes and curled up even tighter, knowing that more blows would follow. Knowing that her life could end like this, right there and then on that freezing Hamburg street at the boot-end of a brick shithouse Nazi thug, just like it had been with countless other Jews or gypsies or 'outsiders' before. It was all very symbolic Anna would later think. You race into battle all fire and fight only to end up on the ground curled up tight into a ball, defeated. But no more blows came that night and her sad and persecuted life carried right on. The NS Youth towering over her simply looked her up and down and turned to his comrades smiling. "Aber die Kleine ist nicht schlecht, oder?" (But the girl's not bad, eh?).

Then Anna heard him unzipping his pants and unbuckling his belt and she knew then that it really was happening to her. He wants to fuck me not beat me. Raped in the street right in front of my father. But all she felt was hot, stinking liquid running all over her. The Nazi thug had broken into a broad grin of superiority and had started to piss all over her, and then her father, with his two comrades laughing madly. Anna tired to struggle to her feet, but the other two pushed her back down and held her while another hot stream of urine hit her in the face. All Anna could do was take it until he was finished and had zipped his pants back up, then the three of them walked off up the street still laughing. Contented - proud even - with their good night's work. There would be other, far more productive and deadly nights ahead for all three of them but for now, this one would do them just fine. They'd collected on the Gypsy Tax.

Anna lay on the ground soaked in Nazi urine. It stung her eyes. She could feel it trickling into her ear and running down her face and over her lips. But she was grateful and relieved. ''This has been a great day,'' she said to herself as she lay on the ground. ''Thank you, God... if you exist. I've had my pride pissed on by a Nazi and nothing worse. I'm still alive to fight another day.''

She struggled up onto her hands and knees but wasn't able to make it any further. The pain from her ribs sliced right through her. She let out a piercing scream into the cold night air. She stayed like that for a moment, on all fours with her head down, like a dog sniffing its dinner and not liking what was in the bowl. Then she forced herself to her feet with as much dignity as she could. She was shivering, and she stank. The urine still stung her eyes, and it dripped off her hair. She could still taste it on her lips. She spat it out into the gutter, wiped her eyes with her coat sleeve then helped her bloodied father up off the ground. His Rat Tax had cost him three back teeth, a fractured jaw, a broken nose, a dislocated finger, a split lip and a small river of blood.

Anna looked around for her girlfriend. But that 'friend' was nowhere to be seen.

***

"I'm in England now. Nothing bad can ever happen to me here," Anna always told herself. But in Guy's apartment above the shop, as Anna's haunted eyes stared down at the note on the floor, that myth was now shattered. It really was always meant to be this way. She could still taste the piss on her lips and the rank smell of stale beer breath; still, see pictures of her bloody father half-conscious on the freezing ground. She could still recall the feelings of pain shooting up from her ribs and through her entire body. "I'm afraid for us Guy," she said.

Guy moved up behind her and wrapped his arms around her in an attempt to comfort her, but it was a gesture which he knew would be in vain. He tried to reason. "That's the first time anything's ever…''

Anna pulled away from him.

"I don't need reassurances Guy. I know this fear. It's what I ran from. I'm a …" She stopped short of finishing her sentence and defining herself as something which surely would have committed her to a very different kind

24

of sentence - a very 'final' kind of sentence - had she not "ran," as she put it. In some bizarre way, Guy felt a sense of guilt. Sure it had been an attack on his window, on his flat, and the message had been directed at him and him alone. Yet somehow, he felt as if he'd been complicit in inflicting even more pain on Anna.

"I'm sorry, but it will be okay," he told her. Who was he trying to fool? Who was he to tell her that? Guy was afraid too. She's come to me for comfort and safety and look at what I deliver! A wall of icy silence built up between them which seemed to stretch into infinity. Guy knew that reason was hopeless. There simply was no justification for what had happened, and Anna had used up all the words she'd ever possess to express the personal horror show which she saw playing out all over again.

She looked over at the broken window, then down at the brick and the note, and then her eyes moved all around the room - although she seemed to be searching inside herself more than anywhere else, looking for a hope which she knew wasn't there. She was an alien at home, and now she was an alien here. Suddenly the room took on the quality of a prison cell. She felt trapped. They stood motionless and stared at each other. The silence built even further. The scene became so frozen it was like a painting, with the only sound that of the wind whistling through the cracks in the broken window. It was Guy who broke first. Aware that he'd been the target that night but Anna had been the real trophy for those bastards down in the street, he moved towards her, arms outstretched, trying his best whilst anticipating only rejection, but that night Anna did need reassurance. Afraid for them both, she reached out and held on tight to Guy in a fractured 'never-let-me-go-moment.

GYPSIES TRAMPS AND THIEVES

The persecution of gypsies, or 'Zigeuner' as they were called in Germany, was nothing new. They'd been shot and burned, hung and drowned, hated, chased and moved on for hundreds of years, and from many more countries than the one which Anna used to call home. And why not? They stank, they were lazy, they were unkempt and dirty. They had sex with their donkeys, and married their sisters and ate their babies, and they'll eat yours too if you don't do something about it and exterminate them all first. They stole, they lied and cheated. They were vagabonds, vagrants and vermin. They all had those evil, pitch-black eyes of the Devil himself. They looked different, they weren't from here, they were from 'over there.' They had no birthright; they were 'outsiders.' You could even say that they'd been born to be persecuted.

"And it could have been worse," Anna somehow managed to joke to her cousin Emma Vieti one evening when they got together in Hamburg. "Just imagine, you could have been a black, Jewish, communist gypsy!"

"Or a handicapped gypsy midget," Emma joked back. "Whose two wooden legs could both have had woodworm in them."

"Do you think they'd waste good wood on rats like us?" Anna reminded her.

"Like us? Like me you mean. You're half 'pure'. I'm sure they'd allow you one good leg."

"Well, that would be good of them!"

'Them' were the National Socialists, the Nazis, who had just passed the second of their Nuremberg Laws, or the 'Protection of Blood and Honour Act' as it was called, which defined who was pure and who wasn't and God help you if you weren't. It stripped non-Aryans of their rights, and the poor gypsies were handed the shittiest end of all sticks, with the very strictest criteria.

Three quarters of the Romanies who lived in Germany perished, with almost every single one of Anna's family being among that number.

"Well, at least they hate us for being something," Anna said, trying to summon up a slice of sarcasm. "Imagine how unfair it would all be if we were being persecuted for no reason at all!"

"We have to get out of here Anna," Emma said to her. Then resolutely she added, "We'll get out one day!"

Strictly speaking, her cousin Emma had been correct. On two counts, one, they both did get out, only it was to very different destinations; and two, she was right too about Anna being 'only' half-gypsy.

Lena Lenz, Anna's mother, had been born in Ahrensburg, a small town about twenty miles northeast of Hamburg, in 1880 and not a single drop of 'impure' blood ever coursed through her pretty little dancer veins and yes, she could show you the proof of it in her Ahnenpass. An Ahnenpass was a small booklet issued by the German Authorities which officially documented a person's family tree and therefore proved their 'Aryan-ness.' It was like a heart if you didn't have a workable one you really were fucked, my friend. So the lusty, licentious, lascivious but only occasionally lovely Lena Lenz became a dancer, met Anna's womanising father in Stuttgart where he ran a theatre, and their affair produced Anna. And plenty of hurt and heartache.

"We'll get out one day." That's what Emma had said to Anna once. It was all that kept them sane, that 'getting out.' But how? Sleep your way out? Read palms? Join the circus? Why not, we're gypsies after all. I'll have to

29

work my way out, and with hard work and a bit of luck - the two things that Anna believed were the base ingredients of any success - that's what she'd put her faith in. So, when she held on tight to Guy that night, that was what she was holding on tight to, all the good things which had got her to Britain and kept her alive and brought her the happiness which she otherwise never would have known and which she feared she was now in danger of losing.

***

In her twenty-three years in Germany, there had been plenty of physical abuse from others - and the scars left by those other beatings would have far greater impact on her - but that icy cold December night in Hamburg when the Nazi Youths had set about Anna was the first time she'd been physically attacked for political reasons. She'd been called names before, especially at school. Children learn things like that fast from their parents, and they are especially skilled at singling out any outsider and inflicting hurt. She'd been shoved and manhandled when she was riding the tramcar with her father, in more than one city.

They'd had dog shit smeared on their front door and had their letterbox set on fire and been turned away from shops, and spat on. But, the morning after the brick had flown through Guy's window, when Anna walked through the main door of Stansfield Street Hospital at seven-thirty with Jane to start their working day, she was all smiles again and what had gone was gone. That's what Anna did well, the art of forgetting. Not forgiving, forgiving came much harder. Pushing out of her mind all the negative, damaging forces which she knew would destroy her if she held on to them - that was what she had chosen to do. There would be occasions when she'd be forced to confront her demons again - like the previous night at Guy's - when she knew she was helpless to keep them out. But she also knew, just like the kicks from those National Socialist thugs, that the wounds would eventually heal. So Anna made a vow to choose the things from her past that she needed, and lock the rest away in a vault in her subconscious and leave them there. That was the theory. It wasn't repression as a way of survival Anna reasoned. It was the art of selection as a way of self-determination. It was choice as a way of getting past all the blind hatred and brutality, the prejudice and fear whilst holding on to what it is to be human in this most inhumane world that she found herself in. She'd decided she'd try to go through life with something else in her heart and she knew she had to get out of the hellhole which Hamburg had become.

Stansfield Street Hospital was a grand old Victorian red-brick building which had become one of the country's leading research units into respiratory illnesses, and Anna's saviour was up on the third floor. Anna and Jane said their friendly good mornings to the doctors and nurses who they passed on their way up the back stairs to room 375, where they knew old Professor Rosenbach would have long started his own day. The Professor had been

Anna's one way ticket out of Hamburg, he was the reason that she was in Britain.

Later, dressed in a long, white overcoat, Anna drew a thin, yellow liquid from a dark brown phial and handed the glass pipette to the Professor, who took it and thanked her without even once taking his eye away from the giant microscope. The venerable Israel Rosenbach was now sixty-nine years old and every bit of him screamed 'professor,' from his thick electric-shock white hair to his intense stare to his painfully sunken cheeks and even the heavy limp which he walked with. But in his eyes, there was also something kind and sympathetic. Anna had been drawn to him from their very first meeting back in Hamburg's University Clinic, in her interview for the job as assistant to the hospital's Head of Research. If I could choose a grandfather, Anna always thought, this would be my choice. The Professor looked through the microscope's powerful lens and brought a thin smear of white powder into sharp focus.

"Did you hear the latest?" He asked Anna in a thick German accent and without looking up from his microscope, "It seems only a matter of hours now before the Germans reach the Channel."

Anna nodded her head and mumbled a depressed "yes" and began to log figures into a thick register while next to her Jane was filling a rack with fresh test tubes.

"I just hope we'll be allowed to finish our work here before the Nazis cross the Channel. We're so close to a breakthrough." He pulled back momentarily from his microscope and shook his head in despair. "I never thought I'd live to see this happen again."

Jane was about to say something but stopped herself. Then finally, "Were you involved...the last time?"

Anna looked up from her register and across at her boss. Germans didn't talk about the war. About any war. Anna knew that much but she also knew that there was another story. He'd told it to her once and she knew that there were scars. The limp was the most obvious physical one but there was another, far more deep and painful wound. One which would never heal. How much did it still distress him to revisit old battles and old loves lost? Rosenbach broke away from his work and looked up at Jane. Anna tensed.

"This old Jew wasn't so old and undesirable back then that he couldn't be put to use on the front line." Then with a sad, ironic smile, he added, "but don't worry. There's not a drop of Englishman's blood on my hands! Only that of us Germans. I served as a field doctor, near Reims. The two longest, worst, wasted years of my life. And I've never been able to look at a bottle of champagne since!"

The Professor gingerly rubbed the side of his thigh, "I got myself a nice little memento to take back to Hamburg. Six pieces of shrapnel... all six still in there!" He smiled at Jane, winked at Anna, and returned to his microscope.

Anna relaxed. What Israel Rosenbach hadn't told Jane was that while he was trying to save soldiers, and at the same time trying to survive a rat infested army hospital tent in Marne, France, his wife and only daughter had both been killed in a fire which broke out in their top floor flat back in Hamburg. No one had told the Professor until he arrived back in Germany, badly injured himself, just three weeks before the Armistice.

Through the microscope's powerful lens the Professor watched the first drops of yellow liquid from the pipette which Anna had given him, hit the white powder, turning it a deep, blood-red colour. He muttered an intrigued and satisfied "Mmmm" to himself and scribbled something down on the note pad next to him.

"Are you seeing Guy tonight?"

"Yes," Anna replied.

"Then be sure to give him my regards," he said, with obvious affection. Then he broke away again from his work for a moment, for what Anna could sense was a 'big' moment for him but an awkward moment. Israel Rosenbach was a man of very few words and never any big scenes. If it wasn't work - which he attacked with a ferocious intensity - then the old Professor approached everything else in a quiet, laid back, matter-of-fact way. But here he was now before her, anxious.

"I-erm, I wondered... if no one else is doing it..."

Anna watched and wondered just what was coming next from the man she'd come to regard as something of a mentor, and whose struggle now was a combination of both nervousness and an uncertainty with the language.

"I'd be honoured to…" He turned to Jane, "how do you say it…walk you?"

Jane nodded and he turned back to Anna, "walk you to the altar?"

Professor Rosenbach had promised himself that he'd look her in the eye when he asked her this but all he did now was look straight down at his feet like a child awaiting judgement from his teacher. Anna didn't need to say a word, she just moved over and hugged him tightly.

***

While Anna was embracing her boss, Guy was standing outside a jeweller's shop in Upper Bexton High Street, waiting for them to open. Some time ago, Anna had seen a ring in the window that she said she loved and Guy had kept that in his head. If I ever marry this girl, he thought back then, this will be her ring. While he was waiting, a necklace of very fine but thin pearls which was draped over a display bust grabbed his attention.

SEVEN

THE NIGHT AT THE CINEMA

Later that day, the 13th of May, Winston Churchill stood before Parliament and gave his first speech as British Prime Minister. By then the German Blitzkrieg had begun, the invincible Wehrmacht was relentlessly powering its way through the Low Countries and across northern France towards the Channel. Against the mighty muscle of the most awesome war machine ever put together, all Churchill could offer the country that day was "blood, toil, tears and sweat."

The weather in England that month continued to be perfect, with tranquil, clear blue skies and nature bursting into bloom. It was England at its finest. It was almost like it was mocking the black horror which was going on in the rest of Europe. It was nevertheless a country full of fear and paranoia, anxious most of all for the thousands of its soldiers over in Europe who were about to feel the full force of the German advances.

"F-f-fuck 'em," Mr Williamson stuttered when Guy called that evening for Anna. He spoke out of the corner of his mouth, the stammer was another tragic legacy of the accident which had half paralysed him. "If I had t-two good arms I'd be over there myself giving the bastards what for. Be happy you're h-h-here and out if it Guy."

"I am Sir, I am."

Jane's father nodded up at the ceiling. "Anna's still upstairs. Or do you want to g-get another g-good hiding at chess from a one-armed genius?"

"Don't you mean a one-armed bandit?"

"Get outta here! Coward!"

Moments later Guy stood behind Anna in front of her dressing table and watched her put the finishing touches to her makeup. She'd already put her hair up and was wearing her new pearls. Then there was that smile.

"I'm so happy that the Professor will... what's 'zuführen'?"

"Give you away."

"I don't come with a price?"

Guy shook his head. "Absolutely free and not even cheap."

"Don't you wish your family could be here?" she asked Guy's reflection, although she knew the answer anyway. This was the biggest of days - a family day - and not having family around, for others if not for herself, well somehow it didn't seem quite right.

"They've made their choice and I've made mine, this is my country, our home now," Guy said, a little surprised that she'd even brought it up anyway. He noticed the swing in her mood. The joy of just a short moment ago had suddenly been replaced by sadness. "Are you okay?" he asked her.

"Yes."

But she wasn't.

"What's wrong?"

"I don't--It's just-- you know that I was happy to lose my chains years ago. I just wish I could keep all of this and change all the rest, make it right. I just wish it was all so different - despite how they treated me..." She could see in the mirror that Guy's mood had changed now too.

"I'm sorry," she said.

"There's nothing you need to say sorry for. Everything's just perfect as it is."

Old, deep wounds had reopened. She thought about her mother's cruelty and brutality, Anna's smile again faded fast. Guy tried his best to lift her. He nodded to her reflection in the mirror, to her fine pearl necklace, and covered his left eye with his hand.

"You know, it's even more beautiful than you are."

She fought to get a hold of herself; remember the good, lose the bad. If you wound easily, then heal fast. Don't spoil the moment Anna, she told herself.

"Actually, I'd say much more beautiful," Guy said. She reached back and gave his leg a playful slap. "I'm only telling you what the camera sees and it never lies, but..." He removed his hand. "With two eyes it's... No, the pearls still have it."

She finally managed a smile. Her mood began to brighten. She was always good at that - at always finding her way back. She became skilled at negotiating the precarious journey out of the dark and back into the light. It was how she survived, and it often needed help from Guy. With her makeup now finished, she let her hair down, shook it loose, and it all looked impossibly beautiful to Guy, although Anna herself never considered herself as beautiful. She hadn't been allowed that privilege. She'd been part of a culture which had a very different perception of what female beauty was, and a dark gypsy girl certainly wasn't it. In fact, she was the polar opposite of blonde, blue eyed, fair featured, curvaceous (and preferably tall if you're compiling a wish list). Nothing about me is right, she believed. Although she also knew the power and the pull that she could have over men. She'd learned that much.

"What time does the film start?" she asked.

"We're meeting Claire and Grant outside at six."

She got up and moved right up close to him, like a raven-haired Gilda - a 'teasing temptress' as Guy called her. "So what do we do till then?" she asked him, which wasn't a question at all but a command.

Guy knew this mood. He knew that look she was giving him. But he would try and play her along a while yet. He attempted a step back. "What about Mrs Williamson?"

"She can't join us. I'm not that kind of girl." Her arm was now around his neck and she was covering him in kisses. Guy was both resisting and giving in at the same time.

"We're...we're not even married yet Miss Vieti."

"What, I'm not allowed to test the goods before I buy them?"

She maneuvered in the direction of the bed... Anna will get what Anna wants.

EIGHT

THE NIGHT OF THE PICTURES

Claire and Grant Pennington-Cooper were already waiting outside the local Upper Bexton Picture House when Guy and Anna crossed the road to meet them. From across the street, Claire Pennington-Cooper looked twenty-five and a lot of class, and from three feet away she looked like someone who had invested a lot of work and time into looking those twenty-five years younger. Because Claire was four months short of her fiftieth birthday and ten years older than her husband but they were nothing but numbers to Claire. She applied her makeup like it was an art form, and wore clothes at least one size too small for her. Yet somehow she managed to pull off the illusion well enough to be described by all of her friends - and there were indeed plenty of friends - as 'eternally youthful' and elegant. There was a heart of pure gold inside the expensively tailored, powder blue suit which she wore with some grace that balmy May night for the date with the Schneiders-to-be. It was Claire who was the undisputed captain of Team Pennington-Cooper and ran the show, which allowed Professor Grant his little indulgences such as the countless hours that he sat alone in his study or at the university library with his art and writing his books. Grant - dark and intense, until just the right amount of drink kicked in and lightened him up - was an inch and a half shorter than his wife once she'd stepped into her high-heels, and had the kind of large and protruding goldfish eyes which made him look like someone who's been looking through too many key-holes. But he had a friendly enough face once he chose to smile and an engaging enough charm. He and Guy were half-cousins as well as being the closest of friends, despite the age difference between them. The four greeted each other with hugs, Claire admired Anna's new necklace, and Grant offered everyone a quick sip from his hip flask before they disappeared into the cinema together.

***

A few hundred yards away in the High Street the blue Morris 10 cruised straight past "Guy Schneider, Photographer's" shop and came to a halt fifty yards further up the road. Adams and his tall, bald partner Eric 'Curly'

Barnes stubbed out their cigarettes then got out of the car and walked the short distance back to Guy's place. Adams rang the doorbell and waited. No answer. He rang again. Barnes looked up at the apartment's cracked window. Guy had nailed a strip of hardwood across the broken part. It would have to make do until the glaziers could come and replace it. Barnes nodded to Adams and they turned away from the front door, walked the few yards to the corner, then headed up the lane at the side of the shop.

***

In the crowded Bexton cinema, the lights were dimmed and the giant screen lit up, and it was welcome to the Picture House of Fun – featuring that night the total collapse and capitulation of Western Europe, starring Adolf Hitler. A woman with an enormous hat, as if someone had transported the Taj Mahal on to the top of her head and left it there, sat down directly in front of Guy just as the British Movietone/Pathé News Bulletin was starting up. Guy dodged from side to side to get a clear view of the screen but it was no good, because every time he moved, the Taj-Mahal woman seemed to move with him in the same direction. Anna tapped her on the shoulder, said something to her with her usual charm, and the woman smiled back and removed her hat. Then they settled back to watch newsreel footage of the week's events and the vast screen filled with images of German panzers rolling over border crossings, while rural villages were scorched by flamethrowers. The fighting in Belgium and the Low Countries had begun. The home team wasn't winning.

The news moved on to the Germans' advance through France, as far as the Channel at Abbeville.

When that was over the next report up on the screen was a series of clips about the marches through the streets of Britain by the growing right-wing/fascist British Union movement, led by Sir Oswald Mosley. His menacing 'blackshirt' disciples were spreading the good word of their charismatic leader with their knuckle dusters and lead filled hosepipes, which the commentary condemned and bluntly denounced. Objective, impartial and unbiased reporting had long been discarded as the media drew up its own battle lines on the home front.

***

At the same time, in Guy's shop, Adams and Barnes had slipped on gloves and were wasting no time raking through Guy's drawers and files, scrutinising as quickly as they were able to each piece of paper and document that they came across.

While back in the Picture House, the Newsreel had moved on to a short report about the growing British hostility towards Germany and the poisonous anti-alien feeling which was spreading through the country. In the darkness of the cinema Guy and Anna turned to face each other and exchanged anxious looks.

In Guy's back office, Barnes held a pile of papers in his hand; invoices, business letters and reminders, orders for cameras and photography equipment. Most were in English, some were in German. He put most of them back where he had found them but pushed a handful of documents into his jacket pocket.

Adams had now moved upstairs to the flat above the shop. In a spare room at the back which Guy used for storage space, Adams opened a drawer to an old, ornately carved cabinet which almost certainly had been imported once from India, and took out a pile of photographs. He started to flick through them. Images of babies; chubby babies, crying babies, laughing babies, sleeping babies, babies with rattles, babies with bottles, and babies who had better things to do with their time than lie still and have their photograph taken by some twenty-six year old half German/half English photographer with a dimple in his chin and endless boyish charm. There were a few portraits, some wedding photographs and a handful of happy family group photographs. Then something that Adams saw stopped him flicking further. It was at the very bottom of the pile and it was two pictures of Anna. In one she was naked, sitting in front of a mirror, putting on makeup; in the other she was slightly less so, sitting on the edge of a bed wrapped only in a Union Jack flag, with a cheeky grin on her face. It was a picture of Anna confident and comfortable in her own sexuality. Adams took a long, lingering look, he liked what he saw. A lot. He searched further, picking up a second pile of photographs, again starting to flick through them as quickly as he could and again; something that he found in that pile was enough to light up his eyes.

***

The sculptured Teutonic features of the Germans' former darling, Marlene Dietrich now filled the screen in 'Destry Rides Again'. The Berlin beauty was dressed as Frenchy, the dance hall queen, and exposed as much leg as she could for the camera as she rolled around the bar-room floor in a vicious cat-fight with Lily Belle. Grant held up his hand to the bored usherette who was passing up the aisle and bought four ice creams.

***

In the backroom of Guy's flat, Adams was looking hard at the photograph of Anna with the airfield in the background - one of the pictures which Guy had taken on their trip to the coast - when Barnes moved up alongside him. Barnes looked at the photograph, then at Adams, and the two exchanged a look which said everything about the case which they'd just stumbled into. Adams placed the photograph back into a packet which Guy had marked "Beach, May 40" pushed the packet into the inside pocket of his jacket, and they headed for the door.

***

Dance halls across the country were booming. The British had chosen to foxtrot or rhumba or hokey cokey their gloomy wartime mood away and Guy, Anna, Grant and Claire took the dancing shoes which the Upper Bexton Ritz insisted its patrons wore, from the cloakroom girl and headed up to the ballroom on the first floor. They'd already tried to get into the more exclusive Gold Lounge in town, where red hot local sensations The Benny Trower Sextet were playing, but it was reservations only there and every table was long gone, and they were turned away despite Grant's attempts at slipping a 'little extra something' into the admission lady's hand. "Don't all breathe out at once" the cloakroom attendant at the Ritz had told them as she handed them their dancing shoes, and they saw why when they entered the packed to bursting ballroom. The place had that intoxicating mix of smoke and perfume, alcohol and sweat. The promise of love everlasting, or the desperate hope of sex tonight hung in the air. A ten piece orchestra was up on stage. The four pushed their way onto the crowded dance floor and went through the motions of a slow, sedate waltz, which ground to a halt when a pencil-thin, weasel-faced smoothie walked up to the microphone and announced the next song and the band went into…

I'll be seeing you, in all the old familiar places,

That this heart of mine embraces all day through…

As he sang, the smooth crooner's eyes scanned the room like busy searchlights, looking at the girls who were dancing with girls, or the girls who were dancing with boys - at basically every and any girl in the room, who he'd later try and get back to his place or to her place or into his tiny dressing room or the back seat of his car. Even the back lane behind the ballroom would do, just as it had countless times before because let's not kid ourselves, he'd even tell you himself in one of his quieter moments, that's the reason he just loved his job. Then old weasel face left the stage, the music changed - the dance too - and only the energetic, the drunk, and possibly the Scots were left on the floor as the band whipped up a lively, lightning fast reel. And still, right in there among the bouncing crowd - now holding her shoes - was Anna. The 'wild, free, barefoot gypsy girl' twirled and spun and twisted to the music with the sheer joy and abandon of a child, loving every second. It was all twirly skirts and sweaty shirts and fun, fun, fun - and if Anna had inherited one thing from her mother ("were a mother and her daughter ever so different, ever so opposite from each other?" she'd always claim), it was the way she could swish and sway and glide so beautifully, so naturally across a dance floor. Guy, Grant and Claire watched her from the edge of the dance floor and exchanged looks which said something along the lines of "isn't she something?" There were plenty of other admirers too. One of them was a half-cut, uniformed service man with chipped black teeth who was pressed up tight against Guy. Servicemen were let in for half price at most establishments during war time, which meant they had more to spend on their beer. The soldier nudged Guy and nodded in the direction of the bar, where someone else had caught his attention. He leaned right into Guy, cupped his hand over

Guy's ear and shouted over the din of the ballroom. "Did you see what she just did?"

"What?"

"The barmaid... just there?"

Guy had only had eyes for Anna and had lost himself in her overwhelming beauty.

"Look, she's doing it again," the soldier said excitedly and tapped Guy's arm.

He was watching the barmaid with the low-cut blouse, who put another beer bottle between her enormous breasts and whipped the top clean off the bottle. The soldier turned and shot Guy a 'how the hell does she do that?' look. But then Guy pointed out the bottle opener which was swinging down on the end of the chain around her neck and was lodged in her cleavage. "That's how," Guy told him and the soldier moved away, disappointed. His place was immediately taken by a smart blonde. All grace and sophistication and four letter words. She leaned into Guy and whispered a selection of them into his ear. It didn't impress Guy. He shook his head and she moved on to pester the next sucker.

Anna caught a glimpse of Guy through the crowd and motioned him over to join her. He shook his head, but a half drunk, sweat soaked Grant put his hand on Guy's back and shoved him off in her direction anyway. He was an awful dancer, stiff, awkward and clumsy. Anna laughed and started to imitate him. Quite well too. "If that's the best you can do the wedding's off!"

"If the wedding's off, so am I." And with a relieved smile he turned and signalled for Grant to take his place.

***

The sergeant on duty at Bexton Police Station that night was PC Francis Dobson, a wall of muscle who was at least six feet four. Wide, that was. When Guy looked up at him from the other side of the desk he seemed to go up forever. He was, without doubt, the biggest man Guy had ever seen in all his twenty six years. Intimidating he certainly was. 'Scary, he certainly is' thought Anna, especially in the dim and somber low watt wartime lighting. But Francis Dobson wasn't a wolf in wolf's clothing. Not without what he thought was a good reason anyway. Perhaps he was grateful for a little distraction that night. Perhaps he'd learned in his twenty one years of duty that it was always best to bring a friendly smile and a joke to the job. Either way, his mood was bright and cheery, despite the fact that he'd been given bad news earlier that day.

"And what was taken?" His voice was deep, like a rumble of thunder, and when he spoke the ground seemed to shake.

"Some business papers. Accounts, invoices, import documents," Guy told him.

Dobson dabbed the end of his pencil onto his tongue and with his tongue still sticking out, he started to write down Guy's details - partly with his pen and partly with

50

his tongue it seemed, as it waggled from side to side across his lips as he wrote in his pad.

"From the shop?"

"Yes."

"And nothing was taken from the upstairs flat? No money? Valuables? Nothing like that missing?"

"No."

"How did they get in?"

"They broke a glass panel in the back door and went in through there."

Sergeant Dobson looked at the top of his notepad. "And the name's 'Schneider'?"

"That's right. Gerhard Schneider."

"'Guy' to his friends" Anna chipped in.

Dobson thought about it. He said the name out loud to himself again, just to see how it sounded. "Ger-hard Schnei-der. You're not British?"

"Half British."

"Which half?" Dobson allowed himself a self satisfied smile. He admired his little joke.

"This one," Guy said, deciding to play along, indicating down the right side of his body.

"And the other?"

"German." Then after a short, silent beat, he added… "Once."

The effect was immediate. The sergeant's smile vanished. His previously concerned, cheery attitude had ended at Guy's answer. He now fixed Guy with a cold look. "I don't think there's much we can do for you, Herr Schneider." There was no disguising it; he seemed to spit out the word "Herr" like it was some kind of poison. "We're severely undermanned at present as it is. There's a war on, you know." If it was Dobson's attempt at sarcasm, it was lost on Guy that late in the evening. Guy just shrugged his shoulders. "I'll try and arrange for someone to come round and see you sometime," Dobson added and put down his pen.

Moments later, at the same time that Grant was being sick all over the new hallway carpet in their new home in Knightsbridge, and a furious argument with Claire was breaking out about his drinking habit, Guy and Anna were walking away from the Police Station with their collars turned up against the cool late night air.

"Do you think the break-in had anything to do with what happened before? With the window?" she asked him.

Guy just shrugged his shoulders again, he simply had no idea, all he could see was Anna's distress. He took off his jacket and wrapped it around her shoulders. Then reached over and put a comforting arm around her as they walked off down the pitch black street together in silence.

Back inside the Police Station, Francis Dobson ripped the page that he'd written on out of his notebook, crumpled it up into a tight ball and tossed it into the waste-bin across the room in a fury. Early that morning, just after breakfast, he had heard that his younger brother had been badly wounded in the fighting in France, although he hadn't been given any more details than that.

***

Over the next few days, the glaziers came - the local CID didn't - and the sun kept on shining. Whilst across the sea, the German tanks thundered ever closer. On Thursday evening, Anna took the bus to Kelsey Park as she did every Thursday, to read German to the blind, eighty-six year-old Hannelore Hildebrandt, once of Berlin, now forty one years in Beckenham.

NINE

THE BIG DAY ARRIVES

Guy was all ready for his big day, dressed in his black suit and tails. His crushed velvet top hat lay on the table in front of him, next to Anna's wedding ring. He picked the ring, looked at it, and then at his watch. The front-door bell rang. Guy slipped the ring into his pocket and went downstairs to answer the door. His Best Man, Grant was dressed just like Guy in tails and top hat. He walked in smiling and shook Guy's hand. They looked just like a couple of conjurers in a Palladium double act.

"Nervous?"

Guy held out a rock steady hand, Grant was impressed. Then Guy held out the other – deliberately shaking it madly. Grant laughed and slapped him on the back. Then he pulled out his hip flask and followed Guy upstairs to the flat.

***

Adams and Barnes stood outside a frosted glass panelled office door. Barnes knocked on the door and an irritated voice from inside barked out "Come in." They pushed in to a room which had the blinds down and was only dimly lit from a single lamp perched on the corner of the desk. The desk was strewn with files and papers, the entire room was cluttered with metal filing cabinets and bookcases, which made the place, appear even smaller and even tighter. Some shafts of morning sunlight had managed to sneak in through the slats in the blinds and threw odd shadows across the room, giving the whole place a mysterious, even sinister atmosphere.

Behind the desk was an intense looking man with thinning gray hair parted down the middle and plastered back with handfuls of Brylcreem. He once had fierce; hawk's eyes but now he wore a patch over one of them. He was said to be in his early sixties, but no one knew for sure and he could well have been older. Without a word, he picked up a thick file from one of the many piles in front of him and tossed it across the desk to Adams, who made the smartest of catches. Then the man with the single hawk's eye nodded his head ominously and Barnes and Adams immediately turned and headed for the door.

***

Up in her bedroom, Anna pulled the veil down over her face. Her heart was racing now. She took a small bouquet of dark red roses from Jane, and they headed for the door - both nervous but excited about the day ahead.

***

At the same time, in Guy's living room, Guy touched glasses with Grant and they both downed their whiskies in one. Guy picked his top hat up from the table and put it on. It felt odd. Perhaps he even looked odd in it. But what the hell, he thought, I'm getting married to my beautiful gypsy girl today. He dipped a hand into his pocket and pulled out the ring and handed it to Grant. Then, deep breath, they headed downstairs to the front door. Grant was first out. Guy was just locking up and was about to follow him out when Adams, Barnes and a policeman the size of a gorilla appeared from nowhere. They shoved Guy back inside and kicked the door shut behind them. Out on the street, Grant - understanding nothing and protesting wildly - banged like a madman on Guy's front door and tried to get back in, but he was pulled back and led away by a second police officer.

***

Picture this: which Anna would do a thousand times over the following few days:

A quaint old Norman church bathed in the late morning sunshine. Faint organ music drifted up from inside the church where the wedding guests had all congregated, although the small church was no more than a third full.

56

Anna stood just inside the main church doorway, flanked on one side by the Professor and on the other by Jane. Anna turned and looked nervously over her shoulder towards the church gates, then back at the Professor and Jane, who were trying their best to give her a reassuring look. They all looked apprehensively at their watches. At the far end of the church, the grey haired vicar stood alone in front of the altar. He lifted the sleeve of his cassock and he too looked anxiously at his watch. In the pews in front of him, some of the wedding guests twisted in their seats and looked back curiously towards the church doorway, where Anna was growing increasingly agitated. Anna once again glanced nervously over her shoulder towards the church gates outside, then exchanged a confused, perturbed look with Jane.

Five more tense minutes passed until an elderly church caretaker appeared from a door at the side of the altar and whispered something into the vicar's ear. The vicar nodded gravely. The caretaker went back through the side door from which he'd appeared and the vicar set off up the aisle towards Anna with a grim look on his face. The congregation turned their heads and followed the vicar's path down through the church as he passed them. As Anna watched him approach, she knew that something had gone very wrong. She realised that her world was about to collapse. Her face drained of colour. The roses slipped from her hand and hit the ground.

* * *

Across town on the High Street, the two policemen led Guy out of his front door. He appeared like a man going to his own funeral, not his wedding. The policemen bundled him into the back of the Black Maria police van which was now parked in the street outside of the shop, then they got in themselves on either side of Guy and the van set off.

***

Outside the church, a light rain had begun to fall. A handful of confused and concerned guests stood and watched Anna climb into a waiting taxi. Her veil had been pulled back to reveal the smile which she had fixed firmly in place to hide her humiliation; to mask her hurt. No one was aware of what had happened on the other side of town. No one had told them, all they knew was that the groom hadn't shown up and the bride had been left standing.

"C-c-coward. I'll give him what for," Mr Williamson yelled angrily out of the side of his mouth after the taxi. Guy himself had become the enemy now, and Jane's father decided that he'd have to deal with Guy even before he'd deal with Hitler's army. He loosened his tie and unbuttoned the collar of his best Sunday/Wedding Day shirt and twisted in his wheelchair to look up at his wife standing behind him. For once there was no smile on her face. "You make a promise you k-keep a b-bleedin' promise, that right Alice?" Alice had nothing to say, she just stood behind her husband and gripped the back of his wheel-chair.

From over her shoulder, a woman's worried voice asked, "has anyone called the Grange Hotel yet about the reception?"

As the taxi made its way back across town, Anna sat and stared out of the rain streaked window. To the outside world, she was still calm, but inside she was raging. She could cry, but she didn't. It was a master class in self control. Her pride wouldn't permit a single tear to flow in public. Opposite Anna in the taxi were Jane and Claire, who held her roses. Claire reached out and rested a comforting hand on Anna's arm.

"What did the vicar say? What did Grant tell him?" she quizzed Anna. She was as concerned and confused as all the other guests, but Anna could only shake her head from side to side disbelievingly and continue staring out of the window at a point which wasn't really there. "Did he say why Guy didn't turn up?" Claire pressed her again. All Anna did was shake her head once more, either she didn't know, or she wasn't saying. Claire looked over at Jane, sitting next to Anna. It was a look which seemed to be asking her ''do you know any more to this than anyone is letting on to?'' But Jane could only shrug her shoulders, as anxious and frustrated as Claire was and knowing just as little.

When the taxi pulled up outside the Williamson's house the rain had already stopped and the sun had reappeared again with a vengeance. Anna jumped out of the taxi almost before it had stopped and raced up the garden path. It was only then that she allowed herself the tears which she'd been bottling up inside of her. It was like a dam breaking, it became an uncontrollable sob. For herself; for Guy; for the dream, she'd had stolen from her and for a future she hadn't the first clue about. There was a tear for every injustice and every violation and hardship that she had ever suffered. For Anna, dreams born under a clear blue sky had died that morning in church.

Up in her room, she ran her arm the entire length of her dressing table, sending her perfumes, brushes and makeup flying. She reached down and picked the photograph of herself and Guy at the water's edge, up off the floor. It had already begun to fade.

***

Guy stood in silence in Upper Bexton Police Station, still in his wedding suit. His top hat was pushed back on his head. There was a look of utter despair on his face. Barnes stood alongside him.

At the other side of the duty desk, Sergeant Francis Dobson had a smile as wide as the Thames. He dabbed his pencil on his tongue and prepared to take down details on his notepad as Barnes explained:

"We're holding him under Regulation 18B."

"Regu...lashun...eight...teen... B."

Dobson said out loud to himself as he scribbled it down.

"What does that mean, 18B? What the hell is that?" Guy protested. "What the devil am I supposed to have done?"

Barnes ignored him and carried on addressing the duty Sergeant. Dobson's tongue was again tracing out what he was writing as Barnes continued. "Under both categories, 'Hostile Origin and Association.' And 'Acts Prejudicial'." Barnes handed a printed, single-sheet document across the desk to Dobson. "That's the Order. We'll have him moved up to London shortly."

"What's this all about? I've done nothing!" Guy protested again, this time louder and this time much more passionately. But no one was listening to him. He rubbed his hands over his face and removed his top hat and ran his fingers through his hair, wondering what in God's name he could have possibly done to deserve this, and on his wedding day too. Sergeant Dobson turned and shouted.

"Hey, Ted. Get yourself in here," to someone in the back of the station. Seconds later an older police officer with a twitch in his left eye shuffled into the front office, grabbed Guy by the arm and led him away. Dobson picked up a thick bunch of keys and followed them. As Guy walked in front of him, the sergeant deliberately stuck out a foot and caught the back of Guy's heel. Guy stumbled into the corridor wall.

Outside the station, the suave Adams was already waiting in his car when his colleague came out. He smoothed down his perfectly-clipped moustache, put his fancy felt fedora back on his head and tilted it to just the right angle, then he started up the blue Morris's engine and drove off.

***

Anna sat on her bed and stared hard into the fast fading photograph. She was lost in its world. There was a knock on the door but Anna didn't look up. Nor did she move. From the landing outside of Anna's room, Jane's worried voice shouted out to her.

"Anna? Can we come in?"

But Anna wasn't listening. She just sat there frozen. Then, suddenly infused with a new sense of energy and determination, she stood up, returned the photograph to its old place on the dressing table and strode purposefully across the room to the door. She jerked it open with as much fury as she'd opened it moments earlier and brushed straight past Jane and Claire without saying a word.

PART 2

COLLAR THE LOT

Guy's wedding suit lay in a heap on the tiled prison floor. His top hat was next to it. Guy himself stood naked in an old, empty bathtub, twisting and contorting his body as a prison orderly hosed him down with ice-cold jets of water.

Ten minutes later an iron cell door slammed shut behind a sorry-looking Guy as he stood and looked around. He was dressed now in shabby prison clothes, under his arm were two coarse, canvas blankets, he threw them onto his piss stained mattress. A cockroach raced out from under the iron-framed bed and scuttled across the cold, concrete floor and disappeared into a crack at the base of the wall. The cell was dirty, dank and claustrophobic. A chipped, shit encrusted chamber pot stood in one corner. A stained wash basin hung off the wall opposite the single bed. The tap constantly dripped. This was Guy's new home. It was the room from hell. And Guy didn't know for how long or why.

***

In tears on the inside, and outside raging, Anna stood in her wedding dress and argued furiously with the tired old duty officer with the twitch who had replaced Sergeant Dobson at the Station. Her face was still streaked with makeup and smeared with mascara; she looked as scary and as intimidating as Dobson had done some days before. She was a tiger unleashed. "What is this...this Regulation 18B? Why has he been locked up? WHY??" Except she had no real enemy to fight that morning. The aging duty officer, only weeks away from his retirement, simply look disinterested and only stood and shrugged his shoulders at her. It might have been indifference, but it could also have been a gesture of provocation. If that was the case, then Anna was more than willing to take the bait. "What are you?" she raged. "Don't you have the ability to speak?" But old Ted still didn't reply and just looked back at her impassively, prepared to patiently sit out the storm. "Mensch, WHAT ARE YOU?" she screamed. "WHY HAVE YOU TAKEN MY GUY?"

Eventually, the old bobby seemed to take pity on her and gave in. "I'm sorry Miss," he said. "With Regulation

64

18B we're under strict orders not to give out any information at all."

Sometime later Anna would say that not knowing was the worst, but that wasn't really true. The ignorance was only one part of the wickedly woven tapestry which made up her and Guy's lives back then-and the lives of many other people too. "They'd taken our dreams away and I didn't know where to. Or why. The country which I had adopted and which I believed had adopted me," she said "… the magic had gone."

THE ROUND UP

A magician stood centre stage in a crowded music hall. A sea of faces looked up at him full of anticipation and curiosity. And then whoosh! he was gone! What about that for real magic? As Barnes and a uniformed policeman dragged him off the stage he protested wildly at the unfairness of it all and tried to resist. His flashing, rotating bow-tie, the magician's trademark gimmick started to turn and blink. Several coloured canaries flew out from inside his jacket. Two rabbits dropped out of his trouser leg and hopped away. At the back of the stage, from an open box with its curtains pulled aside, an anorexic-looking girl emerged from the box's false wall and watched mystified as the magician vanished, his tricks exposed. The bewildered matinee audience looked on, not knowing how to react. Was this a part of the act? One person even started to applaud.

***

Anna trooped through the Bexton streets in her wedding dress, carrying her shoes - defeated, distressed, and devastated, destination home. But where was 'home' now? The people who she passed on the street turned and stared at the bizarre sight of the wandering, teary bride in her bloodied stocking feet.

A young boy standing at a bus stop holding his mother's hand pointed at her and shouted out "look at the funny lady!" Yes, Anna was a funny lady all right. It was a laugh a minute with good old Anna the stand-up act from Hamburg. "Have you heard the one about a man called Guy who hated the Nazis and came to Britain and was arrested for nothing? No? Well, that's okay. No one *should* know that one, but I'll tell you it anyway. Or the one about the Englishman, the Irishman and the Scotsman who went into a bar and all got locked up too for doing nothing? Another 'no'? That's good too. That's how they want it. So thank you and good night, you've been a love-ly audience and I've been Anna Vieti the funny lady from Hamburg."

***

Picture this: a pig farm at the end of a valley in the pretty Cotswold Hills. Idyllic, tranquil, two police officers lead away an elderly pig farmer. His fearful, fretting wife watches them bundle him into the back of a black police

67

car and drive off. Like Anna, the pig farmer's wife didn't know why, where to, or for how long.

***

Earlier that morning a balding, middle-aged man was watching the posters fly off the printing press in his small factory in Birmingham when two policemen entered the room. He stopped the machine while they spoke to him. Stacked up next to the printing press was a pile of freshly printed posters which read: "War Will Cease When Men Refuse To Fight. What Are You Going To Do About It?" The balding man turned off his machine and trudged off with the two policemen, quietly and without protest.

On the second floor of a private school in the Home Counties, a young and enthusiastic teacher nodded a sad farewell to his stunned second year students mid lesson, as two policemen escorted him out. Written on the blackboard at the front of the class was a list of German words for various modes of transport - 'Auto', 'Zug', 'Flugzeug', 'Fahrrad', 'Schiff,' with their English translations written alongside.

A lanky man in a kilt - his long left leg in a plaster cast right up to his thigh - hobbled on his crutches towards a waiting police car. He was flanked by two of Scotland's very finest. Even up in Scotland, the sun was shining that day, but his wife's face was wet with tears as she stood at the living room window and watched him go. The two policemen struggled to get him into the back of the police car - the poor guy just couldn't bend his leg at all. Eventually, they had to send for an ambulance to come and take him in.

A seedy gym above a seedy pub off the Old Kent Road is dark and dingy. Its rancid air stank from old, stale sweat. Lightweight hope 'Fearless' Freddie Turnbull was working away at a heavy leather bag suspended from a beam in the low ceiling. A plainclothes detective approached him from behind and stepped in between Freddie and his bag. "You Freddie Turnbull?" the detective asked.

Freddie moved to within an inch of the officer's face. "Who wants to know?" he asked with an ice cold, killer's stare and a provocative, confrontational stance. No one ever interrupted Fearless Freddie when he was working the bag.

"He does," said the detective and nodded to the man standing directly behind Freddie. Freddie spun around to stare up at the man mountain that was Police Sergeant Francis Dobson. Dobson had been told that morning that his younger brother had died from the horrific injuries which he suffered in France. They took in Freddie Turnbull without any problem.

Up on the top floor of an eighteenth century country mansion, in a small bedroom under the roof, Adams and a policewoman watched a confused twenty-year old housemaid pack a few personal belongings into a bag. Adams looked at his watch and then over at the policewoman; the housemaid simply wasn't doing it quickly enough and time was pressing. The policewoman took the cue and hurried the housemaid up.

**

When Anna, still carrying a shoe in each hand, finally arrived back at the Williamsons' semi in Armitage Street, she just kept right on going to the end of the road and then left down Ripon Street and into the park, past the old ladies feeding the swans and pigeons, the small children playing 'catch,' and the park keeper with his giant lawn mower cutting his perfect vertical patterns on the perfect bowling green. Then out into the wide, tree lined Bolton Avenue, where the rich folk of Upper Bexton had bought their big houses to bring up their rich kids, and then on down the High Street, which should now be 'home' but well, that dream had died earlier in the day. She walked right to the end of the half mile long High Street, straight past Guy's place without stopping - and on... looking neither right nor left. Walking just to be walking.

**

Back in the Cotswolds, the light was now beginning to fade but a big red sun still hung in view between the farm buildings. The pig farmer's wife closed the farmhouse door behind her and walked the fifty yards over to the slaughterhouse. Inside, she closed the door, took a large captive bolt pistol down from a shelf and pressed it hard against her forehead. Then she closed her eyes and squeezed the trigger. The last thing she would ever hear was the dull "thunk" sound as the bolt did its business and she dropped to the ground like a stone.

***

It was late evening and already dark when Barnes knocked on an office door which had the name "Major Robert Walker VC, CBE" printed on its frosted glass panel. The usual gruff voice bellowed out "Come in," and Barnes and Adams stepped into their Boss' main office. The man with the fierce hawk's eye and the black leather eye patch was sitting behind his desk. On the wall behind him was a painted portrait of the King and some old, framed world war one army photographs. A mounted stag's head - a proud hunting trophy - looked down over the Major from its place on the wall above him. It was just one of the many trophies which the Major could brag about, human as well as animal. Robert Walker was the head of British Military Intelligence, MI5. He was a veteran of the Great War, which he returned from in 1918 minus one eye but with a chest full of medals, a hatred of Germans, and a lifelong passion for combat. He was one of those unfortunate and insufferable people who would always find a war to fight. Someone who would always have a battle constantly raging inside of them. Barnes, the senior of the two MI5 Officers, dropped a bundle of files onto Walker's desk.

"They're all in Sir. Or will be soon."

"Good work," Walker said.

Praise came very rarely, if ever, from the Major and didn't come easily at that. Barnes and Adams both knew this and allowed themselves a quiet smile of satisfaction.

Walker glanced up at Adams. "Get that hat off," he barked, and Adams whipped off his fedora and placed it gingerly on the desk. "And off there!" He shot Adams a look which would have sent a chill up Satan's spine.

Adams quickly removed the hat from the desk and held on to it. 'Fuck you, arsehole,' he was thinking. "Sorry, Sir" was what he actually said.

This was a great day for the Major, though you would never know it from looking at him. In fact, you would never know anything from looking at him. There was no smile. Never a sense that he was happy, proud, satisfied, or sad - if he was ever any of those things, that was. Only when he was angry did you know about it. And boy was it ugly. Walker opened the first file in a pile, marked 'Schneider.'

"The photographer here in Bexton?" asked the Major.

"The very one," Barnes said.

Walker took Guy's photographs out of the file and flicked through them. They were the pictures of Anna in front of the airfield on the Kent coast. Anna was an irrelevance to the Major. All he saw were the RAF planes which were coming in to land, the airfield itself and the fortifications around it, and the sea defences at the harbour. If Barnes had sliced off the Major's foot and served it up to him on a plate, Walker couldn't have been more disgusted, or pained.

"Bloody spy!" he spat out. "What do we know about him?" he demanded of Barnes.

"Gerhard 'Guy' Schneider, Sir. Twenty-six, born in Stuttgart. Dual nationality, the father's German, the mother was British, but gave it up five years ago and took up German citizenship. He's been here six years now. There's an older brother in the German diplomatic corps in Lisbon."

On hearing that, Walker's one eye shot up from the photographs in his hand and fixed on Barnes like he'd struck the mother lode.

Then Adams spoke up, certain it would impress the Major even more.

"The Schneider's very good friend and neighbour in Stuttgart is a certain General von Kondertal... of the Luftwaffe."

Walker knew the name, and he knew its significance, he was indeed impressed, but at the same time, he was agitated.

He dropped Guy's photographs back onto the desk and sat a moment in deep thought.

"We thought you might like that," added Adams, with a satisfied smile.

Walker said nothing. He just looked back at Adams, irritated. Then he got up and began to pace across the room.

Moments later, the two MI5 officers walked out of Walker's office and set off down the corridor, quite pleased with themselves.

"Well, that went okay," Curly Barnes said.

"How would you ever know?"

"You're still not too hot on the old man are you?"

"I swear that every time I see that poor stag's face in there, the more I'm convinced that old Cyclops scared the poor fucker to death."

Barnes smiled at his partner. Adams planted his fedora back on his head and tilted it to just the right angle. "They say that the patch is only a distraction, you know?" Barnes said. "He has two good eyes. He only wears that patch to intimidate people."

"It works for me," Adams said. "But I prefer the other version. He took his eye out in France with a heated spoon, removing some poisonous shrapnel that he got in there from a German grenade." While Adams spoke, he made a big show of imitating Walker gouging out his eye.

"Yep, I quite like that version too," said Barnes as he watched Adams reach down into his jacket pocket and pull out the two other photographs of Anna which he had found at Guy's place.

"Not bad, eh?" Adams asked with an impressed smile. Barnes looked down at them and then back up at Adams. "You know that they were the property of His Majesty's Military Intelligence?"

"Not anymore."

Barnes snatched the photographs out of Adams' hand.

"Hey! Steal your own!"

"How much are you willing to pay to get them back?" the tall Barnes said, holding them up at a safe distance away from Adams.

"What're you asking?"

"How much you got?"

"Curly, I'm just a poor servant of..." And like lightning, he reached out and snatched his photographs back.

"You're under arrest," Barnes told him.

"That's fine by me."

Smiling, they pushed through the main door of the dingy MI5 Headquarters and stepped out into the even gloomier darkness of blackout Britain. A bright moon was visible sometimes between the moving clouds and lit up enough of the small car park at the side of the building for them to make out Adams' blue Morris 10 as they headed towards it.

"I'd say that was a good day's work today Alex. A pint at the Crown to celebrate?"

"What time is it?"

"Ale o'clock."

"In that case... why not."

PARLIAMENT DECIDES

Defence Regulation 18B was Britain's response to a so-called Fifth Column or the 'enemy within' as Major Walker always referred to them. They were those British citizens, led by Sir Oswald Mosley, who was sympathetic to the Nazi cause and who the authorities were convinced would do anything within their power to assist the enemy.

"They're everywhere!" Major Walker said, almost in a fever. He was animated and gesturing and stood up to make his point. "We simply have to do something before this 'enemy within' infiltrates us completely and it's too late." He was with two other men in a grand old office with a mile high ceiling and fine old oak furnishings. He picked up one of the files from the thick oak table in front of him and shook it to make his point. "We have hundreds now... hundreds like these. All over the country, all enemies of the State." He looked at the man sitting in the burgundy leather armchair opposite him for a reaction. It was clear that there had already been some tension between the two.

"We simply can't lock away every single one of these 'hundreds' you say it is... these 'enemies of the State' as you call them... without trial and without--"

Walker jumped in abruptly to interrupt him. "We're at war. MI5's concern isn't with any crimes which anyone has or hasn't committed, but with their potential to do so. With prevention, not punishment, gentlemen. What in God's name do you expect us to do? Wait until someone has caused a massive loss of British lives before we can make an arrest?"

The man in the burgundy armchair who Walker had interrupted remained calm. It was his job to remain calm. He was paid good money to keep calm; he was the Home Secretary. "I can assure you, Major Walker, that the Home Office is as concerned as you, or anyone else about the situation," he said. "But there is also the very sensitive question of the invasion of civil liberties for the Government to consider."

Walker could feel himself breaking out in a cold sweat. He didn't like being argued with, and he was a man you either agreed with or you were wrong. A bead of perspiration began its slow journey down the side of his head. It settled on the strap around his eye patch, then it crept under it and ran further down over his cheek. The Home Secretary noticed it. Walker saw him noticing it, which only made it worse for him. He reached for the glass of water on the desk and took a mouthful.

"That's nonsense, and you know it," Walker countered. "There are currently broadcasts going out daily from Germany giving up-to-the-minute reports about the situation here in Britain. Detailed information from all over the country. Information which could only come from an organised infiltrated fifth column of enemy aliens and fascist sympathisers. Tell me, at what point exactly are you willing to take this issue seriously? Precisely how many people need to die first? Give me your number."

Walker sat back down, and the third man at the table spoke up. He wore a dark blue suit with creases down the front of the trousers sharp enough to cut diamonds. A silk, powder blue handkerchief peeked out over the top of his breast pocket. He possessed the charm and good looks of a matinee idol, with skin so shiny and smooth that it looked like it had just been returned to him from the polishers.

All that was missing was the rose between his teeth. "Mosley and his British Union scum are crawling all over the place," he said in his refined voice. "A list of paid-up members we have obtained from Special Branch puts the figure at almost ten thousand and rising."

"Thank you, Sir," Walker said, grateful for a friend.

"Secretary of State for War is the title these days Robert," the third man said.

Walker pressed on. He was on a roll now.

"We've infiltrated their organisations and their meetings. It should be clear to everyone that they aim to assist the enemy in any way it can. The effect on the morale of the country..."

The Secretary of State for War put up a hand to interrupt the Major. It was a gesture of real authority. "The threat and the dangers of further deteriorating an already fragile national morale..." He stopped, took a breath and lowered his voice. He was about to take them into his confidence. He spoke his next few words delicately and carefully as if they were made from the finest Meissen porcelain. "Within hours gentlemen, further legislation will be in place which will make your jobs - make all our lives - a little easier."

Walker's meeting in Whitehall, and the many others just like it which took place during May 1940, were the backdrop to the implementation of Defence Regulation 18B. And on May the 22nd, with the full support of the new Prime Minister Winston Churchill, and a country becoming increasingly paranoid, Parliament passed the Emergency Powers Act, which gave the Government the kind of totalitarian power appropriate to a country at war. That very same evening the Privy Council passed its amended '18B' Regulation - exactly what Walker and MI5 had been campaigning for - and the following morning, which would be Guy and Anna's wedding day, the roundup began in earnest. Oswald Mosley himself was among the first to be brought in.

***

Job done, Adams and Barnes went for their drink at the Rose And Crown. It was a quiet night, with only a handful of drinkers scattered around the dimly lit pub. They sat with their pints of flat pale ale at a table in the far corner, away from the bar.

"Do you reckon there's anything to Schneider's photographs?" Adams asked. "Besides... you know?"

"Besides the good stuff?" Barnes said and nodded towards Adams' jacket pocket. "I reckon there could be something. He's got it all in there, the airfield, the coastal defences, the harbour, the fortifications around it, how things look in the area, the planes in and out... that's all pretty helpful stuff to someone who can use it I'd say - and plenty of it."

"And the connection to get it to the enemy, who knows what he's already passed on?" Adams added.

"Exactly, we know someone is passing on information to Berlin. The old man's not wrong; there's no harm in keeping them out of the way and making sure they're not allowed to do any damage. Better on the inside than on the outside." He picked up his glass and took a sip of flat ale.

"What about the girl?" asked Adams with more than the usual interest, "you think she's involved?"

"I dunno... How innocent does she look to you?" Barnes said, and they both laughed.

But there was clearly something else on Adams' mind. He twisted his glass around and around on the table in front of him, ''cause I was thinking," he said, "About those Lisbon connections that Schneider has..."

"Speak partner, speak," said Barnes full of curiosity.

As Adams began to talk, the loud shrill sound of a bell pierced the air and a voice bellowed out "Last orders Gentlemen, please." Presumably, the two ladies in the bar that night could carry on ordering and drinking right through to the morning.

***

"I don't need a history lesson Grant," Anna complained the next morning, pacing across the Williamsons' living room as Grant tried his best to explain to her what had happened. "Or any other kind of lesson."

They were alone in the room, and for the last ten minutes, Grant had been playing his usual role of Professor Pennington-Cooper, lecturing Anna about the new Regulation 18B. He'd told her that it meant a detainee had been given the 'straight to jail' card and would stay there indefinitely. There would be no trial. No one would judge the case, and no lawyers would be involved. And there would be no explanation whatsoever as to why a detainee had been locked away or for how long. "Lock 'em up first and think about it later," was how the Manchester Guardian described it. "Lock 'em up first and toss the key in the

Thames" was how Sergeant Dobson would have preferred it.

Grant pulled out a dining chair for himself. He sat down and watched Anna continue to pace the room; tormented, heartbroken, confused, angry, and hating her powerlessness. Neither of them looked like they had slept at all the previous night because neither of them had.

"Come on. Sit down. Tell me where everything is, and I'll pop into the kitchen and make us a pot of tea."

Anna ignored him and carried on pacing the floor angrily. "Indefinite detention without trial... it's not even legal!"

"I'm afraid as of yesterday; it is now," Grant said sadly. "The security services have carte blanche to round up anyone they think might pose a threat. All their so-called 'Enemies of the State'. They-"

Anna rounded on him. Someone had to be the focus of her anger.

"ENEMY OF THE STATE!! THEY THINK GUY IS AN 'ENEMY OF THIS STATE'!?"

Grant reached over for the newspaper lying on the dining table, clutching at straws, trying some way to cheer her. "Listen Anna. It says here, "Even though they've had to find accommodation for so many--"

Anna cut back straight in and shouted over him. "I don't care what it says there! Do they even KNOW what or who the enemy of this state is? Don't they know what they're fighting? Guy's done nothing! NOTHING!!"

Grant continued reading "...and may soon have to find room for thousands more..." finally coming to the point he was trying to make: "The detainees are enjoying conditions far more comfortable than those..."

Anna suddenly stopped her pacing and spun round to stop Grant once more in mid-sentence. She'd already stopped listening to him a few words earlier. There was alarm written all over her tired face. "What does it mean, find room for thousands more?"

Grant knew exactly what it meant, and he was aware it had only made things worse. He stood up and put a consoling arm around her. "Don't worry Anna. Full Internment has its opponents in Government. It won't happen. And Guy has a good lawyer."

FOUR

GUY'S ROOM

A black cloud of busy bluebottles buzzed around the plate of untouched food which lay on Guy's bed while he stood at his cell door and listened to the commotion in the corridor outside. A detainee was being led into to the cell opposite Guy's under protest and had grabbed hold of the door frame with both hands, refusing to let go. One of the two warders stepped back and kicked the detainee's wrist free, and they shoved him inside and slammed the cell door shut behind him. "Bloody traitor! If I had my way I'd have the lot of you lined up against the wall and bloody well shot!" the warder screamed at the top of his voice. As he turned away from the cell door with his colleague, the prisoner inside started to sing.

"God Save Our Gracious King. Long Live Our…"

The warder turned back and kicked the metal door hard with the heel of his boot. "Shut it! Fascist bastard!"

The cell fell silent.

Then from the next cell, a fellow detainee took up from where his neighbour had left off. "...Noble King; God Save Our King" he sang out defiantly. Other prisoners on the cell block joined in. Gradually, one by one, the detainees began to sing the words to 'God Save The King' until soon the entire floor was unified in belting out the National Anthem proudly and patriotically at the top of their voices. The warder stormed off kicking each door he passed. "Scum. I have a son in France!" he bellowed out, hardly audible above the singing.

"Me too!" came a voice from behind one of the doors that he took a wild kick at.

"And I have one working in a French restaurant in Bromley," joked his neighbour in a strong cockney accent.

"To hell with you all!" the warder yelled to the closed cell doors as he stormed off.

The singing echoed eerily around the prison. Inside the cell, an emotional Guy looked out at the night sky from between the bars across his windows. Tears welled up in his eyes. Then the lights went out, and the entire floor was plunged into blackness.

But the singing continued.

And so did the incessant buzzing of the damned flies.

FIVE

ANNA GOES TO JAIL

The next morning at a quarter past nine, the prison corridor echoed to the loud, shrill, pounding of stiletto heels on its cold, concrete floor as Anna marched determinedly in the direction of the prison Governor's office. She was angry, and pretty soon someone was going to hear about it. She stormed straight past the surprised secretary sitting in the small outer office, knocked on the Governor's door, and entered without waiting to be asked. Then rapid fire and barely pausing for breath she let loose on the Governor.

"Vieti is my name. I should be called Schneider, but that's another story entirely. I've come here to see Guy Schneider, the man who should be my husband, but I have been stopped from doing so. Despite it being official visiting hours, I want to know why?"

The Governor looked like he'd been cast from the hardest bell metal. He peered at Anna from over the rim his reading glasses.

"Schneider?"

"You probably have him here under the German name in his passport, 'Gerhard'. Top Nazi spy. Hitler's right-hand man." Anna went on, still a lightning fast cocktail of sarcasm and anger, but trying hard to control herself - because expressing yourself at moments like this was one thing, doing it in a language which isn't your own and is still 'foreign' is another matter entirely. She kicked on relentlessly, "but whatever you have him under, and whatever you have him in here for, I've come here to see him and I won't leave until I have done so."

The Governor calmly removed his reading glasses and placed them on the desk in front of him. He could have been either angry or intimidated by something like Anna's bold intrusion into his own little world - the one which lay within the confines of his four office walls - but it was all meat and drink to a man who had seen and heard scenes like this a thousand times before.

"If he's being detained as an 18B prisoner..."

"He's no prisoner. No criminal. And certainly has no business in here."

"I'm sorry, madam, Home Office regulations state that detainees are allowed no visits in the first ten days, except for legal representation."

"What is it? My English or your ears? I said I want to see my fiancé and I'm staying until I do."

The Governor took out an engraved silver fob watch from his waistcoat pocket, flicked the lid and glanced at the time. Anna's two minutes were up, and his patience had been exhausted. He pressed a button on his desk.

"If you want to stay, we have a women's wing. If you'd like me to arrange for you to be locked up too?" There was a short, silent stand-off while Anna took in the implications of what the Governor had said. "Now if you'll permit me, I have important business to attend to."

The Governor's secretary knocked on the office door and tottered in on her heels. They weren't as high or as menacing as Anna's, but they were pretty impressive nonetheless. She looked over at her boss for instructions. The Governor turned back to Anna. "Mrs Jones will see you out."

"I don't think she will."

Bloodied but unbowed, Anna turned on her heel and stormed straight past the Governor's bemused secretary and of out of the office.

***

Before Anna had come to Britain - before she'd met Guy one rainy April day in 1938 when he had come to Stansfield Street Hospital to take photographs for the hospital yearbook - there had been one serious relationship back in Germany. Anna and Ferdinand Constantin were together for nine months. Ferdinand worked as a cook in one of Hamburg's better hotels, he was also a very talented musician and played the trumpet in a local orchestra. He was a good player. A passionate player. All hot lips and nimble fingers. Just like Anna, Ferdinand Constantin had Romani roots, and they had first met at a family wedding. One day Ferdinand went missing. Anna hadn't seen him all weekend, and he hadn't been home for three days, and when he didn't turn up for work on a Monday morning his parents went to the police. "I'm sorry," the Police told Ferdinand's father, "your son was arrested on Friday for drunk and disorderly behaviour and hung himself in his cell on Saturday."

There was no postmortem, with no inquiry. It was how it was. Except Ferdinand Constantin never touched a drop of alcohol in his entire, short life and he never raised a fist in anger. When he was found dead in his cell, he had bruises all over his face and a fractured skull, "It happened in the fight that we had to break up," was the police's explanation. The Constantins engaged a lawyer, but being tribal they went to a Romani lawyer. "Nothing can be done," the lawyer told them after he'd made his enquiries with the local judiciary, and the reasoning "it was how it was" also became his explanation of events. No one ever found out what happened to Ferdinand Constantin. No-one ever found out whether he'd become a police punch bag or whether some local Nazi thugs had used him for some training practice. All Anna and the Constantin family knew was that "it was how it was," which was just a fairy tale that they'd been told. So for Anna, being arrested meant something else. It came with no guarantees, it meant you were gone, and God only knows if you'd ever be coming back.

That was "how it was" in Nazi Germany.

SIX

THE ATTACK

In Upper Bexton High Street, the place Anna should now have been calling 'home,' the wailing air raid sirens fell silent and left an eerie stillness hanging over the deserted street. The residents of Upper Bexton, just like those across the rest of London, had crowded into their corrugated iron, hastily installed Anderson shelters or their local school halls or railway stations in their pyjamas and slippers, or dressing gowns, and overcoats. They sat side by side and knitted or sipped cups of tea, they talked and joked and fed babies, and sometimes they sang or argued - but not too much, because if Hitler's bombs were good for one thing it was bringing the people of Britain together. And they pissed into buckets and they prayed like they had never prayed before, especially later in 1940 when the Blitz finally came to London and those sirens sounded and they could hear and feel the thunderous booms of the bombs exploding above them or close by them. But that early June night there had been no bombs, only a peaceful night sky and an uncanny silence. After the all clear had been sounded at ten to midnight, Anna and Jane finally emerged from the bowels of the hospital where they'd taken refuge and made their way home.

At the same time, in Upper Bexton's High Street, three youths emerged out of the darkness and approached Guy's shop. They began to shout anti-German obscenities, although why they would do that to any empty shop only they knew. One of the teenagers picked up a piece of concrete which had been chipped away from the gutter and hurled it at the shop window. The window shattered. Another youth did the same, this time straight through the upstairs window that the glaziers had repaired. A hail of stones and insults followed. The tallest of the three took a kick at the shop door, then another. The lock broke and the door swung open. They hadn't counted on this, they'd only been game for a little mischief disguised as vented feelings. They stood and looked at each other, surprised that they were now at liberty to take what they wanted from the unoccupied shop. They moved inside and began to grab cameras from the shelves.

The tall one was pushing a small but expensive cine camera inside his jacket when he heard the distant sound of a whistle from somewhere down the street. "Coppers!" he called out to his pals in an urgent half-whisper, half-shout. They stopped their looting and ran out of the shop with armfuls of cameras and photography equipment and sprinted down the street.

Fifty yards away, an aging ARP warden with a tin hat, respirator and an ARP armband blew his whistle like crazy and tried to run after them, but fifty years and fifty yards was way too much for him to make up. As the three youths ran off they screamed anti-German abuse back at him and branded him a "Nazi lover" - as if it somehow justified what they'd just done.

JOHN TIMNEY

Platform two at Upper Bexton's small, picturesque railway station was crowded. Children with signs hung around their necks were being helped onto a train by distraught mothers. It was evacuation day in Bexton and distressed parents were being separated from distressed children for who knew how long. "All aboard for the ten-twenty to London Waterloo," the station master called out - which was the call for Anna's train standing on platform one. Anna jumped on board, the doors slammed, a whistle blew, and a huge cloud of steam blew up from the underbelly of the train as its steel wheels slowly started turning.

At Waterloo, she took two Underground trains to Bank, and a full hour after she had set off she pushed her way out of the crowded station, just a tiny figure among hundreds, and then off up Cheapside. Halfway up the street, she stopped at a building with a name plate which read "Timney, Budgen, Waggott, Solicitors" and went inside.

John Timney was sixty-two years old. He was short - shorter than Anna - and had hair which would once have been red-blond but was now getting thinner and had faded to grey over the years. He wore thin horn-rimmed glasses and a conservative but smart black double-breasted suit. John Timney was elegant. He was a gentleman, and when he spoke in that soft voice of his you knew it was the voice of reason. He was indeed the calming influence and safe port of call in the eye of Anna's storm. He put down the phone and looked across his desk towards Anna. He was disappointed, but there was no way he would let her see or know it.

"The Prison Governor was correct Miss Schneider."

"Vieti,'' Anna corrected him.

"'Vieti, sorry," Timney smiled at her and carried on. "Damned Government rules I'm afraid, but he assures me that Mr Schneider has been separated from other criminals and is being afforded excellent living conditions and extra privileges, and he has free access to Council." Then he sat back in his leather chair took a breath. "And if you believe all that, Miss..." He stopped, suddenly unsure what to call her. "You can stay with Schneider if you like?"

Anna thought about it. She liked the idea. And she liked the kind-faced John Timney. "Vieti is fine," was what she said.

"If you believe in all that Miss Vieti, you'll also believe in the idea that justice and human freedoms can survive in times like these."

***

Guy stood at his barred cell window and peered out into the moonlit, upside-down world outside. Behind him, a pot full of piss stood in one corner, no one had come to take it away. The cells were cold, they stank, the mattresses were like beds of nails. Rusty nails. There were damp patches all over the cell walls and the plaster had peeled away everywhere. Someone had scratched the words "Mitch + Jimmy" into the wall under the flaked plaster and next to that, almost as an afterthought, they had drawn a small heart. Guy wondered who Mitch was. Bed bugs had taken up residence, the cockroach which had greeted him on his first day had returned and it had brought along many friends. The jails were full now and filling further by the day, with detainees as well as the cockroaches. Staunch fascists had been put in with staunch communists and, best of all, Jew haters alongside Jews. 'Excellent conditions'? 'Wonderful freedoms'? Sure Mr Governor. If paradise was only half as nice. I'm a very lucky man. I'm so grateful to you. And all because

96

of... because of what exactly, Guy asked himself time and time again. What have I done wrong? Why am I in this God forsaken place? What kind of evil are these bars protecting the world outside from? "That's how it is with 18B," John Timney had told Anna. "They don't tell you why and they don't tell you how long. They don't tell you anything."

Guy now had a new cell mate, who lay curled up on his mattress in a foetus-like position, rocking uncontrollably back and forth, back and forth the whole day and all night, with his hands covering his ears. His World War One veteran's medals were pinned to his chest and they were covered with food and vomit stains. He stared off wide-eyed into nothing, truly out of it - the tragic victim of shell shock. He just lay there and let out one mad scream after another, which sliced right through Guy and made him jump every time. Guy had no idea why the veteran had been detained. He didn't talk. Guy just left him alone and tried to imagine that he was on his own in the room, and let his mind turn one crazy circle after another.

Then there was the blackbird which came and perched on the window ledge outside the cell. Guy stood and watched it peck away at something it had carried there to eat. "Whatever it is, it'll be better than what we get" Guy thought. Then the blackbird stopped and looked into the cell directly at Guy, and for a moment they shared a staring contest. The Blackbird and the Prisoner. Eyeball to eyeball, the first one to break dies. Then the bird turned, shook its wings a little and, almost as if it was provoking him - "here, just look what I can do" - it took off. As Guy watched it fly away, for the first time in his life he wished he was a bird. In fact, he wished he was anything at all, just not 'Guy Schneider, Felon,' but a bird would be nice. Fly away, Guy. Up, Up, oblivious to the crap of the world. No locks, no keys or walls to keep you inside Mr Jailbird. Someone should write a song about you one day, Guy thought. "Jailbird fly; into the light of the dark black night."

***

Anna and Jane took the number twelve bus and got off at the stop at the very end of the park, just as they did every working morning, and made their way up Cresswell Road. A Police van with its bell ringing raced past them as they walked. Someone had decided to kill someone else very early that day.

"How soon can you visit him?" Jane asked.

"Not for another six days, but the lawyer said he'll try and get in to see him tomorrow or on Thursday."

"Is there a chance he can get Guy out? I mean... what's he supposed to have done?"

"We still don't know."

"But they can't just say nothing at all. You can't just lock someone away without a reason."

There was nothing Anna could say to that. They walked on in silence, with their minds racing. A weather-beaten old man in an old, flat cap the shape and colour of a large cow pat and an even older, tattered and torn rain-coat which had been soaked in blood and whisky greeted them with a cheery 'Good Morning' and a smile which showed off his only tooth. Then he took out the morning's newspaper which he'd found over at the railway station, spread it out on a bench, and lay down on it to sleep the morning away. The headline at the top of the newspaper that day was 'German Army at the Channel.' The sub-headline read 'British Forces Forced To Retreat.' The old man didn't care about any of that. It was only a blanket to him, precious because it would protect him from the early morning cold of the hard, wooden bench. Anna and Jane turned the corner into Stansfield Street and up towards the Hospital. Jane opened her mouth to say something. Then she hesitated. Do I trust myself to say this? Finally, she knew it was something she had to ask.

"What- what if Guy actually has done something?"

Anna thought about this for the very first time while they walked in the direction of the hospital.

"I've..." Anna started to say but stopped dead: walk-ing as well as talking. Her answer was left suspended in the cool morning air as they stood and looked in horror towards the main hospital entrance. The police van which had sped past them was standing outside the hospital with its rear doors open. Next to it, propped up against the hos-pital's outer railings, were two black push-bikes. From thirty yards away Anna and Jane watched the Professor shuffle sadly out of the main hospital gates and towards the police van, flanked by two uniformed officers. A handful of people had stopped to watch the action. Anna dropped her bag and set off at a frantic sprint, Jane followed her. They reached the van just as its doors were closed on them, and on the poor old Professor inside. One of the policemen banged his fist on the side of the van and shouted to the driver up front. "Okay, take this scum off to jail." Then he jumped on his bike as the van pulled away. Anna stood distraught, frozen to the spot. Jane reached out and grabbed hold of the policeman's sleeve and stopped him from setting off, she pleaded with him furiously.

"He's no enemy. He came here to help us! To help everyone!"

The officer said nothing. He pulled free from Jane's grasp and took off on his bike. The second policeman took his own bike from where he'd left it, propped up against the railings, turned and said grimly to Jane "Orders, Miss." Then he set off too.

From the van's small rear door window, the Professor looked back sadly at Anna. Her heart was breaking, she was watching another big part of her soul slip away. She was distressed for him and afraid for herself. As she watched the van disappear around the corner, Rosenbach could almost read her thoughts, "How long before it's me?" With tears falling, she turned and ran off down the street in the direction from which she'd come, picked up the bag which she'd dropped, and kept right on running -

right back up the street towards Cresswell Road. "To hell with them all!" Anna yelled out loud, while the voice inside her was screaming out to no one but herself 'He was here to heal! He was here to help! Why can't we all be judged on who we are and what we do?'

In the spring of 1940, such thoughts were worthless.

EIGHT

ANNA LEAVES

Israel Rosenbach, like Anna, had been categorized by the Home Office as a class C enemy alien, which meant that they'd been deemed by the authorities to be harmless and posed no danger to the British war effort. They were therefore left to enjoy their liberty. Until that is, a Government order was made to detain all German and Austrian males over the age of sixteen and under the age of seventy, meaning that five short weeks later the Professor would have to celebrate his seventieth birthday in a British prison. The majority of the popular newspapers had become increasingly xenophobic - especially with the British Army on the run and about to get its nose badly bloodied at Dunkirk - so the press warmly welcomed the decision to take more enemy nationals off the streets, despite the reality that very many of them, like Anna and Professor Rosenbach, were refugees who'd fled to Britain to escape persecution by the Nazis and were themselves anti-fascist and hostile in the extreme to the German ideology. "Every German is a German first and an ideologist afterwards" was what the Daily Mail wrote. Or as one northern newspaper headline put it more bluntly, 'Lock 'Em Up.' It was the wisest thing - no, the only thing - to do in the circumstances they reasoned. No one cared that most of the so called enemy aliens in Britain came carrying weight, or how deep their scars were. No one considered the contributions they were making to the society which they were being taken out of, no one cared that brothers or mothers. And in Anna's case a father, three aunts, six cousins and two uncles had been taken and worked to death in a camp; or murdered in a gas chamber or experimented on and had the teeth pulled out of their head and the gold pulled out of their teeth or their eyeballs sliced open or their babies cut up or their organs removed or their bones transplanted. And how about this Mister Emil Vieti, we'll do it for you without an anaesthetic. They had electrodes attached to their genitals and were wired up to a machine to see how much pain they could take before they finally gave up and died. They were boiled and frozen; they were gassed and burned, poisoned and tortured. They were playthings and it all would have been Anna's fate too had she not got out in time with the Professor. But the establishment was nervous, it was on edge and shaking in its boots. Even the War Cabinet themselves concluded that "Alien refugees are a most dangerous source of subversive activity and the numbers allowed in to Britain must be cut and kept under closest surveillance." Give them a chance to sabotage things and they'll take it was the sentiment, although there wasn't one proven case of any German or Austrian committing any act which was hostile to the British war effort, like Guy, the Professor was now gone. Except in Rosenbach's case, he knew why he had been detained. Guy didn't. Not yet, anyway.

***

Anna and Jane were up in Anna's bedroom packing the last of Anna's clothes into an enormous, battered old red suitcase – the one that she'd moved to England with three years earlier.

"They told me I'll be starting on ward eight tomorrow morning," Anna said.

"On Emergency?" asked Jane.

Anna nodded.

"In the office. The Ward Sister has been pleading for extra staff for weeks."

"They've kept me in Research. With Professor de Villiers."

"That's good." Anna, still hurting, stopped and looked at Jane for an emotional moment. "I knew I'd be moving out... But I never dreamed it would be like this."

104

Jane held Anna's sad look. It was a heartbreaking moment between two close friends about to go their separate ways. "I'm going to miss you," she told Anna. Then she moved towards her and held on tight, until Anna, almost in tears, pulled away to distract herself in her packing. "At least you'll be safer and closer to the prison," Jane said to her. She had picked up the ruined photograph of Anna and Guy at the beach, the one that the perfume had faded, and was about to drop it into Anna's case.

"Leave it," Anna told her. "I'll replace it from Guy's. I know where he put all the originals." Then she added, a little nervously, "I have to pick up some things from there anyway."

Jane knew that the idea of Anna returning to the scene of the two attacks scared her. "I'm going with you," she said and put the photograph back down on the dressing table.

When they got to Guy's, Anna let herself in through the back door. The glazers had already been back and replaced the smashed shop windows, and a thick metal bar had also been extended across the front door to add extra protection, even though the shop had been cleared out and there was nothing of any value left in it to take.

They went upstairs to the flat and into the back room, where Jane stood and watched Anna rake through Guy's photographs - nervously, quickly, aware that at any moment someone could come in and find her there - in fact, in exactly the same way that Adams had done some weeks earlier. The packets were neatly filed in chronological order; Guy was that sort of ordered person. He was part German after all. Anna looked confused that she wasn't able to find what she'd come for. "I just don't understand it," she said, "I watched him put the packet here."

She quickened her search. Anna felt anxious and uncomfortable to be there, Jane did too. They both jumped when they heard the front door bell ring. It was accompanied by a loud knock. Anna and Jane froze and locked eyes; they've come back! They know we're in here and they've come to get us! Anna thought. They didn't dare to move. The bell rang again. The caller knocked again. Neither of the two girls even dared to breathe. Then they heard the sound of something being pushed through the letter box downstairs and the sound of someone walking away. Anna crept downstairs while Jane went to the window, the old ARP warden was heading off up the High Street. He had called to confirm that the flat was currently unoccupied. Those air raid lists of his had to be kept up-to-date. Anna raced back upstairs to the flat and continued to rake through the photographs, even more hastily now.

**

Anna struggled with her big red suitcase and another bulging, heavy leather bag along a busy Knightsbridge street, with its sea of anonymous faces. Her head was down, she looked so lost, so alone, and oblivious to the person who ran straight into her, sending her suitcase flying out of her hand and onto the wide pavement. Anna turned and for a split, inert, frightening moment, she was staring straight into the face of 'the enemy.' Two soldiers in uniform stared right back at her. One of them apologised politely, bent down, picked up her case, and held it out for her.

"That's a heavy case you've got there 'mam, can I help you with it?"

But all Anna could do was shake her head and grab hold of her bags. She tried to summon up an awkward "thank you" but it didn't really happen. Then she turned and with her head back down again, she pressed on down the street with only her own shadow for company, passing a newspaper stand where the seller was shouting out the headline from the paper that he was holding up, as if he needed to prove that he was shouting the truth and nothing but the truth. "Read all about it. German and Austrian men in the latest round up." His words sliced deep into an already wounded Anna, who was now looking at the city streets of the country that she loved through the distorting lens of fear.

Five minutes later she was standing outside of the Pennington-Coopers' impressive new home in Rowlandsgill Gate with a faraway expression on her face. She carried her heavy bags up the three outside steps of the fine Victorian town house and then stood for a moment to catch her breath. She looked up at the white stucco-fronted terraced building with its long French windows and its front balcony with the ornate wrought iron railings, and then turned and took in the pretty garden square which ran right down the middle of the quiet road. Its roses and rhododendrons and pretty white hydrangea were already in glorious full bloom. It was all quintessentially English. Grant and Claire have certainly bought well, she was just thinking to herself when the front door swung open. Claire had been expecting her. She welcomed her inside with a warm smile and held out a helping hand to take her heavy red case from her.

Anna's new bedroom was a spacious, high ceilinged room on the top floor. Its furniture was in keeping with the grand facade of the house. Classic and stylish. At least for someone who likes that sort of thing. It had a marble corner fireplace with a black limestone hearth, and a freshly polished herringbone parquet floor you could slide for miles on. Each wall in the room had several large prints of paintings hanging from its high picture rails in a variety of styles and artists from Monet and Pissarro close to the door, back through Manet, then Raphael and finally to the old Dutch masters hanging at the other side of the door. It was almost like a journey around the room from the present into the past and from the light into darkness. An easel with an unfinished landscape painting stood in one corner. It might have been an image of the Tuscan countryside, but it really wasn't so good nor the image clear enough to know with any certainty, and its perspectives and proportions somehow weren't quite right. The long French windows looked out over the street and the picturesque little garden-park opposite. The Pennington-Coopers had only moved into the place two months earlier, but Claire had already made it feel homely. They had bought it with money that Claire had inherited from her wealthy parents, and also from the royalties which Grant had earned and saved from the art books which he'd had published.

Whilst Anna was unpacking her suitcase, Claire fussed about with towels and blankets, trying her best to make Anna feel at home. "The guest bathroom is right there across the hall. I'll get Grant to take that away," she said, looking over towards the easel with the 'maybe Tuscany' painting in the corner, "It's one of his many abandoned efforts at... well, not greatness, 'ordinariness' would be more appropriate. Grant's talent lies in explaining art, not in doing it."

"It's okay, he can leave it there. The room's big enough to take us both. I'm just so grateful to the two of you for letting me stay here until things get sorted out" she said, clearly touched by Claire's generosity.

"After what happened, we're only too glad we can help," Claire said with a mix of anger and dismay. "But you must be exhausted. I'm sure you'll want a little time to yourself." She smiled sympathetically at Anna then turned and left the room.

As Anna watched Claire close the door behind her, some "time to herself" looked like the very last thing in her sad and chaotic world that she wanted. She slumped down onto the bed looking as lost and lonely as Guy had done in his own prison cell. She felt just as trapped as he had done. She looked up and the ceiling seemed to be coming down on her, the walls began to close in. The room was becoming smaller and smaller. It was crushing her. She couldn't breathe, she shut her eyes.

She opened them again in Hamburg. She was five years old and in a crammed, cramped room which stank that day of old fish. It was a living room, bedroom and dining room all in one to the Vieti family. The five-year old Anna sat at the table with her mother and father. Lena Vieti was now several pounds over her best fighting weight and her once stunning good looks had started to give way to deep lines and a blotched skin and tired, hooded eyes and puffed cheeks, her dancer's figure was now only a dream she once had. It was evening. An empty bottle of cheap Schnapps stood in the middle of the table, Anna's father was drunk from it. He was slouched to one side on his chair. Anna pushed her half eaten plate of repellent fish slop masquerading as human food away from her, she wasn't going to touch that.

Her mother shoved it angrily back in front of her, "Eat it! And you'll finish it too!" She picked up a thick leather belt from the floor next to her and waved it at Anna; a forewarning of what to expect if she made the wrong decision. Anna defiantly pushed her plate away again.

"I'm not hungry."

Anna's mother's temper exploded. Anna covered her head from the blows which she knew would follow.

A moment later in the yard at the back of the building, a thick wooden door opened on a small, pitch black concrete hole not much bigger than a dog kennel. Anna was slapped across the face and flung with venom into the hole. She landed with a hard thump on the concrete floor, the door slammed shut behind her, plunging her into blackness. She heard the key turn in the lock and her mother's angry voice shout at her from outside, "we'll see how you manage without food." But as she turned away from the door, there was a wicked smile on Anna's mother's face.

Inside, Anna screamed and kicked at the thick door. The back of her hands bled from punching at it. Her right ear bled from the belt buckle, her face stung from the slap, her heart was torn into pieces. Anna's kicking and banging and screaming were all in vain.

***

There's an old Chinese proverb: "Hit your wife every day. Even if you don't know why, she will." Even that sick and twisted perverted logic didn't apply here. Anna's mother loved the power she held over her only daughter, she took pleasure in the sordid beatings and she relished the sight of Anna flying into her black hole from hell. There was a sadistic smile on her face when she heard Anna's screams and her futile kicks at the door. The smile got even wider when the screaming and kicking stopped because Lena Vieti knew then that she had won. What she'd won she wouldn't have been able to define but Lane knew it felt oh-so-good, and it was merciless. She took joy in locking up and scaring to death her only child, she delighted in cultivating Anna's nightmares. It was torture, physical, emotional, and psychological. It was meant to break her spirit. More often than not, Anna would be her victim for no other reason than her mother 'felt like it.' Put it half down to the drink if you like, but only half. The other half was Frau Vieti alone. She needed to project and unload her own anger and built up frustration and yes, her self-hatred on something or someone, and Anna became that outlet. Anna represented youth and vitality, optimism and innocence, and all the things that her mother had lost along the way and knew wouldn't be coming back. It was a toxic brew of the fiercest jealousy, of thwarted ambition, of bad decisions taken and wrong roads travelled - and the realisation that so much of it was self inflicted - mixed in together with a raging and insatiable lust for retribution. She was purging herself of her sins and losses by inflict-ing pain on someone else, just as she relished telling her husband Emil about her latest sexual conquests. It was invariably with any old tramp that she would drag in off the street, but when she told it, her tramp became a prince. I should have been a star she told herself, I should have danced myself across the world's great stages. I should be living in luxury. It's all Anna's fault. WHACK! And I also married a gypsy. WHACK again and get in that hole, you pathetic little bitch! And the remarkable thing, Anna realised much later, was that despite all the cruelty which her mother had inflicted on her, it hadn't made Anna hate her mother more, it had only made Anna love herself less. Why, Anna would ask herself, am I so bad that I can never win her approval?

Eight hours after she'd been tossed into her black hole bunker, the darkness which had seemed infinite finally became light. A single shaft of sunlight picked out Anna - her anger long spent - lying shivering on the damp concrete in a pool of her own urine. She held her stomach and cried out to no one "Why Mama? What have I done to deserve this?"

**

Anna only managed to survive those torturous hours in the cellar by inventing a series of mind games. She counted up as far as she could - once to eight hundred and eighty-eight - and then all the way back again to zero, picturing each number as it appeared in her head. She would also go right through the alphabet thinking of names that you can give to cats. She recalled the surnames of all the children in her class and the names of the streets where each one lived. After that, she recited to herself the fairy tales and fables which they had read in school. She tried to remember only the happy ones - the ones which she liked the best such as "Hans Im Glück" about a young boy who starts out with a big golden nugget only to lose it and finally end up with nothing, except for the realization that you don't need much in this world, and certainly not a gold nugget to find true happiness. But it was all the bad ones and the sad ones which forced their way into her head, like the tale about the kind old fox who sacrifices himself in order to save the frightened young rabbit from the hounds, or the one where the wicked witch decides to boil her illegitimate daughter and feed her to the wolves. It was only those little meisterwerks of mental gymnastics which got her through the night – what she would later call her "Sturmflutwehr" – her very own flood barrier which she built up around herself for protection in the same way that they used to put up their makeshift barriers of sand bags back in Hamburg each year when the river Elbe broke its banks and threatened to flood the city. Anna's Sturmflutwehr was what kept her from going under, but only until the point where the pain returned, as it always did - the aching little heart, the brittle body; and always the vision of her mother's wretched violence.

"Why Mama?" Anna cried out in the blackness and screamed into the abyss. "Who am I that you hate me so much?"

'Why do they hate me?' 'Who am I?'... Anna was asking the very same questions all over again more than twenty years later in the stillness of her new room at the Pennington-Coopers.

NINE

WHO WAS ANNA VIETI AND WHY DID THEY HATE HER SO MUCH?

Anna Vieti was born in Hamburg in 1914, only days before the curtain went up for the opening act of 'World War One,' the money spinning prequel set in France. Anna was German, her mother was German, and her father Emil was also German. Emil's grandparents had moved to Germany from an old, faraway land and Anna's father was therefore classified as a gypsy just like them, which made Anna a gypsy too. She'd never travelled, never sold clothes peg or read a tea leaf, never ridden bareback on a white wild pony or seen the inside of a tent or a caravan. But she was a gypsy.

How could she deny it with those sexy, sultry dark looks and those raven-black curls which she'd inherited from both parents? Then there was her Ahnenpass of course - the official record of an individual's origins. Anna's father had run a theatre in Hamburg where her mother came to work as a dancer. Boy meets girl? Not really. Randy-old-boss-who-wants-to-screw-his-way-down-the-chorus-line meets pretty young thing, ambitious enough to believe that a night or two with the head honcho might smooth her way on to the next bigger and better job... possibly in his place, but preferably somewhere else. Except that little Anna came along. In 1921 they closed the theatre and the Vietis really did have to become gypsies for a while as Emil took the family from Hamburg to Kiel, to Bremen and then back to Hamburg - looking for, finding, and then losing again whatever work he could find. The last job he ever had was down at the harbour in Hamburg, loading the barges before they set off on their journey up the river Elbe.

With the rise of National Socialism, Emil Vieti graduated from unemployed to unemployable but that was no problem; he'd simply drink his depression away, just like his wife had done. Drink and screw around. And why not? Back then the Vietis drank like fish and they screwed around like rabbits and they fought like cats with poor little Anna caught in the crossfire; a sort of human collateral damage. Several times she'd tried to run away, only to get dragged back by her mother and brutally beaten.

'Why?' Anna thought. My mother doesn't even like me, she can't even stand being anywhere near me. What perverse existence this is? Why Mama?" Anna would plead with her mother through her tears. "Why am I always hit and kicked and thrown into that pitch-black hell hole?" WHACK! was the answer. Then WHACK! again. The great thing about being an only child was that she never had to share anything with anyone. The pain was hers and hers alone.

Then on the day that Anna turned thirteen, her aunt Marlies came and took Anna back home to live with her. You'd think that Anna's mother would have flown into a rage when she saw her daughter being taken away from her, that she would have wanted to hit out and hurt someone. The sad truth was that she couldn't possibly have cared less, she didn't even miss her. Losing a daughter simply wasn't the same as losing her looks, her figure, or her glorious, golden future. She had taunted Anna mercilessly about how she wanted to give her away as soon as she was born, a baby left abandoned on the hospital steps. An unwanted infant dumped in a basket outside the local orphanage, and she'd tell her that it was only her father who had stopped that from happening.

"I should have aborted you!" she would scream in her very blackest moods, like the morning she flew into a rage and picked up one of her husband's heavy winter boots and hurled it clean through the living room window and out into the yard and the snow came in and everyone froze for a week until Anna's father was sober enough to repair it.

Marlies was Anna's mother's older sister and the polar opposite of the one time sexy but now permanently drunk and degenerate dancer who would sleep with a garden gnome if there was no one else around to screw with. Marlies was the 'anti-Lena' who Anna's mother hated with a passion, although it was Marlies who had generously given Lena a place to live when Anna's mother first came to the big city to work. She was a widow, after the love of her life, Heinrich Stadelmann, had been declared missing in action in 1916, and although Marlies knew that she was destined to spend the rest of her life lonely and forever in mourning, she nevertheless prayed and dreamed and hoped beyond hope that one day there would be a knock on her door and when she went to answer it she would find Heinrich standing there smiling and they would pick up their perfect life together once again. The truth was that Marlies needed someone to fill the big, fat, lonely void in her life and the bottomless hole in her heart every bit as desperately as Anna needed a savior and a mentor. In that respect, you could say Anna and Marlies was a marriage made in heaven.

Before her aunt Marlies came for her and gave her a new home, Anna had lived her short life in the emotional, spiritual and even physical darkness in which her mother had imprisoned her so she began to look around her for clues - for lights to show up her path through life, for a road map to guide her. She studied how to dress, what to read, how to act, how to behave towards those around her. She vowed to work hard at trying to become the opposite of what she had known. It was Marlies who taught Anna the merits of discipline, order, education and respect for others. She drilled into her the fact that nothing which had happened to her had been Anna's fault, and crucially for someone of 'ethnicity,' that she should never allow other people's perceptions of her to become Anna's own perception of herself.

"Your life has dignity, Anna. You have worth. Everyone's place here has value." She instilled in Anna the concept of love over hate and the power of a book over the power of a bottle. "Learn, learn and never stop learning Anna." Marlies told her. Substitute, or add if you will, the word 'love' for 'learn' and there was Anna's mantra right there. Learn and love, work hard and you'll get your rewards. "And don't wait around for fate to determine your destiny" Anna heard regularly. "Be bold." She learned from Marlies and her teachers and later from the Professor when she went to work for him. Let the haters hate, Anna thought. I'm ready.

Anna was always close to her father. In his kinder, more sober moments he had always been the 'love' to her mother's 'hate' but by the time Anna had gone to live with her aunt Marlies, her father was just drifting. Just another broken soul washed up on the rocks of fascism. The Vietis were divorced at the end of 1936 and two and a half years later, Emil was among a group of 'ethnics' rounded up and taken for a train ride to oblivion. Anna's cousin Emma and the rest of the Vieti family were also on that same train. When Anna's mother heard that her husband had been taken away, all she felt was relief.

Lena Vieti died a year later. She was having sex in the back seat of a car with the City's deputy Registrar when the car slipped its brake and rolled backwards over a cliff and onto the rocks two hundred feet below. They both died instantly and with their pants down. This at least would have pleased Lena Vieti and was certainly how she would have wanted to bow out. Whether a smile was still on her face when she died remained unknown.

TEN

THE BROTHER

Anna wound her way through the fine streets of Knightsbridge to the Underground station. Next to the entrance an old, olive skinned organ grinder had set up shop and was grinding out "Yes We Have No Bananas." He had attached a big sign to the side of his barrel organ which read, "I'am Britich and the monky is from Afrika."

"Good Morning pretty Miss," the organ grinder said as Anna passed. Anna took out a halfpenny from her purse and dropped it into his hat. She knew hardship.

"Thanks you Miss," the organ grinder said and took a nut out of his pocket, handed it to his 'monky,' and the monkey clapped for Anna. She smiled. Then she disappeared inside the Tube Station and again took the train to

Bank and then walked the two hundred yards up Cheapside, passing men in bowler hats and women in their summer dresses, and into John Timney's chambers.

"I saw Mr Schneider yesterday," the lawyer told her as his secretary poured a cup of tea for them both. He pushed a small plate of plain biscuits across the desk and invited Anna to take one. She did. In times of rationing, a free biscuit was like mining gold.

"Thank you. How is he?"

The lawyer took off his glasses, rubbed at his tired eyes and made one of those 'not good, not bad' gestures with his hand, but in a way that Anna could sense meant 'not too good.'

"What's wrong with him?"

"He's in prison is what's wrong with him. And the not knowing."

"Will you be able to get him out?"

John Timney had to smile at her naivety. "The only way out of a Detention Order under 18B is by appealing, and then going in front of the Advisory Committee."

"Have you appealed?"

John Timney nodded, "we will."

"How does it work?"

Timney put his glasses back on. "The detainee has to go before the Committee. There are usually three, maybe four members who sit and hear each case. They'll ask Mr Schneider their questions, and then they'll make their decision. They'll have a report from MI5 laying out the

122

reasons for the detention... but the detainees themselves won't be given any information. I'm-"

"What?" Anna jumped in. "They still won't tell Guy anything at all?"

"That's the way it is I'm afraid. I'm not allowed to represent Mr Schneider. He'll be in there alone. He has to go in and persuade them that he's absolutely no threat."

Anna was indignant. "Of course he isn't a threat."

"I know that but I think MI5 are suspicious of his Lisbon connection."

"His what?"

"His brother there."

Anna had absolutely no idea what the lawyer was talking about. "Guy has no brother."

"In the German Embassy?"

John Timney looked across the desk for some form of recognition from her. She must surely know something about the brother in Lisbon? Anna fell silent, she looked vague, vacant. John Timney was suddenly aware that this had become awkward. "I'm sure Mr Schneider will be able to explain it all to you himself." Then he tried his best to lift her. "It won't be long now before you're allowed to see him."

Anna wasn't listening, she was distracted, full of her own doubts and suspicions. "Just what did they tell you?" she asked.

"Nothing. As I said, that's the way it is with Detention. Neither the detainee nor Council are told anything. We can only make assumptions from the questions that he's been asked. I only know what Mr Schneider has told me."

"And they asked about this... this brother?"

"Yes."

"Guy told you this himself?"

The lawyer gave Anna her answer without saying a word. Anna shook her head, understanding nothing anymore. John Timney could see her distress. With his warmest, most reassuring smile, he reached over and gave Anna's arm a reassuring squeeze. "Don't worry; it will all work out fine."

ELEVEN

ANNA RETURNS TO PRISON

Two days later, Anna sat opposite Guy at a wooden table in the prison's small visitor's room. A few feet away from them, at another table, an older couple sat with nothing to say to each other. Maybe they were comfortable that way. Or maybe they'd had nothing to say to each other for years. The male detainee just sat and fingered his thick grey beard and looked at his wife to say something but she just looked down at her feet. Or over at the two hefty prison warders who stood next to the door, keeping their watch. Guy looked tired and drawn. Anna tried hard to hide her thoughts; that the man across the table from her truly is suffering badly from his incarceration.

"Are you getting enough to eat? Do they allow you to have exercise?"

Guy shrugged his shoulders. The question was as irrelevant as any answer he could give.

"Jane's cousin has cleared the shop and boarded it up for now, and changed the name... to Taylor. We got Strothers to make a new sign for the shop front."

Guy could only sit and shake his head in disbelief. Then finally he said, "Thank God you're safe with Claire and Grant."

Anna said nothing to that. She swallowed hard. She knew that what would follow would be a question she was compelled to ask, and possibly an answer she dreaded hearing. Eventually, she asked, "Why have you never told me you have a brother?"

The question rocked Guy. He shifted in his seat while he thought about his answer. Then, after a tense, silent moment had passed, he gave his response. "I have no brother."

"The solicitor said…"

"I don't care what the solicitor said."

"So, it's not true?"

More silence from Guy. He looked away from Anna and over at the wordless couple at the next table.

"Look at me."

Guy only shifted his look to the two warders, having a conversation of their own over by the door.

"Look at me Guy!" Finally, he turned to face her and she asked again, "do you or do you not have a brother in Lisbon?"

"Claus is dead for me. He's a Nazi. Like the rest of my damned family."

"So it is true?"

Anna managed to look both deceived and at the same time after the shock had settled, relieved.

"Why did you never tell me this?"

"Why should I? I haven't seen him in years. He doesn't exist for me. They - in here - they claim I send him stuff regularly, using the diplomatic bags at the Portuguese Consulate." He was now looking directly into her eyes. "You know me, Anna..." And she could see the passion now raging in him. "You know that working for the damned fascists" - he almost spat out the word - "is the last thing in the world that I'd ever do."

For the first time, Anna almost managed a smile. Almost. Guy rubbed at his red eyes. He looked dreadful. It pained Anna to see him like that.

"You have to get out of here," she said and stretched out her arm to touch him. From across the room the meaner looking of the two warders, the one known in the prison as 'Lashem,' who would spend every working hour of every day trying to impress the inmates that he was as hard as the blade of a shovel, barked out.

"Hey!" and gave her his sternest look. The rumour was that he'd been given the name 'Lashem' by his colleagues because he would "smash 'em, bash 'em, thrash 'em and lash 'em" - "em" being any prison inmate who dared to step out of line.

Anna jerked her arm back.

"So... so how are things out there?" Guy said finally.

"They've taken the Professor up to Liverpool."

Guy shook his head disbelievingly. "What about your job?"

Anna shrugged a despondent I don't know, then added, "they've given me something else for now." She glanced across at 'Lashem' - the tough guy Warder who had shouted at her and who was now back in his own quiet conversation. Then she reached out to Guy again, needing him desperately. ' Lashem' saw it out of the corner of his eye and started off towards them. His colleague stopped him and made a gesture with his hand, 'leave it, I'll handle this.' Then he walked the few yards across the room. Anna's hand was now desperately holding on to Guy's across the table. She didn't move it one inch. Instead, she looked defiantly at Guy as the warder got closer. She looked directly into Guy's eyes. Her grip tightened. "I'm not afraid. Not anymore." She could sense the warder almost up to them now. "And if they want to tear us apart by force, I'm not letting go, Guy. I'm not letting go."

The warder positioned himself directly behind Anna. "Just watch it, Miss. There are regulations."

She reached out her other hand and ran her fingers over Guy's unshaven cheek. "Perhaps if they'll allow this..." She nodded down to their hands, "they might also allow this," and they both leaned across the table and moved towards each other. They were less than an inch away from a "you and me against the world" kind of kiss when the shout came from 'Lashem,' who was still over at the door. "Okay. Time's up," and the warder behind Anna took a step forward and put his hand firmly on her shoulder and pulled her back. Her hand slipped out of Guy's. Their eyes met despairingly across the table. Then the warder took Guy's arm and led him away.

The 'silent' visitor at the next table stood up and headed for the door with a look of relief which screamed out 'thank God that's over.'

THE JOB

The days in early June when Stansfield Street Hospital received its first intake of Dunkirk evacuees were busy ones. They took twenty three casualties on the first day, and many more would follow. Anna helped out on the ward itself however she could. She wasn't a trained nurse - she had qualified as a dispenser and had worked in a pharmacy before she got the job as Professor Rosenbach's assistant - but still, she tried to make her contribution where she could, by fetching and carrying, cleaning up, making tea and serving meals. Like everyone else on the ward, it was Anna's very first experience of the direct ramifications and consequences of war and it shocked and deeply disturbed her. All the bloodied and burned and broken bodies. It wasn't pretty, and it wasn't exactly the kind of distraction which she wanted or needed, but it did serve for a while as a diversion from her own troubles. Two of the injured soldiers who they treated that first week were from the once formidable French First Army. They both spoke no English, no one on the entire ground floor of the hospital could speak any French, but the Frenchmen were both from the Alsace region and they could speak good German. So Anna was asked to interpret for them. One was a Captain in the Tank Corps who had been badly injured when a shell hit the jeep in which he was travelling in, just south of the Belgian border, and the blast had shattered his arm. The bone had shot right through the skin and pierced the thick material of his jacket sleeve. He had managed, with some of his Battalion, to stay alive and ahead of the advancing German army, but gangrene had set into the wound on the chase across northern France and they'd been forced to amputate his arm from just above the elbow in a spontaneous operation carried out under the cover of some trees west of Lille. The unit had managed to make it to the Channel and joined up with the retreating British army, and they'd been picked up off the beach at Dunkirk with them. The Captain was in constant pain which was being dulled with heavy doses of morphine, and he floated in and out of consciousness. What was extraordinary about the tall Captain was that he had six toes on his left foot. Every time Anna attended to him and saw them poking out from under the blankets she counted them, just to

131

make sure she wasn't the one hallucinating. Sure enough, every time she counted, they always added up to six. The second Frenchman - who was in the bed next to the window at the end of the ward and opposite the Captain - was a cheeky young fresh-faced infantryman from Strasbourg. He had already lost his two older brothers to the war but had somehow managed to maintain a cheery demeanor. He also liked Anna. A lot. He had several broken ribs and his right knee had been shattered when the supply truck which he was driving skidded off the road in a night time storm and hit a tree. Only when he'd arrived at Stansfield Street did he have his injuries treated when, the previous night, they had set his leg in a plaster cast and fitted a corset to protect his broken ribs. Anna stood next to his bed alongside the ward doctor, who was reading the infantryman's chart.

"So what are you? German, English, or something else?" the wounded soldier asked Anna in German but with a strong French accent while the doctor scanned his chart.

"I'm German and something else."

"Something else? What does that mean?"

"It means nothing's ever very easy."

"Where are you from?"

"Hamburg."

"So why are you here then?"

"To translate for you."

"No, why in England?"

132

"To translate for you," Anna repeated with a smile.

The doctor finished reading the chart and hung it back over the end of the soldier's bed. He said something to Anna and she turned to the soldier and said in German, "the doctor would like to know how you're feeling this morning, and if the plaster cast is okay for you?"

"Tell him I'd like to know your name and if you'll agree to be my personal nurse in here? And maybe afterwards too?"

Anna just smiled at him again and turned to the doctor.

"He says everything's fine."

A nurse entered the room and called to Anna, "Miss Vieti?"

Anna turned around. "Yes?"

"So it's Fräulein Vieti. Well that's a start," said the Frenchman, without being invited to speak, "and the first name?"

The nurse then addressed the doctor.

"The Director would like to see Miss Vieti straight away." Then she turned back to Anna, "If you'll come with me."

"Hey, we haven't finished yet!" the Frenchman shouted after them as they left the room.

With its white washed walls and ceiling to floor windows, and with the early summer sun again streaming in, the Director's office was brilliantly bright but the Director's mood was dark. He shifted awkwardly in his seat as he faced Anna across the desk. He looked genuinely sad. He looked embarrassed.

"I'm terribly sorry Miss Vieti. But now that the Professor is no longer with us..."

"But there is plenty of other work here. I can do that work. You need people." Anna protested, "I'll do anything you want me to do. I just want to contribute."

"I'm sorry, but my hands are tied in this."

"Who tied them? Tell them I'll work and tell them I'm good. Ask anyone here."

But the Director only shook his head from side to side and repeated, "I'm sorry, there's really nothing I can do. The decision has been made."

For Anna, it was yet another blow; yet heartbreak. You're out Anna. You were down before, and now you are out. And there's nothing we can do. How about that? "The decision has been made," he said.

God had spoken.

THIRTEEN

THE LETTER

The elaborately carved grandfather clock which stood at the end of the Pennington-Coopers' long hallway was striking eight when Anna came down for breakfast the next morning. She was half an hour later than usual getting up. The night had been a bad one - it must have been well after three o'clock before she finally fell asleep - and even then it was only a troubled night's rest that she got. She was about to enter the dining room, where Claire always set the table for breakfast when she stopped. From the other side of the door, she heard two raised voices. It was her own name that she heard mentioned first.

"Anna's our guest. What's wrong with inviting her?" Claire said with more than a little anger in her voice, "It's a housewarming party and your fortieth for God's sake. Not a political rally." Claire and Grant were sitting having breakfast. Or rather, they were just looking at the food on their plates and twisting their tea cups around on their saucers now that tempers had become raised.

"I'm... I just don't feel comfortable," Grant said. And it was true. He didn't look comfortable.

"With what?" asked Claire, trying to control her emotions, but not really managing it too well. "The cover of her passport? It'll be your colleagues from work. People from the art college. People you know. Our friends. What problem could they possibly have whether there's a German or a Jew or an Eskimo here?"

"People have their prejudices. That's all I'm saying."

"And you? Do you?"

"Don't be ridiculous," but he appeared to have been stung by the wasp's nest that Claire had poked a finger into, "I just don't want any delicate situations."

"Who with? Who would give us a delicate situation? Tell me Grant because I'd love to know. Exactly which prejudices are we talking about here and who could possibly share them?"

Grant shoved his plate to one side, got up from the table and stormed out - bumping into Anna outside in the hallway. "Morning," he mumbled to her, rather sheepishly. Anna nodded and mouthed an awkward, almost silent "Morning" back to him, and moved into the dining room. She was about to say something, but before she was able to, Claire had picked up an envelope from the breakfast table and held it out for her. The envelope was addressed to her, but it had no stamp on it and had a deep crease right down the middle.

"Morning Anna. This arrived for you."

Anna, full of curiosity, took the letter from her.

"Here," said Claire, and held out a knife for Anna to open the envelope with. She took out the two page letter, which had been written in pencil and folded tightly into quarters. She unfolded the pages and smoothed them out. "It's from Guy," she said, breaking into a broad smile and, still standing, she began to read. She was probably no more than five lines down the page before Claire couldn't stop herself from asking, "So what does he say?"

Anna looked up from the letter with a hopeful smile. "He's asked the lawyer to see if we can get married in prison." She returned to the letter and carried on reading it out aloud. "John Timney was in to see me today..."

***

Two days earlier Guy lay on his prison bed and wrote the words which Anna now read at the Coopers.

"John Timney was in to see me today. He told me that Military Intelligence wants to speak to me again tomorrow. I have no idea what they want, but it can only be a good sign. There are restrictions on sending letters, although no one has yet been able to tell me what they are. And we aren't allowed any uncensored mail, in or out. In my wing, we've even been denied the use of pen and paper. But I have met someone who can smuggle letters out. It's someone I work with. So if you get this, then it's thanks to him and his contacts."

Guy's letter smuggler supreme was twenty-five year old merchant navy seaman Duncan Carmichael from Portsmouth. He had thick, black hair which he had slicked back into an enormous quiff, and was painfully thin but tough looking, with a deep two-inch scar down his left cheek and a large tattoo which vaguely resembled a serpent with seven tails running all the way down his left forearm. It looked like it had been inked on by a ten year old in a dark and dingy Shanghai back alley in the middle of an earthquake. And possibly had. He had been arrested on the same day as Guy while he was back home in Portsmouth on a short three-day leave. Duncan Carmichael was fiercely patriotic and had become a member of Mosley's British Union fascists seven months earlier. He had a homemade radio transmitter up in his bedroom, although it hadn't worked for some time and he vehemently denied having ever used it for political reasons. Guy met him while they were in the prison workroom stitching mailbags. "Duncan knows people and he has a certain way with one of the warders here. You know what I'm saying?" Guy wrote. What he meant was that his prison pal was of 'other' sexual orientation, although as Guy said "you would never guess by looking at him," Guy had made it plain to Duncan that "I'm sorry but there's nothing here for you, friend," when he felt that Duncan once tried to make a play for him.

The day before Guy wrote his letter he was in the workroom alongside Duncan, who scanned around the room, first to his left, then to his right, and then when he was sure that neither of the two warders over by the door, nor any of the other dozen inmates in the workroom were watching, he slipped his hand deep into Guy's trouser pocket. Guy didn't move an inch. After two seconds Duncan withdrew his hand and carried on with his stitching.

A moment later, Guy reached down into the same pocket and nodded to Duncan; so far so very good. Guy looked around the room; everyone was still either occupied or bored, except the shorter and heavier of the two warders, who were then staring straight at Duncan.

Duncan got up from his seat, walked over to the warder, gave him the slightest of nods, and disappeared out of the door towards the toilet.

Guy watched the warder follow, and as soon as they were out of the room, he pulled out a few feet of the thread which he was using to stitch his mailbag and tucked it inside the front of his shirt.

Back in his cell, Guy reached down into his trouser pocket and pulled out a small, stubby pencil which was wrapped in two sheets of writing paper and a folded envelope. It was the paper and pencil which he would use to write Anna's letter. He smoothed out the pages, lay down on his bed, and began to write.

"The old war vet who I told you about when you came to visit - well Anna, I'm still sharing the cell with him. It's driving me crazy, all his wide-eyed gawking and his wild antics all day and all night. I actually felt sorry for him at first. But he muttered something the other day –it was the very first time he had spoken since he came in here - about how only fascism could defeat the communists and how the Nazis were the only ones with the answer. God help me but I could have put my pillow over his face and kept it there until he stopped breathing."

In the background, while Guy was writing, his cellmate rocked and stared madly and the saliva continued to dribble out of the side of his mouth and down his chin and the sporadic ear splitting screams just never stopped coming. Guy told Anna all about Duncan Carmichael and about the torturous sleeplessness that he was suffering, and the rumours that they put Bromide into the detainees' tea and in their soup to suppress any sexual urges that they might have. "As if!" Guy wrote. He told her about the damp and how he permanently felt cold - "and in June too"- and about the rock-hard bed and the terrible back pain which he had from it.

"There's also a rumour that Mosley himself is being held here, in another wing, but no one has seen him. And do you remember that magician we saw last year at the Palladium? Well, he's in a cell at the end of the floor. Can you believe that? Let's see him conjure his way out of this one Anna."

Someone had told one of the inmates - they called him Black Dog but nobody knew why - that Guy was German and during one of the short exercise periods which the detainees were allowed Black Dog had blindsided Guy and landed a haymaker on the side of his head.

"It could have been much worse, he was really in the mood to finish me if Duncan together with his cellmate hadn't stepped in and stopped him. But you know what the strangest thought of all is about this horrible experience? You almost feel guilty just by being in here. In fact, I could swear I have actually done something."

Then he did a very odd and for Guy a very unusual thing, he wrote the following in German: "Wir alle haben in unserem Leben..." ("We've all done something in our past that we regret. We all carry a secret something around with us.") Finally he went back into English to say "I just have to get out of here Anna."

When Guy had finished his letter he added a 'PS' at the very end:

"Don't write back to me at the prison Anna. I don't want to give them the privilege of reading even one single word of my mail."

He sealed the envelope and added Anna's address at the Pennington-Cooper's. Then he wrapped the mailbag thread which he had stolen from the workroom around the envelope and knotted it securely. He went to the cell window and pushed the envelope through the bars and started to swing it from side-to-side by the thread. When its arc became high enough for it to reach the window of the cell next to his, a hand grabbed it and the envelope disappeared quickly through the bars. In the cell next door, a fellow detainee pushed Guy's envelope under his pillow next to three others. The prison's 'pony express service' had slipped into action.

In Claire's dining room Anna was still standing, reading her letter.

"I am lonely in here without you. It will always be lonely without..." She stopped short of reading the rest out aloud and with a shy, nervous laugh she ended with "And so on."

She sat down at the breakfast table still holding on to her letter. What she had in her hand certainly wasn't great news. It was definitely strange - but it wasn't too bad, and right then "not too bad" was also okay with Anna. There was also the meeting with MI5 which surely offered some hope at least. She looked a little more relaxed and a little relieved. But Guy's "We've all done something in our past that we regret" still confused her. And in German. Guy never even spoke German, never mind wrote it. And what did he mean by 'we all carry a secret something'? It disturbed her. He must mean the brother he never told me about - yes, that will be it, Anna tried to convince herself. Still, Guy's words nagged away at her and the same question kept repeating itself; why in German? She was still lost in all the jumbled thoughts which raced through her mind when Claire broke the spell by pouring her a cup of tea and asking, "how about you help me prepare for to-morrow night?"

***

Whilst Claire and Anna were getting ready for the party, Barnes and Adams had taken Guy to the prison Governor's office for what they called "a serious chat." Guy looked even more tired and even more drawn from yet another sleepless night. They sat him in the Governor's leather chair then they pulled their own chairs right up to within a couple of feet of Guy. They looked long and hard into his face and studied him with heron-like intensity.

"We're not going to blow smoke up your arse Schneider," Barnes said. "Just think of the money you're losing while you're in here."

Adams shifted his chair even further in towards Guy. It was a little intimidating - and it was meant to be. "And think about that pretty little bride of yours," he said in a menacing tone.

There was a short silence while Adams let that sink in, then to drive the point home he added: "You don't look after her, then somebody else out there certainly will." His eyes penetrated into Guy. Is this the key which will unlock him, Adams wondered?

They watched Guy twist and shift in his seat, a picture of pure uncertainty.

"Look at me Schneide," Barnes said but Guy only twisted further. "Look at me. You don't get a better deal

143

than the one we're offering you." He turned his partner. "Am I right Alex?"

"You just don't get another deal full stop," added Adams. "Come on Schneider. Do yourself a favour. There's only one decision to make."

"Well?" asked Barnes.

FOURTEEN

THE COOPERS' PARTY

Every room on the first floor of the Pennington-Coopers' new house - and there were a lot of rooms - was full to bursting with characters, colour and chaos, with music and madness. Grant and Claire's party was in full swing. It was Holly Golightly's party only wilder and twenty years early, or it was one of Gatsby's mad extravaganzas eighteen years on. This was a world - the art community of London, or at least those who hadn't already headed off to America - that the austerity of wartime England had not yet touched. At least that's how it appeared that sultry night in early June. In the living room - the largest room on the floor - there was music blasting out from a gramophone in the corner, there was drink in every glass and laughter on every face. Some couples were dancing together in an area cleared for just that. Some of the characters were rather 'offbeat,' others were the suave, sophisticated, London intellectual elite in their Bond Street and Saville Row suits and their expensive cocktail dresses.

It was a collection of the weird and the beautiful. Claire had squeezed into a flowing green silk dress at least one size too small which she had bought especially for the occasion and was pushing through the crowded room past the fun and the flirting, the dancers and the drinkers, the lecturing and the lechery, with a bottle of red wine in her left hand and a bottle of white in the other, topping up her guests glasses with wine as she passed - even if the guests didn't want it or the glasses didn't need filling anyway. Pressed right up behind Claire and clinging to her as tight as Claire's new dress was Anna, who Claire introduced to each new guest they passed. Her spirits may have been low and her anguish might have been at odds with the happiness and the celebrations going on all around her, but Anna looked a knock-out that wild party night in her blood-red gown. She followed Claire into the adjoining room, the lounge, where a man in a paper Christmas party hat was playing the piano. He had a drunken crowd gathered around him who were all singing along and were being conducted by Grant with a paint brush. In the middle of the room a balding, middle-aged man had his trousers rolled up to his knees and was pretending to be a bull, charging at a girl who was playing

Matador for the night. She held out a bright red towel and lifted it to cries of "Toro" every time the 'bull' brushed past her. When Claire and Anna came close to him the 'bull' noticed the red of Anna's dress and charged at her instead. Anna gracefully turned with him like the finest Matador and allowed him to glide past her.

Someone had been following Anna closely and intensely all that night as she passed through the rooms behind Claire. Someone was taking a very keen interest in her as she followed Claire into the hallway, where some girls were playing a game of hopscotch using the patterns on the carpet, and then into the library. A young man with an ostrich feather stuck into an orange headband sat blind-folded near the door and was sketching portraits of his models by feeling their features and tracing the contours of their faces with his fingers before transferring it to his canvas. The portraits were remarkably good. When Anna passed him he was sketching identical twins, who were dressed in Japanese kimonos. One of the twins was pulling faces and twisting her features to try and trick him.

No one at the party spoke about the war. This was a night to leave their depression at home or else pour it into their work. The talk was all about who is painting what or who is painting who and have you read that novel by that still obscure but brilliant French novelist Patrice Lenclud who "will do for words what Matisse did for colour" insisted one of the guests - and of course everyone claimed they knew Lenclud, even if they didn't. The only person who spoke about the war was the effeminate conscientious objector who wore thick eyeliner and had a lipstick heart painted on his cheek and was dressed like a master of ceremonies character from a 1920s Berlin cabaret scene in a tight black suit with tails, a black bow tie, and black velvet bowler hat. He had corralled a pretty young thing who might have been a girl but also might have been a boy and had her/him pressed up tight into a corner of the room and was delivering his lecture on war and how his father had been executed at the Somme for disobeying orders by refusing to go 'over the top' - while all his pretty androgyne friend wanted to do was dive into the bouncing masses and get himself/herself a piece of the action and who knows, maybe a willing body to drag off home with him. Or her.

Claire's had now emptied both of her wine bottles, so she headed off to get refreshments and left Anna in the library with one of her male guests, the Soho sophisticate from the outskirts of Paris, Anton Le Trayas. He was tall and slim with a long neck and red-brown hair, which Anna thought made him look like a giraffe. He started up an intense conversation with her about a surreal painting on the wall next to them.

"It's called The Dream," he told Anna in a heavy French accent.

"Look closely at the imagery and I promise you'll not only see it you'll feel it," he said as if he was letting her in on his best kept secret.

"I'll let you be in my dream if I can be in yours?" A voice from behind them said. Anton and Anna both turned around at the same time.

"Oh, Mark. Didn't see you," said Anton. "Ca va?"

Markus Hermann was in his late thirties. He had sharp, piercing brown eyes and a lean, athletic figure which his black clothes simply hung on. His black hair was longer than was fashionable at the time and longer than what was acceptable, and it was swept back over his head. He would have belonged to the 'offbeat' at the party by appearance, although his cool, sophisticated manner could quite easily have also placed him with the others. Actually, Markus Hermann – one time Impressionist painter - no longer belonged to any one group. He held out his hand for Anna to shake.

"Hello."

Anna took his hand but it was more of a polite and quick 'touch' that she gave it rather than a firm squeeze, and she said her own quiet "hello."

"I hope you aren't allowing this old conformist to fill your head with his notions of good art," Mark Hermann told her in his light French accent, and almost as an order.

"The only art in painting is in selling them. Just you remember who has made you famous," Anton replied and exchanged a smile with Mark.

"He was just explaining about surrealism to me," Anna said.

149

The painting they had been looking at was an image of burning and melting bowler hats, stylistically similar to what Rene Magritte would make famous. Mark gestured towards it.

"It's old hat! Or... if you'll please excuse us 'Salvador'...?" He slapped Anton affectionately on the back and dragged Anna through the crowd to another part of the room over by the balcony doors. "Those kinds of paintings, they're all just...' He carefully and deliberately pronounced his next three words, because he knew they would resonate with Anna: "Snow from yesterday!" He waited for Anna's reaction. She got it immediately.

"That's German!"

"So are you."

"How did you know?"

Mark touched his nose. "I can smell it a mile off." Then off her confused look, "Beauty, I mean... naturally. I heard it in your accent."

Anna suddenly became self-conscious. They can all hear it. The voice of the enemy, I'm trapped.

"And what else does your nose tell you about me?"

He moved right up close to her and put his nose against her neck. It was bold and it surprised Anna, but for some reason that she didn't quite understand why she didn't stop him.

The party's vibrant mood and high spirits had finally infected her too.

"Some people judge beauty only by what they see," Mark said as he took in her scent. "There are other senses."

They were suddenly interrupted by a loud commotion in the street outside, where there were loud shouts and bangs and the shrill sound of whistles pierced the still night air. Most of the party guests in the room rushed over to the balcony windows next to Anna and Mark and crowded round to watch the action. It had been another fine early summer day and it was still light outside at close to ten o'clock. Someone opened the balcony doors and a handful of people even went out onto the small front terrace to look.

Down below them in the street, a group of about two dozen men, ranging from late teens through to early thirties, were chasing a second group of around a dozen males who, from their appearance, the way they were dressed and their shouts, were obviously Italian. Some of the Italians had jumped the garden-park fence and were trying to flee across the lawn and through the trees in sheer panic. A handful had been caught by their pursuers and were being kicked and punched and beaten with iron bars. One Italian had his head cracked off the pavement by a thug wearing knuckle dusters and he lay unconscious in a pool of thickening blood. Five or six of the Italians had taken their chance and turned and confronted the attackers, and a violent fistfight had broken out in the middle of the street. One Italian had pulled a knife and was keeping two of his attackers at arm's length with it, waving it madly from side-to-side. A policeman had followed the chase on his bicycle, but he was powerless to restore any kind of order, and in the face of such a ferocious outbreak of violence he had been reduced to the role of a mere helpless onlooker. Then a Police van turned the corner into Rowlandsgill Gate, closely followed by two Police cars.

Behind Anna and Mark one of the guests, who was wearing a double-breasted beige suit and a yellow tie, said: "What can you expect, now that Italy is about to declare war?"

A second Police van and another Black Maria arrived at the other end of the street and blocked off the road, and a dozen officers were immediately out and sprinting towards the brawling mass halfway up the street. The fighters were now trapped between advancing police officers from both ends of the small street, but a few still managed to vault the park fence and escape before they could be rounded up. The police quickly had the situation under control, but they ignored the attackers and concentrated instead on the Italians, who they rounded up and frog marched to the end of the street, where they manhandled them into the back of the police vans. Three of the Italians were badly injured and lay motionless on the ground, including the one whose head had been bounced off the pavement and who was now out cold and barely breathing. As the Italians were herded into the vans they protested their innocence. While up in Grant and Claire's living room a second party guest watched them being driven off and said with great contempt in his voice "Even more lock 'em up first, think about it later" and he walked away shaking his head.

In Rowlandsgill Gate, the attackers had been allowed to disperse freely and were by now well away from the normally peaceful little Knightsbridge street.

Anton watched appalled from the balcony as the police vans pulled away. He turned to the couple next to him. "First the fascists, then the Germans, and now the Italians." Then he directed his next comment at the guest with the yellow tie. "You watch out or it might be the artists next." He turned away and moved off the balcony, giving Mark a friendly squeeze on the shoulder as he passed him, "eh, Mark?" Anton went inside, joining the other guests as they drifted away from the balcony, leaving Mark and Anna together.

"They just let them walk away," a short, moon-faced dandy in a red cravat and matching red rose in his buttonhole complained to Claire about what he'd just witnessed while he stood in the kitchen and watched her struggle to open a fresh bottle of red wine in which the cork had snapped. He was chief Arts and Culture editor for a leading Sunday newspaper. "This business..." he said aloud to the others in the kitchen, "who are the good guys and who are the bad guys... it's so complicated even the London taxi drivers don't have a solution!" He watched and was waiting for the laughter which he felt his little party joke deserved when Grant staggered into the kitchen, followed by the guest who had played the role of the 'Bull.' "Ah the birthday boy!" old moon-face said when he saw Grant. "When's the new book coming out then Grant?"

"Oh hello, Barney. When I write one." Grant said, matter-of-factly, desperate only for refreshment for his empty glass.

"So what's this one going to be about then?"

"Devils and angels and a passionate affair, out next month."

"You wish!" chipped in Claire, losing her fight with the cork.

"Devils and angels, that's what I'll tell Charlotte to tell her readers."

"Then tell her it's Cowboys and Indians, all blood and mayhem. Where is Charlotte anyway, I haven't seen her all evening."

"The last time I saw her she was downstairs with her sister, getting their portraits done."

Grant's new book would be his third, but the first not to be about art - 'if' it were ever to be finished. Claire had been a little unfair when she had told Anna that Grant wasn't a natural talent when it came to art. It was certainly true that he couldn't paint any better than a trained chimp from Regents Park zoo, but he did have a special talent for explaining the subject which he loved so much. No one was better than Professor Grant Pennington-

Cooper at articulating what Art with a capital 'A' meant, and his two previous books, 'A Culture and its Paintings' and 'The History of Modern British Art', had not only sold well but had become standard text books in every university which taught the subject. The reason Grant could do it so brilliantly was that he had a deep passion for art, the keenest interest in history, and most of all, he loved artists. But his third book had come not just hard, but increasingly impossible to him, and he was convinced that he would never finish it. It was meant to be a novel, and Grant's attempt finally at conjuring up something creative himself.

He'd only written three chapters, and each of those at least a hundred times. In fact, he could have carpeted the entire county of Kent with the paper that he'd pulled out of his typewriter in disgust and tossed angrily into the bin next to his desk. He hated himself and his inadequacy. No matter how much he sat in silence at his typewriter the words just wouldn't flow and a second problem had now started to kick in with a vengeance; drink, because the more Grant didn't write - and there were millions of words that he didn't write - the more he had to drink.

Grant started to feel like a failure. A charlatan. He realised that he would never be able to create like a true artist and that he was destined forever just to feed off them and live off their backs. I'm not worthy, his inner voice told him.

"Come on Claire," said Grant impatiently.

The 'Bull' had now moved alongside him and he held out his empty glass with the unspoken order to Grant to 'fill this up.' It was Claire who grabbed a fresh, open bottle of white from the table and poured it for him. The Bull didn't thank anyone, he just barked out an annoyed

"I hear there's a German girl here tonight. I thought you two would have shown a bit more loyalty than that!" Then he turned and wandered back into the party. Grant followed him, shooting Claire a half-cut 'Well? What did I tell you?' look. Claire turned away from him and took her anger out instead of the cork she was fighting with.

"They should raise the legal drinking age to sixty," she said under her breath and Barney the culture king giggled.

Back in the library, Mark stood next to Anna, both sickened by what they had witnessed in the street. "And there was I thinking we were in the presence of beauty," Mark said, not taking his eyes off her.

"An artist, not a warrior, right?"

"Something like that. I'm Swiss Miss...? I never got your name."

"I didn't say it!"

And with that, she shot him an enigmatic 'Mona Lisa' smile, turned on her heel... and ran straight into...

The 'Bull'.

"Toro," he blurted out, "fine beast." He peered over Mark's shoulder towards the street outside. "I hear I missed all the action. Too bad it wasn't the bloody Germans getting a good hiding, eh?" He spat out of the open window. Grant, alongside him, just stood passively and took another swig from his bottle.

"Bastards!" shouted the Bull in the direction of the street.

Fragile that night and all out of fight, it cut right through Anna. She looked to Grant and took in his drunken indifference. Suddenly, she felt very foreign; aware that she was absolutely and utterly out of place there. Every face in the room now seemed to be staring right through her. Every pair of eyes burned into her. She fixed a smile on her face, in the same way, she had done on her wedding day outside of the church and headed for the door with stoic dignity, apparently immune to the barbs. Mark brushed the 'Bull' out of his way as he moved off after her.

Moments later, one floor above, Mark knocked and entered Anna's bedroom without waiting to be asked. It was dark in the room and the heavy curtains had already been drawn, but he could make out Anna on the bed, buried under her blankets, just a little girl shutting out the evil from her world. He stood a moment, unsure of what to do when Anna's voice broke the silence. She was calling out in the dark for someone. Tonight she needed a friend.

"Don't go. Just don't say anything.''

She lifted her head from under the blanket and was surprised to see who was standing there.

"Oh... I thought it was Claire.''

Mark started to move towards her. But he froze when the dim bedroom light went on. Claire had entered the room. She walked straight past Mark and headed directly over to the bed to comfort Anna. "I heard what happened. I'm so sorry Anna. Are you all right?"

Mark turned and slipped out of the room - it was as though he had never even been there - leaving Claire and Anna alone.

FIFTEEN

A NEW DAWN

Guy stood in front of the mirror which hung above the sink in the corner of his cell and stared at his tired, pallid features. Over the years the mirror had become cracked and warped, so for Guy, it appeared as if he was looking at his reflection in the back of a dirty, pock-marked spoon. He slapped cold water on his face, picked up a rusty old razor, and began to shave. Yet another piercing scream from behind him made him jump and cut himself. Then the old Vet let out an even louder groan like a cow being slaughtered. Guy stood and watched the blood trickle slowly down his chin and drip into the sink. Then he threw his razor down and just gave up.

***

Anna sat in the passenger seat next to Grant as he drove across the city. It was a wet Sunday, the first rain that London had seen in days, and the streets were quiet. Grant was nursing the mother of all hangovers.

"You acquired a very enthusiastic new friend last night," he said to her with a slight smile on his face. Anna didn't react. She just stared out through the windscreen and the 'swish, swish, swish' of the wipers at the road ahead, lost in her thoughts.

"He certainly wanted to know everything about you… Ow, ow, ow," he put a hand up to his pounding forehead, then added, "Mark has an extraordinary talent. I could hate him for it," he joked and turned quickly to look at Anna. She said nothing, all she did was tighten the grip on the handbag on her lap. Grant went on, "he could paint the sound of a teardrop falling… I think that's what I once wrote about him. Or the noise a cloud makes as it passes across the sky."

"Or a picture of someone who doesn't want someone else staying with them?" Anna put in, "could he paint that?"

Grant turned his head and for a short moment glanced across at her.

"What is that supposed to mean?"

She turned in her seat to look directly at him. "It means... you have a problem with me, don't you Grant?"

Her question left tension between them. It all suddenly became most awkward.

"No."

"No?" Anna pushed further, "you're okay with me staying with you?"

There was a long strained silence in the car, which told its own story, while Grant thought about what to say. Or what 'best' to say.

"I promised Guy I'd look after you, and look after you I will. That's what a friend does. Besides, where else can you stay now that the Williamson's have rented out your old room?"

She sat for a moment and thought about Grant's answer. It fell well short of providing any reassurance. There couldn't have been more distance between them as they drove on in silence, which was only broken when Grant's car eventually pulled up outside of the prison.

"Say "hello" to Guy for me," Grant said to her as she got out.

***

Guy looked dreadful; like he hadn't slept in a week, and was at the very end of his nerves. There was thick dried blood on his chin from where he'd cut it with the razor.

He cleared his throat and rubbed at his eyes before he told Anna, "I saw the two MI5 guys yesterday."

"And?"

"And we talked."

He glanced over at two watching prison warders. They were more interested in the private little conversation

161

which they were sharing than on the eight detainees in the room with their visitors.

"They said that the Committee would throw out my appeal. But..." He hesitated. Anna could see that he was eager to say more. He looked nervously around the room - first at the warders who were still occupied with themselves, and then at the other detainees and visitors. Then, almost in a whisper, he said to Anna in German: "Sie haben mir ein Angebot gemacht. Sie lassen mich frei... wenn ich ihnen helfe Jemandem etwas anzuhängen. Jemandem ganz oben im Verteidungsminis-"

(They've offered me a deal. They'll release me... If I help them set someone up. Someone high up in the Ministry of Defen-)

Anna jumped in before he could finish. She was incredulous. She also spoke in German, but not in as quiet a whisper as Guy had done. "Was! Du sollst für sie spionieren?"

("What! They want you to spy for them?")

One of the warders spun around. He had heard something 'unusual.' He moved closer to Guy's table, straining his ears to hear. Guy returned to English and turned to a different topic entirely.

"They turned down our request to get married." It was one more depressing, but not unexpected, blow for Anna. She took in the implications of the news as the warder turned and walked back over to join his colleague, and Guy returned to his other 'news,' quietly, and staying in

English. "It's that... or this." He looked around the dingy, depressing room and its single, narrow, barred window, "they said they want to talk again."

Anna looked at him like he'd lost his mind.

"You're not going to accept?" This was no question at all, but a command.

Guy shrugged his shoulders, noncommittal.

"Guy..." She was pleading now. "You can't for one minute consider it." But she could see that he was.

"What choice do I have? Look at me. Look at the shop. Look at us," he came back at her.

"These people have locked you up in here... for what? That's exactly what we left behind us. You're not going to work for them. Ever," she spat out, disgusted that he would even consider it, "you're a better person than that."

"I'm not. And they'll throw out my appeal."

"Why would they? You're innocent."

After a tense second Guy moved closer to her and said quietly, "I don't know what they have on me."

"What can they possibly have on you?"

There was yet another silence while Anna watched Guy shift uneasily in his seat, just as he had done with Adams and Barnes, and looked off at a point under the table. And the question which Anna had just asked - 'what can they possibly have on you' - slowly became one not only for him but also for herself.

"What aren't you telling me, Guy? What do they have?"

"Nothing. But... the war could drag on for years. Is this," he looked around the four prison walls again, "what you want? For us? For you? They'll come for you next - and this way, I can prevent..."

"Stop this. Stop it!"

It was her turn now to twist and shift uncomfortably in her seat. She wanted to get up. To pace around the room but she fought hard and managed to control the urge.

"Someone spied on you Guy. Or someone invented something. Is that what you want to do? To buy your freedom by selling them someone else's? Someone probably just as innocent as you?"

Guy simply looked like that was exactly what he had in mind.

"How could you live with yourself?" she pleaded desperately, "how could we both live with that?"

Guy remained silent. His eyes were everywhere now but not on Anna.

"Scheiße! Oh, Gott, Scheiße!" she said and her hands shot up to her face.

"Time please!" went up the call from the back of the room.

Guy's parting shot as Anna got up to leave was, "if you don't like it you know what you can do."

#

When Guy was taken back to his cell after Anna's visit he found it empty. The World War One vet had been taken away. All that remained of his presence was the filthy, stained mattress that he had rocked back and forth on and the pot that he had pissed into. Guy asked one of the warders what had happened to the old man, but the warder wasn't speaking or answering questions that day. Maybe he was just deaf. Either way, he slammed the cell door shut without a word and left Guy alone in the room to watch the blackbird outside on the window ledge and re-live the conversation that he had just had with Anna, and for the hundredth time, the one which he'd had with Barnes and Adams the day before.

Those conversations were still spinning around in his head when, a half an hour later, the cell door opened and a five-feet-five bundle of pent-up muscular energy with a boxer's profile and a street-scrapper's scars strutted in like a proud peacock.

It was Fearless Freddie Turnbull, the Lewisham light-weight hope who Sergeant Dobson had helped bring in. Once the cell door was slammed shut and locked behind him, Freddie stood and glared at Guy with his ice-cold assassin's eyes. Then without a word he threw his few belongings onto the free bed, got down onto the prison floor, and went through a routine of two hundred and fifty press-ups followed by two hundred and fifty sit-ups and squat-thrusts, all at lightning speed and with the greatest of ease. When he was finished he stood up, shook his head from side-to-side to loosen up his thick neck mus-cles, then he lay down on the old vet's mattress. Guy had no idea how to take his new cell mate. But once he had finally finished his impressive routine Guy decided to approach him with his arm outstretched.

"Hello, I'm Guy.''

The boxer simply ignored him, closed his eyes and went straight off to sleep.

Three hours later Freddie Turnbull woke up. Guy was taking a leak into his pot at the time. Freddie rubbed his eyes and looked Guy up and down as he was zipping his fly back up.

"So wot they got you banged up in 'ere for?" he asked Guy.

"They're not saying."

"Fuckers. You're not BU as well then?"

Guy shook his head and muttered, "No." Just the sound of those two letters, B and U, made Guy wary.

Then 'Fearless' Freddie got up, approached Guy with that threatening strut of his and said, "I'm Freddie... Freddie Turnbull." Guy held out his hand to shake, but Freddie let it hang in the air. "That your clean hand or the filthy one?" he asked.

"Clean," Guy said and Freddie broke into a laugh. "I'm Guy. Guy Schneider."

Freddie thought about the name. "German?"

"Half British, half German." Even before the words had left Guy's mouth he was angry with himself for saying it.

But Freddie nodded his approval. German seemed to be fine with Freddie, and finally, he took Guy's hand to

166

shake. Then an afterthought hit him. "Yer not a fackin Jew-Boy are ya?"

Guy felt anxious. He wanted to say something but thought better of it. There was something intense, something dangerous behind Freddie Turnbull's steely eyes. Guy knew that 'Fearless' could demolish him, eat him up, spit him out and afterwards pick his teeth with his bones if he wished. He wasn't undefeated in his weight division for nothing. Guy smiled instead and said, "No. But I think if I was... I'm not too sure I'd admit it in here."

"Good decision pal," said Freddie. "But a fascist, right?"

Again Guy thought about his answer.

"I'm a photographer... so, yeah," and they both laughed at that.

"You're okay Schneider," Freddie Turnbull said. "You from round 'ere then?"

"Upper Bexton."

"Never been. I'm Lewisham," Freddie said and tapped his heart with his fist in a show of pride and a strong sense of belonging. "The awld nutter I shared with daan the corridor, he woz Lewisham too. Facking gypo he was. Stank. And screamed and shouted awl noit and day. I coulda killed 'im a dozen times. They put him together the geezer wot woz in 'ere wif you and shifted me in 'ere."

Then the cell door opened and a warder brought in two bowls of crap masquerading as food. Freddie took one disapproving look at it and gave the warder the same intimidating glare that he'd given earlier to Guy and told him where to shove his stinking bowl of shit. Then he lay back down on his bed, closed his eyes again, and went off back to sleep. Guy went back to staring out through the barred cell window with his jumbled thoughts occupying him further.

SIXTEEN

MORE COMPANY

Claire was carrying a silver tea-tray up the hallway towards the living room when the front door opened and Anna drifted in like a ghost, back from the prison. "Anna, we...." Claire started to say something, but she stopped when she saw Anna's distress, "what's wrong? Has something happened to Guy?"

Anna looked at Claire for a disquieting moment, not knowing what to say. Then she twisted her head away and opted for something else to explain away her anguish.

"They refused our request to get married."

Claire set the tray down on the hallway table and moved towards Anna. She was just a moment away from tears. Claire wrapped her arms around her and gave her a consoling hug. "I'm sorry Anna." And with as much of a hopeful, sympathetic smile as she could summon up, she added: "I'm sure something will work out soon." She released Anna and picked up the tea tray. "I've made some tea. We have a visitor. If you want, come in and join us?"

"Let me freshen up first.''

Minutes later, she came back downstairs looking brighter. She knocked politely on the living room door and entered the room, and was surprised to see that the visitor sitting on the sofa was Mark Hermann.

"Hello," Mark said with a warm smile.

Anna took a seat in the armchair opposite him, "hello."

From another room came the sound of the telephone ringing.

Claire got up. "Excuse me a moment," she said and left the room.

Mark waited until Claire had gone then said to Anna, "I suppose I should apologise for Saturday."

"Accepted. But I don't know why. You were the perfect Gentleman."

"Oh. In that case, I *really* must apologise," Anna looked across at the cool, unusually handsome and char-ismatic bohemian sitting opposite her and a slight smile crept over her face. "Have you had any more thoughts about my offer?" he asked her.

"Your offer?"

"About your dreams, remember?"

"Ask me something else."

Anna's thoughts truly were somewhere else.

170

Mark looked at his watch. "Okay. Entirely honourable. How about you walk with me through the park to my bus? Then you could tell me all about those dreams... Which you don't have of course." He looked hopefully at her, anticipating the answer.

"Well?"

But Anna was in no real mood for games at that moment.

"Is that a yes, or a yes?" he pushed her.

"Begins with 'N' in most languages."

"Next time?"

"I think the question says more about you than the answer does about me. I'm sorry I've..."

Just then the door opened and Claire came back into the room. She looked at Mark, "It was Grant. He said he's sorry he'll be late."

"It's all right. I can't stay anyway. Tell him to bring the prints round sometime." He stood up to leave.

"You haven't finished your tea," Claire reminded him.

"I think abstinence and denial is the message of the day anyway." He shot an enigmatic smile at Anna as he got up from the sofa and followed Claire to the door. "Next time," he said over his shoulder to Anna as he left the room.

***

Barnes and Adams were back in the prison governor's office with Guy. The morning had been a hot one and the top of Barnes' bald head had caught the sun badly. It irritated him and didn't help his mood. He drummed his fingers on the governor's desk and looked hard into Guy's eyes. "We'll set you up as an RAF photographer. You tell him about your Lisbon connection and that you have a secure and guaranteed way of getting information to the Germans. He'll check it out and fall for it like a fish on a hook."

Guy said nothing. He just looked vacantly at Barnes and rubbed his fingers tenderly over the lower part of his jaw where a tooth had started to hurt.

Then Adams leaned in close. It was almost a whisper, for effect, "then you say you'll use your connection to pass on detailed aerial photographs... of British coastal defenses. We'll give you something to pass on, and you give him your price; Ten thousand pounds."

The two MI5 officers tried to mask their impatience as they sat and watched Guy fight the two voices in his head. The devil was on one shoulder whispering softly, "Do it" and the other voice was Anna's screaming, "Guy, you can't!"

Eventually, Guy shook his head. It was a weak and uncertain "no" and his tired eyes were saying something very different. He knew he was in trouble. Adams exchanged a look with Barnes, got a nod, then knowing it would seal the deal said to Guy, "you'll keep half of the money."

"Come on Schneider," added Curly Barnes, "five thousand, and a pass out of here...?"

Guy sat and continued to struggle with the voices in his head.

***

Back in the Pennington-Coopers' living room, Anna emptied the last drop of tea from the teapot into Claire's cup. Claire opened a thick art catalogue to a certain page and turned it so that Anna could see. The page she showed her was an Impressionist-style landscape painting. Anna tried to look mildly indifferent, but she wasn't very good at it. It was a wonderful painting she thought, and it's truly beautiful. Claire flicked the page to another, similarly Impressionist painting of bright, vibrant colours and shades. "That's how Mark used to paint. But Grant says that for the past couple of years his work has changed radically."

"In what way?"

"I don't know. I haven't seen any of it. It's Expressionist. Abstract. Dark and pessimistic, Grant says. And certainly no-" (quoting from the catalogue text) "peaceful celebration of the exhilarating beauty of life." She closed the catalogue and put it down on the table in front of her.

"Why did he come here?" Anna asked.

"To collect something Grant has for him. Some prints I think."

"To London, I mean."

"Mark taught at Munich University. After the Nazis came to power he got out - like all the artists. He came to London and found a job here at the University. That was four years ago. Then when his paintings started selling, he was able to concentrate on that."

Anna picked up the catalogue and looked at the cover. It was a catalogue for an exhibition by Markus Hermann. On its cover was a painting of a wide sweep of coastline. She looked over at the wall behind Claire. The original of the painting was hanging there. Like the others in the book, it was light, bright, peaceful and radiant. And it was dreamy. But a lonely girl was walking the empty sands.

***

Back in his cell with the light now fading, Guy looked into his cracked, marked mirror and felt with his fingers into the back of his mouth. He pulled out a piece of the tooth which had broken off and looked at it disgusted.

From another cell down the corridor came the echo of a haunted scream, and from somewhere in the night sky above the prison Guy could hear the faint drone of bombers somewhere south of the prison, followed by distant explosions. That night, London received its first calling card from Hitler when the German Luftwaffe dropped its inaugural bombs on the city, near Croydon. Right then Guy didn't care about any of that.

SEVENTEEN

GOVERNMENT HELP

Guy's solicitor John Timney's philosophy was that there is never such a thing as a wasted call or a wasted hour with anyone if there was just the tiniest percentage of a chance that it might help a client. Guy was in jail and he'd be in there indefinitely so when John Timney went to meet with the Right Honourable Maurice Percy, Member of Parliament for Upper Bexton, he reasoned that he had nothing to lose. He couldn't come out of the meeting with less than he'd gone in with. Guy would still be incarcerated. That Maurice Percy would help was a long shot, Timney knew, but it was one he considered well worth trying.

"Mr Schneider's imprisonment is without grounds and a total denial of our system of justice which, as a lawyer, I represent and am powerless to challenge," John Timney opened his argument once the small talk had been dispensed with.

Maurice Percy, who had been Upper Bexton's representative in Parliament for twenty seven years, already had his plastic smile fixed firmly in place long before John Timney had even sat down in his plush office with the deep, thigh-high pile carpet and the finest ornate British Colonial furnishings. He was a professional deal maker, ring kisser and handshaker and all-round good guy. He had been a child of privilege who had a lot more money than he'd ever had to work for and he meant to keep things that way. If as a by-product he could make the world a better place... then that would be okay too.

"Firstly, Mr Schneider has my full sympathy," he said in his refined accent, and really looked like he actually believed what he was saying, "but the Emergency Powers Act is, as you have said yourself, beyond challenge. I'm afraid there is nothing that I am able to do."

"As Guy Schneider's MP we need your lobby in the Commons," John Timney pleaded.

"You know how high feelings are running in the country. The constituents who I represent simply won't accept my campaigning on behalf of a German," and he said all of that with that wonderful, winning smile of his still in place. "We are at war with Germany," he reminded John

176

Timney in a patronising tone as if the fact had totally passed the lawyer by. "And secondly..."

"One of your constituents is sitting in prison for nothing," Timney interrupted heatedly, "and he's a lot more British than he ever was German. Indefinite detention without trial can't be right and if we have to challenge the law so be it. The Commons is the only body available to us to do this."

"I represent all the people of Upper Bexton Mr Timney. Not just the one," Maurice Percy said and fiddled with the expensive gold and diamond cufflinks at the end of his expensive shirt sleeves, which were poking out of the arms of his expensive jacket. He was starting to lose patience but compensated for it with forced politeness. The smile got wider and even more teeth were on show now, "I can't campaign for one at the cost of fifty-three thousand others who simply wouldn't tolerate it." He could see John Timney's frustration. He went on," but I'll put myself in your shoes for a moment. I would want to fight for the client who was putting money in my pocket. I respect that." Timney opened his mouth to say something but Maurice Percy only raised his voice and ploughed right on to prevent the lawyer from stopping his flow. "Now you do the same. Imagine you had a mandate from an eighty-two percent majority in your town. Eighty. Two. Percent," he repeated the figure for effect. "But not even one single person of the remaining eighteen per cent would want to jeopardise the war effort. Not one. 'Victory at all costs' is what our Prime Minister has said. And if one of those costs is detaining the enemy until the war is won then that is what we will have to tolerate.''

"Guy Schneider hasn't been incarcerated because he's the enemy. He hasn't been interned. He's in prison under Regulation 18B, which denies him the right to a trial and therefore denies him a fair and proper defence. That's not right and you know it. You should say so in Parliament."

"The War Office has decided that it's part of the battle we have to win. Think of what we're fighting for!" insisted the MP.

"Think of what we're fighting against," countered Timney and looked directly into smooth Maurice Percy's eyes. "You know what Mr Schneider is accused of? Then great, tell me. Then let's put him on the stand and see what a jury makes of it. That is how a system of justice works." He shook his head in helplessness and began to get up out of the soft leather armchair.

He lowered his voice and spoke softly and his words seemed to carry even more weight. "You know, you might be right, you are powerless. But if the law stinks, it stinks. As a lawmaker who refuses to challenge it, you and your other local jokers might just deserve one another."

Just as he'd reasoned beforehand, John Timney came away from the meeting with nothing - but also nothing less than he had gone in with.

***

While his lawyer was making his plea to his local MP, Guy lay on his bed and wrote another letter using some more paper that Duncan Carmichael had acquired for him. "Life in prison is life in suspension," he wrote to Anna. "One without purpose and without meaning." He talked about how Freddie Turnbull had spent his time making up for lost sleep and hadn't bothered him at all, but he had attacked a Jew in the exercise yard and when he heard that Duncan Carmichael was homosexual he promised to 'sort him out too.' Freddie Turnbull didn't know Duncan or even know what he looked like but he would see to it at some point that Duncan would be taught his lesson. The Jew who Fearless Freddie hit was Hans Leibnitz from Dresden. He had managed to escape from a Nazi concentration camp and found asylum in Britain, but for Freddie, he was fair game. Hans Leibnitz never even saw the lightning bolt of a left hook which broke his jaw. He mumbled to the prison medical staff through his smashed teeth that the injury happened when he slipped in his cell and fell against the metal bed frame. Most of the detainees around Guy were depressed, lonely and afraid. "It's a prison of broken men," Guy wrote, "some are broken by fear, some are broken by anger, and others by shame." One poor internee wrecked his cell in protest at his loss of liberty and was given an additional three months for it. There were plenty of pro-fascist/anti-Jew prisoners, and most worrying, a few who had become indoctrinated while they were in there. An inmate three cells down from Guy had become fascinated by Hitler and by fascist ideology from the time that Hitler came to power. The detainee claimed not only to know Lord Haw-Haw personally but also to having slept once with Mosley's sister-in-law after a political rally which they had both attended. He spoke with a lisp but had managed to persuade his fellow cellmate to "give thum theriouth thought to the benefith of right-wing politicth," and how for the hard working man fascism was the only fair and correct way of organising a society. Pretty soon his cellmate was vigorously spreading the message to others in the style of the finest orator, persuading them that "we need a new world order. The discipline, heroism, camaraderie and patriotism which won us the war in 1918... surely it can be harnessed to the good in peacetime to create a better and more harmonious society? Think about it. We need something finer. Something nobler." The third detainee in their cell might even have agreed with those sentiments, but for very different reasons. He was a shipyard worker from Southampton who was a shop steward and a member of the communist party and he was head-over-heels in love with the sound of his own voice. "It's an imperialist war and does nothing for the common man - in either country," he tried to argue forlornly, "this war is unjust and unlawful." He preached as if all it needed was a handful of Europe's best lawyers to put their heads together to stop it.

"I'll buy you a ticket to Berlin," one of the inmates in the exercise yard proposed one morning when the shop steward kicked off again with his monologue. "You can piss off there and tell all that to the Nazis." A far more common response though was "Go fuck yourself."

They weren't the exact words which Guy used the day the shop steward managed to corner him in the workshop but the sentiment was similar. "The employers in this country are using this war to increase their productivity and their profits," he droned on, "they're exploiting their workers with longer working hours and using women and cheap labour in skilled men's jobs to lower their costs. They've been allowed to completely ignore the Factory Act which was imposed to protect the workers' rights," he said as if it was a personal insult before he delivered his killer line, "we're even denied the right to strike." Guy just nodded, faked an urgency to get to a toilet, and slipped away, bored.

Like the Jew, the shop steward had been given a taste of Fearless Freddie's impressive right hook on the way back from the workshop. Yet no matter which flag they chose to march under - whether they were politically Right or Left, Jew or Christian, rich or poor, pacifist or soldier - every detainee claimed to be a Patriot with a capital 'P.' Even the fascists. All everyone wanted was a 'greater' Britain. A better, finer Britain. Which presented many of them with a problem. They were suddenly conflicted because their admiration of fascist ideology - which bordered on the fanatical and the religious - and their obsession with Germany and Italy, was at odds with their sense of patriotism and nationalism.

EIGHTEEN

THE GERMANS ARE HERE

"If The Invader Comes" the booklet was titled. Like every household in Britain, Grant and Claire received theirs on the morning of the 13th of June. In the booklet there were seven rules to follow, should the worst ever come to pass. Rule four stated "Do not give the Germans anything. Do not tell him anything. Hide your food. Hide your bicycles." Rule seven instructed everyone to "Always think of your country before you think of yourself." It was a country on edge and afraid. Britain wasn't winning the war, Dunkirk was the reality, and now the Italians were in on the side of the fascists. Even the Queen was being taught daily how to fire a gun.

Claire dropped the booklet into the rubbish bin before she knew Anna would be able to read it once she got back from visiting Hannelore Hildebrandt.

Because of circumstances, Anna hadn't been to read German to the blind eighty-six year old for three weeks. When she arrived at her house near Kelsey Park in Beckenham, Anna found Hannelore unwell and a lot more fragile than at their last meeting. She'd had a cold which had developed into a bout of bad bronchitis and when Anna arrived she was coughing from somewhere deep down in her lungs and having great difficulty breathing, but still, she insisted that their session with her beloved Schiller, Goethe, and Heinrich Heine should go ahead. After ten minutes, when Anna looked up from her book, she found Hannelore Hildebrandt fast asleep and her chest wheezing and heaving up and down, up and down with each hard fought for breath.

When she had first started to go to Frau Hildebrandt's eighteen months earlier, Anna had felt uneasy. Blind people had always made her nervous, she believed that they were in possession of an innate, mystical gift which allowed them to see things which mere mortals cannot. They possessed another dimension. Something beyond the visual. Can they see deep into my soul and recognise some evil residing down there? Anna wondered, and how can they evaluate things? How can Hannelore Hildebrandt evaluate me? Surely she can never know if I'm happy or sad, angry or depressed without me saying it. It confused

Anna, and those feelings were only heightened when Hannelore told her once "you have to go into the darkness sometimes to see things clearly Anna." Into the darkness was the very last place Anna wanted to return to. Somehow, blind people gave her the creeps. She hated herself for thinking that way so she hated them for what they could make her feel, which was cheap and bigoted and discriminatory and all the things that she of all people should know better than to tolerate. But Anna grew to adore the old German widow who had come to London in eighteen ninety nine when her husband Oskar got a job lecturing in Germanistiks at the University of London, and she knew that Hannelore liked her too. I can't be all bad then Anna reassured herself. In her prime, before her eyesight failed her, Hannelore Hildebrandt had been a cantankerous, rebellious, feisty old warhorse who loved nothing better than to rattle cages, especially cages which she felt deserved to be rattled. She had taught German herself and fought like a tiger for better conditions for herself, for her colleagues, and even for her students. In fact, for everyone and anyone who she felt was being short changed by the powers-that-be. She had led a strike at her first school for better pay for her female colleagues, for which she was dismissed, and encouraged a walkout by students at her second school - the first in the school's one hundred and twenty-five year history. Anna could only imagine the fire and fight which the old girl once went into battle with, and she loved hearing her stories

184

and her radical, left field theories such as her conviction that if the men who waged wars would only spend more time having sex then there would be no wars. "As my Oskar always used to say, more fucking would equal less fighting, do you understand Anna?" she asked in her immaculate German, which contrasted starkly with the coarse words that she was speaking, and a split-second after recovering from the shock of the old German woman's free and explicit language, Anna responded with a vigorous "yes."

Anna put her book down and left Frau Hildebrandt to sleep on, and busied herself instead with tidying up the house and mending a tear which she saw in the dining room curtain. When Hannelore finally woke up Anna made her a cup of tea and a sandwich out of some sliced meat - which was all she could find in the sparse, near empty pantry - and made sure that she'd be fine until her daughter arrived an hour later. Her daughter lived close by in Bromley and called in at her mother's twice a day to do the things that her still stubbornly independent mother wasn't able to do. Anna had wanted to tell Hannelore all about Guy and the wedding and losing the Professor and her job and the move to Rowlandsgill Gate, but she could see that the old girl really wasn't well so she left it for another day. She was curious to see what Hannelore Hildebrandt would make of the whole sorry story. But the trip out to Beckenham and having someone else to fret over, however brief it was, occupied Anna enough to distract her from her own troubles for a short while.

On the way home from Hanelore, Hildebrandt's Anna could have sworn she was being followed. First, to the station at Beckenham Junction by two men, then again when she got off her bus in Knightsbridge, but this time by only one. She kept turning around and looking, but each time she did, her followers were nowhere to be seen. You're crazy Anna, she told herself. Where do you think you are? Back in Hamburg? With two Gestapo monkeys after you? Get a hold of yourself. That man with the fancy felt fedora... why, he's just a figment of your wild, runaway imagination.

"Get out of my head. Leave me alone," Anna's inner voice screamed back at her errant, inane thoughts.

NINETEEN

THE PRINTS

The next morning Anna was coming down the stairs just as Grant was picking up his briefcase to leave for work. "Don't forget to drop those prints off at Mark's," Claire shouted to him from up the hallway.

"I really have no time today. I'll try to…"

"I'm going to the city. I can take them." Anna said.

***

"I'm sorry Miss... what was the name again?"

"Vieti."

"Miss Vieti, But it would be very difficult to employ you under the circumstances."

What the circumstances were they weren't saying, but it was Anna's first rejection when she called in at the Little Sisters Infirmary in Pimlico. She had written to them a few days earlier to see if they had any work for her. She would do anything, she told them. She'd heard nothing back from them so thought she would just call in speculatively because you never know, Anna thought.

And "I don't know" were the exact words at the second place she called in at - St. Andrew's Hospital in Chelsea. Again it was just a hopeful knock on the door in passing. The hospital official who she spoke to was the only one available who could talk to her and he was in way over his head so far as recruitment was concerned. "I'll have to ask. Leave your details and someone will get back to you." was how he left it.

"Should I be doing this?" Anna asked herself after the second hospital. Is it bold? Or is it desperate? It doesn't matter. It's practical. I can't live off the Coopers or off Guy forever. I want to pay my way. I need to work. I'll do anything they have for me. I'm desperate to make my contribution.

"We're not taking on any more full-time professional staff at the moment," was what Anna heard at the third place - a small private clinic in Westminster - from the red-headed receptionist who had applied a little too much lipstick that morning. "We're fine with the current numbers and the extra volunteers who have been helping out. You can volunteer if you wish?" Anna told her that she 'did wish' and she left her details for someone to get in touch with her. "It will take a week or two," they told her.

Undeterred, Anna set off with Grant's large package under her arm and tried a fourth and fifth. Her qualifications 'weren't right' at the hospital across the river in Lambeth (in other words, she was the wrong nationality), where the receptionist who she spoke to looked at Anna as if she had no business at all being there. At the hospice close by which she also tried, there was no one free that morning to see her except a young ward clerk who was under time pressure and could only spare Anna a rushed couple of minutes. "Where did you say you're from?" the ward clerk asked Anna.

"I didn't."

"But the accent... you're Polish, aren't you?"

"Yes."

"I thought so. My new neighbours come from Danzig. Why not try the Army?" the ward clerk suggested, "they're looking for people."

"Of course," said Anna to her politely and thought to herself 'what, as target practice? As a human shield?' Look, there's that funny lady again - the crazy German gypsy in the British army. Anna even had to laugh herself at her own joke thoughts. "You have to laugh or else you'll cry," as old Mrs Williamson was always saying.

**

Mark Hermann lived on the first floor of a terraced, three-storey Victorian house in Fulham. He also had the very top floor in the building - the attic - which he had made into his atelier, and when Anna called that was where he had been working. He came downstairs to answer the front door with paint smeared all over his fingers and hands and streaked across his black work shirt. Someone had followed him downstairs to the door - Roland, a tall jack-the-lad character who Mark was in the process of showing out. When Mark opened the door and saw just who was standing there, a smile as wide as the horizon broke out over his intense features. "Well hello Miss 'Next Time,'" he said, beaming.

"Anything else you need, you know where I am," Roland said to Mark as he left.

"Thanks, Roland."

Roland nodded an informal 'hello' to Anna and crossed the road with a keen look back over his shoulder at the attractive, olive skinned girl who was standing on the doorstep and holding out a large wrapped package for Mark.

"The prints from Grant. I was passing and... well, here they are."

Mark was unable to take them from her on account of the mess on his hands and gestured to her to "come in." He led her upstairs, past his flat on the first floor and up to the next, where she followed him into a bright room flooded with light from an overhead window. There were paints, easels, canvasses and brushes lying all over the place. "Put them down somewhere... wherever you can find space," he said, referring to the prints that she was holding. In the corner of the room was a female shop window mannequin which Mark had once used as a model. Now, layers of his own clothes were draped over it. Anna nodded towards it.

"The wife or the girlfriend?"

"An ex-girlfriend… who I had embalmed."

"I don't know what that means."

"It means you kill them and then you stuff them."

"And you suffocated her with shirts and coats?"

Mark smiled. He was starting to like her even more, "I killed her with love. And kindness."

Anna found some room between two easels for the prints, leaned them against the wall, and looked at the painting standing on the nearest easel. It was dark, abstract, and full of sharp lines and grotesquely distorted figures. They were difficult to make out, but in the foreground the painting had two disfigured men, holding rifles, marching forward but appearing as if they were being driven backwards. One of the men appeared to have had his insides blown out. The landscape behind them was bleak and menacing. It was all in total contrast to the paintings in the catalogue which Claire had shown her. Mark saw her looking at the painting and made an "And?" gesture at her.

"There's something missing," she said, trying to act less interested than she actually was.

"Oh, an art expert now?"

Anna scanned the picture further. "Beauty. That's what's missing."

"I paint what I see." He watched her look deeper into the pitch black vision of his unchained imagination. "I told you," he said, "there are other senses."

Anna turned to look at him. "Wouldn't you like to paint beauty? Again?"

There was no answer to her question. He simply looked at her looking at the painting; lost in her over-whelming beauty. Then he said, "I'd like to paint you."

It neither shocked nor surprised Anna. She remained cool and impassive. "You have the wrong colours," she said and gestured towards the depressingly dark painting. "The wrong shades."

"You think so? I think they would do. Right now."

"Am I this dark?"

"No. Only the parts I can see." He picked up Grant's package and took it over to the table. "I learned all I know from an old, blind man," he told her as he unwrapped the parcel. "He used to sit in the corner of a cafe in Paris which we always went into."

"You lived in Paris?"

"I studied there for four years. That old blind man, Remi he was called, taught me to look beyond the visual... and get to the essence of a thing. 'Look for the meaning in everything' he told us. 'Tear right through to the heart of your subject... see what you can find in there and describe it' he said. So I did. I tried to look beyond the physical." ('And then along came Anna' he thought to himself, but he didn't say it.) He raised his eyebrows. "So...?"

"So what?"

"So do I get to tear right through to the heart of this particular subject in front of me?"

She tried to lighten up, even warming to their little game. "It will cost you." Then, off the look that he was giving her, she added playfully, "I'm desperate for money these days."

"Only for money?"

But Anna wasn't taking the bait. She simply stood and looked up at him, momentarily unsure how to react. He fixed her with a with a "well, what comes next?" look. She glanced down at her watch. She wasn't late, but it was all she could think of to do. She scratched at something which didn't itch and looked back up at Mark. She felt uncomfortable, worse, she felt confused. She found herself wanting to go and wanting to stay at the same time. Mark finally broke the spell by saying "Thanks for the prints." Anna gestured a 'you're welcome' to him and, just as she had done at the party, she turned away with her cool, Mona Lisa smile and made an exit.

***

After she had left Mark's place, Anna went to see John Timney. She knew he had been to see their local MP the previous day and she called to hear the news - which was what she had been told to expect, but not what she had hoped for. It will have to be the Appeals Committee, John Timney had told her. The Committee would be Guy's only way out. And no matter how well he could prepare Guy

"You just don't know" he warned her. "It's like all good battle plans; perfect... until you go up against the enemy."

Anna walked off down Cheapside towards the Underground station with John Timney's parting words still ringing round in her head. "Justice and the law have nothing to do with each other these days Miss Vieti. It's just a game they play," he had told her grimly. While over in Hamburg that same morning the local Nazi Party leader stood on the city hall steps and proudly announced to a large, cheering crowd that the city would very soon become a "Juden und Ratten freie Stadt" a Jew and gypsy free city.

TWENTY

ANOTHER LETTER

Unable to sleep, Anna lay on the bed and stared, tormented up at nothing. She ran her fingers through her hair and squeezed them so tight that her knuckles were almost white. A crumpled letter lay on the floor next to the bed. Guy's words on the page echoed round in her head:

"A starving man can't always be an honest man, Anna. His choice is simple. Survive... Or die."

The day Guy had written his letter was the day that someone got out of jail. Guy heard a commotion in the corridor outside the cell door and he jumped up from his rock-hard prison mattress to join Freddie Turnbull, who already had his ear pressed hard up against the door. On the other side, two warders were passing by, carrying a dead detainee on a stretcher. The poor bastard had managed to hang himself with his belt in his cell seven doors down from Guy. Just as Guy had suspected, conjuring up his liberty had proved to be beyond the illusionist's magic powers. Shame. Hopelessness. Isolation. Depression. They were just four of the things which had got to him. Just as it had so many of the other detainees. As the warders passed Guy's cell both of the magician's arms poked out from under the blanket and hung limply over the sides of the stretcher. Word had spread quickly from the other end of the corridor by way of the inmates shouting out the news to each other, and from every cell on the floor came the ear-splitting sound of metal cups being banged on metal doors. Guy and Freddie grabbed their mugs and joined in. One of the inmates a few doors away let out a deafening noise that sounded like a wolf howling - 'A-Whoo-Hoo' he roared - which even sent a chill down Fearless Freddie's spine.

"Until you have experienced hunger you can never say that you are completely honest," Guy wrote, "you don't know what you'll do."

The magician had been the second detainee to take his own life. Guy hadn't known the other one but the word in the exercise yard was that it had been an ex-policeman in another prison. "They're in a better place now," he told Anna.

That night Guy lay on his bed in the dark and, like Anna, stared up at nothing. "I don't know how much more of this I can take. I have to get out of here Anna," he had written.

Anna tossed her body from one side of the bed to the other, as if the pain which she felt was physical. Her mind was racing. Then she buried her head in her pillow, shutting out the voice which was now haunting her.

"Principles won't buy him freedom," Guy had ended his letter with. "I have to get out somehow. We have to get away Anna."

While Anna had her sleepless night, Guy finally managed an hour's sleep, but it wasn't a good hour. His head spun with frenzied, crazed, corrupt images.

Picture this, just as Guy did: Anna standing in a crowded pub - up close to a handsome doctor from work - she leans right in close - whispers something into his ear then stands back to see his reaction - he nods his head and smiles - she takes him by the hand and drags him away grinning - they're in her bedroom now - she kisses him - they start to tear at each other's clothes NO, STOP!! MAKE THIS IMAGE GO AWAY Guy's voice screamed, and the doctor disappeared, leaving Anna alone in the room, naked. But a second doctor comes into the room and takes the first one's place - he's taller, stronger, RICHER, even more handsome - Anna grabs down at his belt buckle - goes down onto her knees and... STOP! STOP! Anna hears Guy shouting and turns to see him watching her - she's angry as hell at him - she storms over and pokes her finger hard into him...

197

"Shut the fuck up Schneider!" Freddie Turnbull stood right over Guy and dug his finger into Guy's shoulder. Guy opened his eyes and stared right through Freddie as if he was made of glass. His moans and groans had woken Freddie from his deep sleep. "You okay camera man?" Freddie asked. Guy just continued to stare. He was still seeing Anna. Worse still, he knew it had been no dream. It was his new reality.

***

Someone was watching Anna from across the street when she left the Pennington-Coopers' house the next morning. At the other side of the small garden park which ran the whole length of Rowlandsgill Gate an immaculately waxed and freshly polished blue Morris 10 was parked at the kerbside. Inside it was the silhouette of a fedora. Adams sat and watched Anna leave the house, then turn right at the corner of the street and out of sight.

Zamborano's, the Italian restaurant next to John Timney's offices in Cheapside, now had a sign in the window which read 'The Proprietors of these premises are British and have two sons in the British Army' which didn't stop an attempted arson attack however two weeks later. Anna walked past the restaurant and into John Timney's office building.

Ten minutes after she'd gone in, Adams approached the same building furtively and looked at the nameplate on the door. Then he quickly moved off when he saw someone approaching the door from the inside. He swiftly darted into the entrance of Zamboranos restaurant just as Anna walked out.

Shortly afterwards she was standing at a bus stop. She looked on edge and picked nervously at a loose seam on her handbag. She was second in line in the queue. Four people behind her stood Adams. As the bus approached, Anna stepped out of the queue, turned, and walked directly up to him. Adam's face was a picture of surprise. Hers was full of mischief. "Well fancy meeting you here. Where's the car today? Left it outside of the house?" Then she leaned right in to him and quietly but forcefully whispered into his ear "Stop following me or I'll scream and let everyone know you tried to rape me, okay?" Then she stood back from him and remarked out loud "Nice hat." and reached up and flicked the brim of Adam's fedora with a finger. And with that, she was gone, up to the street. Leaving an intimidated Adams in shock - and perhaps a little in love.

TWENTY-ONE

PICTURE THIS: IF ANNA HADN'T RUN

Anna's cousin Emma Vieti looked up and straight into the cold killer eyes of the camp doctor. "One day you'll all have to answer for this, you know that don't you?" she managed to say to him in the weakest of whimpers. She knew what would follow. She had already been stripped naked and strapped to a cold, wooden table. Emma was always a pretty girl. She had a rounder face than Anna and had much bigger and rounder eyes and perfect teeth. But none of that was left six months after she'd arrived at the camp. She was now so skeletal-thin and emaciated and her eyes so sunken and devoid of any signs of life that Anna would hardly have recognised her.

Ewald Baumgärtner, the camp doctor, ignored her question and picked up a shiny curved scalpel. Emma's eyes widened as he moved the scalpel nearer and nearer to her left leg. He stopped briefly to clear his throat before he sliced into her thigh and meticulously scraped the skin and muscle fibers apart. Emma's screams echoed around the windowless room. Baumgärtner raked around inside the wound for some time. Then he dosed the cut with a cotton swab covered with bacteria, and after that, he took some sharp wood splinters and bits of grit and dirt and shoved them deep into the open wound just to make sure that the infection would spread even further and even faster. Only then did he answer Emma's question.

"One day science will thank us for all of this," was all that Baumgärtner said to her.

Then he took a drill from his portly male assistant and started it up. It made a high-pitched whirring noise. He pressed it against Emma's right kneecap and slowly began to drill into the joint, pressing deep down through the flesh until the drill hit the bone. Emma's screams became earsplitting. He kept on drilling right down into the knee-cap. Blood and skin and tissue and fragments of shattered bone flew all over the place. A piece of sharp bloody knee cap hit Emma under the chin. He drilled right through the knee and only stopped when he smashed into the base of the femur. At which point he twisted the end of the drill around to enlarge and widen the hole in the kneecap as much as he could. Then he withdrew it and carefully packed the hole with tiny shards of broken glass and old metal chippings. When he was finished, his assistant wheeled Emma out and into an adjacent room. By now she had long passed out.

One day science and the Fatherland would indeed be most grateful to Emma Vieti and her band of happy fellow 'volunteers' for helping to establish which drugs were the best to use for treating the wounds of German soldiers who'd been injured in battle.

So take a bow, Emma.

Or rather, take a bath. Because seven weeks after her legs had been sliced open and drilled she was again stripped naked and this time dipped into a vat of ice-cold water. A probe had been pushed high into her rectum to measure the drop in body temperature. Emma was lowered into the vat and began to freeze. Like most victims, she lost consciousness and died when her body temperature dropped to twenty five degrees Celsius. Who would ever have thought?

And these things really happened.

In the end - it has to be said - Emma Vieti welcomed her own death. If death meant no more camp, no more worse-than-living-hell-on earth, then she was happy enough to finally fulfill her wish and "get out" that way.

Five years later and some weeks after the war had been lost Ewald Baumgärtner managed to evade the Allied military police and escape south to Rome, where a leading Italian Cardinal arranged a new ID for him and letters of transit to get him first to Rio de Janeiro and then on to Paraguay where he lived happily and healthily until he was ninety six years old.

"One day you'll all have to answer for this" my freezing-cold ass.

***

Anna herself never knew what happened to her cousin back in summer 1939, or to the rest of the Vieti family rounded up with her. But it was all meticulously documented and recorded for posterity so that the past wouldn't be lost for the future.

So picture this: If Anna had never managed to escape from Nazi Germany and hadn't run into the safe and comforting and welcoming open arms of...

Well, that would have been a different story. Just another one of the quarter of a million untold disappearing gypsy stories.

The world never got to hear a single one of them.

TWENTY-TWO

THE WAR OFFICE

They met in a private room that afternoon in a gentlemen's club in Mayfair. The décor fitted the mood perfectly - dark and somber. There was a bottle of gin and a bottle of the very best malt whiskey on the table but it remained unopened and next to the two bottles were three empty glasses. Major Walker, his adversary the Home Secretary, and the Secretary of State for War would all remain clear headed and sober for this.

"There's anger on the streets," Walker spat out. "We've all seen the violence which is happening in every big city throughout the land now. Apart from avoiding mass civil unrest, it would also be safer for the Germans and Austrians living here if we take them out of harm's way. This is not only about the security of the country but also security for them." Walker argued with the logic of a parent who beats the crap out of their child and then tells it 'now look what you've made me do!' Yes, that's it. Why did nobody point this out before? Guy and the others are in a better place. A safer place. They should actually be grateful. 'Thank you Mr Government' they should be happily saying while they're down there on one knee.

"It would be a gross overreaction and an affront to civil liberties," the Home Secretary countered, although he knew even while he was making his pitch for reason that his argument no longer carried any real weight.

"Not that again!" Walker rolled his eyes, "why are you more concerned with foreigner's rights than with the safety of our own subjects?" He was growing increasingly exasperated. "Your mandate is from the British people, not those who we are at war with."

"I can assure you, Robert, that almost every single German living here is more anti-Nazi than the British. They've witnessed the horrors of fascism themselves firsthand. They have come here seeking refuge. They hate what Germany has become."

Walker threw the Home Secretary's own words back at him. "Almost every single one - but not every single one. If there are German agents out there - and there are - we need a net big enough to catch them all."

"We can't cope," the Home Secretary replied. "The prisons are full. The camps are filling. We must have more support. And more time."

"We need them all in," Walker repeated firmly, sensing that he was now holding the better cards. "You know that I know that, the Government knows it."

They both looked over to the Secretary of State for War, who looked back at them impassively. This could go either way.

***

That afternoon Guy and Freddie Turnbull received a new cellmate. The warders first took out Guy's bed and installed a bunk bed in its place, and a few minutes later they led in a sad-looking Ulsterman with red hair, bloodshot eyes, and a ginger wizard's beard thick enough to nest a dozen sparrows. He had been brought in from a smaller prison out in the suburbs which had taken in more detainees than it could cope with. Freddie Turnbull wasted no time in telling the new man that he would sleep on the old vet's crap-heap of a mattress and Freddie would take the top bunk for himself. When he said to Guy "That okay with you?" it was again no question but a pretty firm statement; that's how it's going to be. "You look like shit Cameraman," Freddie Turnbull added. And he was right.

***

"They think I'm a monster," Major Walker said to his wife when he sat down at ten thirty that evening for a much later than usual dinner, "a belligerent buffoon." He shook his head, exasperated. But his voice carried a hint of sadness along with the frustration. "They just don't understand. I've been closer to war than any of them."

206

His wife put his plate of boiled beef and steamed cabbage and carrots down in front of him. The Major looked over her shoulder at the photograph which was hanging on the dining room wall. Seventeen proud officers of the British IV Corps lined up for the camera before going into action at Langemarck at the Battle Of Ypres. Only five of them, including a wounded Robert Walker, would later return home alive.

The Major turned to his wife. "This is my battlefield now. Here, helping to protect these shores. Every drop of British blood which flows here on my watch as a result of any enemy activity is blood on my own hands. You understand that, don't you Elsie?"

"Yes. I do," Elsie Walker nodded her head sympathetically, "of course I understand." She sat down across the table from her husband, put her hands together, and prepared to say grace. "Dear Lord, for the… "

The Major's voice cut in over her. "Why can't they understand?" He was on his own direct line to God. He was making his own personal plea. He looked across the table at his wife and lowered his voice, "this is a war we simply have to win. No matter what the cost."

"I know dear," his wife said, then pressed on. "Dear Lord, for the food you have put on our table, we are thankful. And please help us all to live our days with thankful hearts and loving ways. Amen."

"Amen," echoed the Major and again muttered under his breath, "no matter what the cost."

That evening, just for one fleeting moment, Major Walker almost became human. But only until the next day, when the old protective shield of myopic fury and raging, heartless ruthlessness would go straight back up. Just as it would do every single day of his discontented and melancholic life.

***

That night, several hundred miles across the North Sea in Hamburg, thirty two more German gypsies were rounded up, together with a further two hundred and seventeen Jews, and taken to Altona station where a train was already waiting for them. Two more of Anna's cousins were among them. They were herded into three stinking cattle wagons and taken off to a death camp in the east. Not a single one of them would return home.

Freddie Turnbull knocked out titleholder Lew Jenkins in Madison Square Garden in New York to become the new Lightweight Champion of the World and celebrated by tap dancing his way around the ring. But it was only in his dreams. In the bunk below him, Guy didn't dare dream at all. He did⁻ ⁻ ⁻ ⁻ ⁻ ⁻ ⁻ ⁻ asleep.

TWENTY-THREE

ANNA'S LUCKY DAY

Three days later Anna put on her favourite beige suit – the one with the belted jacket and the brown suede collar and pencil skirt – and took an extra few minutes with her makeup so that it was all just perfect. Then she fastened on the pearl necklace which Guy had bought for her. She was visiting him that morning and wanted to look her very best. When she thought she was finally ready she regarded her reflection in the dressing table mirror. 'You're fine today Anna' it smiled and whispered back to her. Then she picked up the four leaf clover from the day out at the coast and pushed it into her handbag. 'I don't know why but I feel lucky today' she said to herself and the clover was extra insurance on that good time feeling. This is my day and no one else's. When she came downstairs there was a letter waiting for her. It was from St. Andrew's Hospital in Chelsea - one of the places she had called in at by chance earlier in the week. They said they had a vacancy for her and "we would like to formally invite you for an interview" they had kindly informed her. It's my day. It's the four-leaf clover. It's the pearls. It's all the stars aligned in Anna Vieti's favour she told herself.

"That's wonderful news, Anna," Claire said to her before she set off to visit Guy.

She had to take two buses to prison. On the second was a woman who Anna had seen before in the prison visitor's room. The woman took a seat next to her. She recognised Anna too and they struck up a conversation. The woman was a Londoner, like her detained husband Max, but she told Anna that they had lived in Leipzig for three years before the war. Max still corresponded with old friends which they had made in Germany and she thought that must be the reason they had locked him up. "They told him it was for 'Hostile Origin and Association' and for 'Acts Prejudicial'… or something like that," she told Anna vaguely. "That's all we can think of." She was "angry as hell," she said, and indeed she sounded 'angry as hell.' Her husband was a watchmaker and they'd had to shut up shop since the day he was arrested. So they obviously had no income coming in and she'd been forced to live off their savings "and the charity of others" she said with more than a hint of shame as if she was confessing in church.

'The same with me' Anna thought to herself but kept silent.

"Are you two married?" The woman asked, and Anna spent the rest of the ten minute journey answering questions about the sorry tale of the wedding day that never was.

"That's awful. Just awful," the woman said as they walked through the main prison gates together, followed by a highly pregnant young woman with red-rimmed eyes, who looked like she'd spent the entire past six weeks crying.

***

The woman from the bus took a table at the far end of the visitor's room from Anna, who sat facing Guy across the table. Next, to Anna, the pregnant woman had already burst into tears long before her youthful looking husband was led into the room by a warder and took his seat a few short feet away from Guy.

Guy was just a ghost now and looked a whole lot worse for his incarceration. His hair hadn't been so much cut as sliced off indiscriminately in clumps. The bits which had survived had taken on a life of their own. He was unwashed and unshaven. His skin had a yellowy, unhealthy pallor, and there was now a large sore on his lip. His eyes were tired, sunken, defeated. Once only six months older than Anna, he now looked double her age. He'd fallen into the abyss. A lost soul.

Anna steeled herself. She was determined not to let him see her distress at his appearance. "I have a job interview," she said with the same cheery optimism that she'd started the day with. Guy showed no response, no interest, and just looked down at the table. "I was at the lawyer's on Friday," she tried again, still with the same hopefulness in her voice. "He's sure the Committee will have to recommend your release." But Guy had long since stopped believing, and his eyes told Anna this. "It's true Guy. You have to believe it!" she pleaded.

"Why should I wait for some Committee to release me?" he snapped back.

"You have to. Just six more weeks to your hearing, that's all Guy. And when they release you we-"

"They're not releasing me," he cut her off.

"Of course they will. You'll convince-"

"I'll convince no one," his voice had got louder. One or two of the other inmates and their visitors turned to look. He lowered his voice, but it was with a defiant, angry growl that he said, "If I don't take the chance I've been given I don't deserve any better."

"No one knows why they've locked you up in here, but it isn't because you are German. And you're giving that up. You're British. You've done nothing. And whatever else might happen out here that will keep you free.

Maybe keep both of us free." She reached out to take his hand but he jerked it back and out of reach.

"So that's it? That's what she's after. Pretty Miss Righteous hasn't come here to save me, but to save herself," he snarled. He was convinced now that he had finally seen the light.

"Oh Guy, stop it. How can you say that?" she could see now that it wasn't only his appearance which had changed. It was a very different Guy who was sitting opposite her.

"Why do you want to keep me in here anyway? Found someone else have you? Is that it?" His imagination was now running wild. She looked across the table at him. He was now a stranger she no longer knew. There was something in his face now which scared her. "Little Anna found something better now, is that it?" Each word was like a dagger through her heart. "Whore!" he spat out.

"What?"

"You heard. Whore."

She stared at him disbelievingly. "Why are you saying this?" she said over him as Guy ploughed on relentlessly.

"Who is it? One of those doctors at the hospital? Any rich, safe, steady pair of hands just waiting to grab a piece of cheap and easy gypsy slut who's ready to turn a trick in return for her free ride to freedom?"

She was truly shocked to hear him talk this way and the first signs of tears began to form in her eyes. But she fought them and tried once again to reason with him.

"There's a war on. So fight Guy. Fight! You'll get out. The right way."

He looked at her with total contempt. "There is no right way. If MI5 want me to set up another fucking spy, what the hell do I care? He won't be the first. And he won't be the last.''

"What do you mean?"

Guy ignored the question. He looked away and over at the two warders.

"What do you mean 'another spy'?" she asked again.

Guy turned back to her. "I mean, you're not the one in here. But you know what?" He seemed to be relishing this now; this pain he was inflicting on her. "You could be soon."

Anna should have been afraid.

He was confronting her with her greatest fear, but she barely heard him as she sat and struggled to take in the change in him. Her own mind was now racing; trying to put two and two together; her suspicions beginning to grow. Perhaps it's all beginning to make sense now, her inner voice was screaming.

"Those missing photographs... they mean something, don't they?"

Guy just continued to shoot her a look of pure loathing.

"What did you mean when you wrote about the secret we all carry around? What's yours Guy?" She sat back in her seat - the penny had finally dropped. She was starting to understand more than she ever wanted to. "MI5 does have something, don't they?"

"Yeah... let's see them lock you up, eh?" Guy said, ignoring everything she'd just said to him. There was something sinister, something even sadistic in his voice now. "Then we'll talk again about how fucking easy this is. Then you'll understand. And we'll see just how far you'll go to get yourself out."

Anna could only stare in disbelief and shake her head from side to side. "How can you use such words Guy? Oh, Guy. I don't want to see you like this.''

"Then get out. And don't come back.''

There was a long, tense silence while they stared at each other across the table. There was a solid wall of ice between them now.

Her eyes searched all over Guy's face, almost pleading for a sign that none of this could possibly be true. But all she could see was the hatred in his eyes.

Finally, she broke the silence. "Do you really mean all that?"

He didn't really need to answer; the ice-cold look in his eyes told her that he did. "If that's all you've got for me - fuck off! And don't come back. I don't need that. I don't need you."

Anna sat for a stunned moment. She had no idea what to do. The man across the table was no longer the same man who had gone into prison four short weeks ago.

Guy got up out of his chair. "Fucking ignorant, disloyal bitch," he snarled at her, and every person in the room turned to look at them.

Anna stood up, wiped away a tear, turned and left the room. As Guy watched her leave in her half-run half-walk and with her hand over her mouth, there was pure anger in his eyes as he called out one last time after her. "Don't come back! It's over!"

***

In Rowlandsgill Gate, parked in the shade of the tall garden-park trees, Adams sat in his blue Morris 10 with his newspaper spread out across his steering wheel. A young squirrel hopped up onto the garden-park railing right next to the car and stared in at him. He looked bored. Across the street at the Pennington-Cooper's nothing at all was happening. He stifled a yawn and turned back to the sports section of his paper. The young squirrel hopped back down from the railing and scuttled off into the bushes.

***

Anna was lost in a daze as she walked away from the prison. Extracts from her conversation with Guy echoed around in her head - "she's come to save herself... there's no right way... they're not releasing me..." - all drowned out by Guy's louder voice screaming at her "It's over." Suddenly she stopped. She got control of herself and her emotions. She turned right around and headed off hopefully and purposefully back in the direction of the prison. This wasn't over yet.

Back in the prison visitor's room she sat anxiously and waited, bearing her heartbreak with dignity. The chair opposite her where Guy had sat a few short minutes before was empty. While she waited, one of the warders let himself into Guy's cell. The warder said something to Guy. Guy shook his head vehemently. The warder tried again, but once more Guy grimly, stubbornly, angrily, shook his head, spat out a few vicious words, then turned away from the warder. There were fury and defiance in his eyes. He had already abandoned himself, and now he was forsaking everyone else in his life.

And right then Guy really did hate her with a passion (he hated the world).

He really didn't want to see her ever again (he didn't want to see anyone).

He really could have put a knife right through the middle of her heart.

He had become Anna's mother. It was now time to detest what he once claimed to have loved. His loathing was genuine. And despite Anna not daring to believe it, she could palpably sense it. She had been loved. Now she was unwanted. It was, as Guy himself said, all over.

Detention Without Trial wasn't just winning the race now, it was way out in front and cruising.

Back in the visitor's room the warder stood over Anna and gave her the bad news. "He says it's over. He says... I

217

don't want to repeat the other things he said, Miss." Anna sat there distraught, taking in the implications of what was happening to her. "I'm sorry Ma'am..." the warder went on - "If I can give you some advice... You deserve someone better than that." Anna sat for a moment, shaken to the core. Then she collected herself, got up out of the chair, and for the second time within minutes, she left the room - rejected, hurt, utterly humiliated. And once again, just as she had done with her mother, she turned the blame in on herself. She wasn't good enough. She hadn't been strong enough. It's me, she told herself. And then she gave up thinking for a while.

***

Anna stumbled down the busy High Street close to the prison. She didn't know where she was and she didn't care. Her world had collapsed. Once again, those dreams born under a clear blue sky had died, but this time in a British prison. She looked pale and unwell. She was unsteady on her feet. She began to keel over to one side. She shot a hand out to grab hold of something to steady herself. It was a newspaper advertising board in the middle of the pavement. She stared and stared at its headline: "ALL ENEMY ALIENS TO BE INTERNED." Everything seemed to slow down for her. The bustle around her became a dull, hollow echo. She looked over at her image reflected in a shop doorway. Her entire life had just fallen apart - and now this. And that was what she saw in the face reflected back at her. Anna looked utterly defeated.

She looked sick. She once more looked so terribly alien here. And now very, very afraid. She stared again at the newspaper headline, barely able to draw breath. Guy suddenly wasn't her problem anymore. She fought desperately for air. She was fighting her demons. And now facing her past. She closed her eyes and squeezed them tight to shut out the image of the advertising board, but she couldn't erase the pictures which had haunted her all her life. She was back in Hamburg, standing on an embankment close to a railway station watching the masses of Jews, gypsies and assorted good-for-nothings herded into the trains and the doors slamming shut behind them. She saw the eyes full of fear and defeat as they took their last look at Hamburg through the wooden slats of the transporters taking them to their death. I have to get out before it's me. I have to get out. She saw her boyfriend from Hamburg, Ferdinand Constantin's battered face and limp body swinging in his cell. Then she was little Anna watching her drunken mother fight her drunken father. It was especially vicious. Her mother was out of control. It was a master class in rage and fury. "Bastard!" she was screaming. A bottle was thrown. A pair of scissors was picked up. In Anna's memory, she can't remember by whom. But she does remember moving in between them, screaming at them to stop. She'd never forget the fist that inevitably came down hard on her head, and then another. Nor flying into her black cellar prison and watching in horror as the door was slammed shut on her. There she lay gasping for air. Blood ran from a deep cut on her head. She covered her ears to block out the sound of the continued fighting from somewhere up in the building. She screamed and kicked out at the locked door.

A hand tapped her on the shoulder and the spell was broken. She was back in the busy High Street close to the prison in late June 1940.

She spun around and stared straight into the face of a friendly policeman. She stood frozen to the spot - a rabbit caught in the headlights, pale and trembling, staring vacantly up at him.

"Are you alright Miss?" Anna was unable to react. Afraid that an accent would give her away. The policeman nodded down towards her feet. "Your jacket belt. It's trailing the ground." Without a word, she picked it up, turned and was off down the street, leaving her reflection behind her, frozen in the shop door - grotesquely distorted by the angle of the glass. It stared back out at the world, torn and haunted.

In Knightsbridge, Anna turned the corner to see a blue Morris 10 car parked across the street from the house. She knew that car and the man in the fedora who sat patiently with his newspaper. She turned straight round and ran off in the direction she had come from, towards Kensington Road.

Moments later, a few miles away across the city, John Timney sat in his office and held the phone to his ear. "Where are you now Miss Vieti?"

"It's safer I don't say. Just..." her voice was weak and shaky. She stood in a small phone booth in a hotel close to Knightsbridge underground station. She'd squeezed herself so tight into the booth that it looked like she wanted to disappear into its walls.

As she spoke she nervously fingered her necklace. Her voice was a low whisper. It was heartbreak speaking. She looked increasingly unwell and massaged the sides of her forehead while she spoke. "Just - please take care of him for me. I-I can't anymore." Then in tears and with her voice nearly breaking, she put the phone down and left the phone booth.

"Miss Vieti? Miss Vieti...?" the lawyer shouted into the phone desperately. But it was to no one.

***

Picture This:

A middle aged waitress is escorted out of a Manchester restaurant by two police officers.

A fireman is arrested during a routine fire drill in Bristol.

A pregnant young woman in Hull is led off towards a Black Maria waiting in the street outside of her house.

A dentist in Sunderland is just about to extract a tooth. A detective knocks and enters the room without an invite.

A frail old man in Crewe packs a suitcase whilst a policeman stands and waits.

Two teenage schoolboys are helped into the back of a police van parked in the grounds of Gordonstoun School.

Their crime? Being German. The world had just been simplified to a plain "us" and "them."

The great roundup had begun. Again, and Anna was to be one of them. She knew she couldn't let that happen. But where do I go? How can I stay free? Because Guy was right, I would never be able to take it. Being locked away will finish me. I could never rise above it. Never conquer that dark part of me. She believed that prison - just like money, and war - didn't change or form character but reveal it, and what it would reveal would be the worst and the weakest and the most hateful part of herself. She wandered down Kensington High Street like a shock victim stumbling through the rubble after the last bomb had dropped. She turned a corner and ran straight into a small crowd of people who had gathered to shout anti-German abuse at a family of four who were being packed off into a police van by two police officers. The mob were vicious, and they were after blood. German blood. Someone hurled a rock, which ricocheted off the police van and hit Anna. Mortified, she had to gasp again for air, as if a rope around her neck was tightening. Then she pushed desperately through the crowd to get where she was going. And that certainly wasn't to prison or to any camp.

***

A little perspective here... No one ever wants to be locked up. And no enemy alien or British subject living in the United Kingdom in 1940 welcomed internment or detention without trial. But even as they were heading to the prisons and the camps which were hastily set up in the summer of 1940 to accommodate them, every German and Austrian national who had sought refuge in the country would have readily agreed that life in a British internment centre was nothing compared to what their fates would have been in the concentration camps of Nazi Germany. Most were prepared to dismiss it as a 'necessary evil' - an aberration in an otherwise noble and exemplary British war effort. They put it down to a consequence of war, and to being born the wrong side of the line, but for others who were denied their liberty for the duration of the conflict that was like telling a person who has broken his back and will be paralysed forever 'that's good news because at least you haven't got cancer.' You don't want one and you certainly don't want the other, and being the lesser of two evils didn't make it tolerable. Anna didn't want either. One would have killed her, and the other would... well, it will kill her too she believed. She had witnessed up close the horrors of incarceration and its ugly sisters: the beatings, the torture, and the slow, slow death. She also had her very own personal experiences of being caged up to draw on, she might have been as anti-German and pro-British as the next man or woman. But she would do what she had to do in order to avoid capture.

It was while she was on the bus going past a row of neat gardens on her way to Upper Bexton, slumped as low as she could in the back seat where she believed no one could see her - overwhelmed by her greatest fear and with panic now kicking in - that she remembered someone from home, a gypsy just like herself, who had hidden away for two years in his employer's garden hut. The police had called twice and searched high and low but had found nothing. The gypsy's employer promised the police that he hated Jews and gypsies with a passion and that he would certainly report the stinking gypsy's whereabouts if he ever heard anything. His act was good enough to convince them and they left him alone. So Anna knew it was possible to hide and survive. But locked in a tiny garden shed? Her? Never. This war could last for years, the last one went on for four. Who would provide for me? And what do I live from? Rations are at a minimum anyway. Whose share would I be taking and who would have to go without? And then there's the winter. She shook her head. I simply won't survive the garden shed or anywhere.

Her thoughts were getting wilder as her desperation increased. All she knew was that she couldn't be locked up. She didn't have what it took to survive that. 'Oh God I feel so sick,' she thought.

She got off the bus at Dorset Avenue and set off for the Williamsons,' and sanctuary. I'll survive there. They'll take me. They'll hide me away. Fifty yards short of the house she stopped.

A Black Maria police car was already waiting outside the house. Barnes sat in the passenger seat and flicked cigarette ash out of the open car window. Anna turned and ran back towards the bus stop.

Hannelore Hildebrandt's house had all the curtains drawn when Anna arrived there an hour later. It was two in the afternoon. Anna was walking up the garden path past Hannelore's small rose garden when the front door opened and a middle aged woman came out and locked the door behind her. She turned and saw Anna standing in the middle of the path. "Have you come to see Mrs Hildebrandt?" she asked with a sad and broken tone to her voice. Anna just stared at her for a moment. What do I say? Whatever it is my accent will give me away. Do I turn and run? That's a give-away too. I'm trapped.

"Ja," Anna heard herself saying. But what she really said was "yes."

"I'm Grace's sister-in-law..." She could see Anna was vague. "Grace is Mrs Hildebrandt's daughter. I'm afraid Mrs Hildebrandt died last night in the hospital. Did-"

Whatever she said after that Anna didn't hear. She had already turned and started her half-walk half-run away up the street.

She wandered in a frenzy around nearby Kelsey Park for a while. When anyone came towards her she immediately changed direction and shot off somewhere else. She was a wanted criminal. She was a fugitive. I am the enemy! There's a swastika tattooed on my forehead. I'm the most German person you've ever seen in your life. Her paranoia was running wild. A fever was boiling up inside of her. She wandered a little longer, around and around the small lake where two ducks stood and watched her

225

bend over and throw up into the water. But nothing came up, there was nothing inside her to come up. The ducks looked at her like she was a bad impersonator. Is that the best you can do? Get out of here. Then they flopped into the water and paddled away to the other side. Anna took a handkerchief out of her handbag and wiped at her mouth. She thought about poor Hannelore and began to cry. A little old lady feeding the birds came over and asked her if she was okay. Anna nodded her head. Then she asked if she could help her in any way and Anna this time shook her head and turned away. The old lady watched her walk off, staggering unsteadily from side-to-side, wondering if the problem was that Anna had lost her tongue somewhere in the park. She felt faint and was getting weaker by the minute. Her forehead was covered in perspiration and pounding. She was unwell, and she was on the run. But where to? She didn't know. But she did know that she had spent her last drop of energy, and she'd used up her very last ounce of hope.

TWENTY-FOUR

GIVE ME SHELTER

Mark Hermann opened his front door and, just as he had done the first time that Anna had called, he broke into a broad smile when he saw who was standing there.

"Well, well. Miss-" but before he was able to say another word and pick up on their little game he stopped. He could see that something was badly wrong. Her skin had a pallor which alarmed him. Her eyes were sunken. A film of perspiration covered her brow.

Anna removed her hand from her mouth just enough to say in a weak voice which was almost a whisper "They--they were waiting..." She looked dreadful. She looked like this really had been the worst day of her entire life. And she looked like she was about to collapse any second.

"Who was waiting? Anna... what's happened?" Mark asked, immediately concerned.

Before she could answer she had brushed straight past him and rushed up the stairs to the first floor, with her hand back over her mouth. Mark closed the door, and as he took the stairs after her he could already hear the sound of her being violently sick. He got to the bathroom just in time to see more vile, yellowy contents of her stomach fly into the toilet bowl and watch her collapse onto the floor, too ill even for tears. The perspiration was now pouring out of her and raining down the side of her face. She was gasping for breath. Her skull felt like it was splitting in half right down the middle of her forehead. Then her whole body convulsed again as she retched and vomited. But all she could bring up was a thin mixture of watery, slimy blood which dribbled down her chin and dripped onto her beige suit. Mark went over to her. Her hands were trembling and her body was still shaking. He swept her hair out of her face and lifted her head and cradled it in his lap. He grabbed some sheets of toilet paper and wiped the mess from her face and chin, then he reached over and ran a towel under the tap and dabbed it tenderly over her forehead. Finally, he lifted her up and carried her into the bedroom.

At eight o'clock that evening Mark stood in the public phone box at the end of his street in Fulham. Heavy rain was lashing against the phone box's small square window-panes - a brief interlude in an otherwise perfect

228

early-summer. He listened to Claire at the other end of the line.

"I'll call the doctor," she said, with clear worry in her voice. "I'll be straight over."

"No. And no doctor. It's too dangerous for all of us. I'll look after her."

"You can't Mark. You don't know-"

"I don't know any doctors who will break the law for her and neither do you," he jumped in and cut her off. "I'm her only chance." And before she could protest he added, "when it's safe, I'll send someone over for her things."

"No doctor would turn her in to the authorities. She needs professional help!" Claire pleaded, but it was to no one but the ringtone. Mark had already hung up and, rain-coat collar turned right up, he was braving the summer storm on his way back to the flat.

Anna lay in the pitch blackness of her cellar prison. She was gasping for air. Her throat was closing. She grabbed at it. She had to get air... Had to get it. She kicked out at the cellar door and it flew wide open. Brilliant sun-light filled the tiny room - so bright that she had to cover her eyes. Then water flooded in through the door. Loud, crashing waves of water and Anna was drowning. She floated and twisted through the foam and the bubbles and the swirling white water, gasping desperately for air and saw rocks coming towards her far too quickly. Sharp, jag-ged, terrifying rocks, and she knew that if she hit them she would die. A hand reached out to her. I'm saved. She grabbed at it. Frenziedly. As the fingers were about to meet the hand was pulled away from her. Guy, with crazed, menacing eyes, laughed sadistically as he watched her float back down. She called out frantically to him. "Nein! Guy...BITTE..." but she knew that it had been her very last breath and she let herself go. Then a hand was behind her head, lifting her up to the water's surface, and she crashed through it, screaming.

Mark raised Anna's head and wiped the perspiration from her fevered brow as she woke from her nightmare. Delirious and panic-stricken, she looked up at him. Then her eyes rolled to the top of her head and they closed again. To Mark, it all seemed like she was a heartbeat away from death. Strewn around his feet and across the bedroom floor were Anna's pearls. She had ripped her necklace apart when she was choking and had grabbed at her throat. He bent down and began to gather them up.

***

That night, the man who had bought those pearls stood at the window of his moonlit cell and stared out, knowing that he was in a nightmare all of his own makings. He had stood at the crossroads - one where a decision had to be made, and a direction followed. One where a question had to be asked and answered: which takes the most courage? To change course? And therefore stay faithful to Anna? Or to stick with what I deep down believe in? Which means do a deal and regain my liberty. The liberty which is my right. Hating himself more than he hated the world, he turned, picked up his full chamber pot and flung it violently against the wall. The contents slid and streaked down the flaking, filthy wall just above his new cellmate. The Irishman jumped up and squared up to Guy and they stood puffed-out-chest to puffed-out-chest. The Ulsterman stepped back and threw a punch and Guy was sent reeling back against the wall. Freddie Turnbull was down off his top bunk like a shot and landed his notorious left hook on the side of the new man's hairy jaw. He dropped like a stone onto the prison floor. Then Freddie grabbed Guy by the shirt and flung him across the room towards the fouled wall. "Clean that up!" he yelled at him.

***

Ever so gently, Mark sat Anna up in bed. Her Lazarus' heart was pounding. She was wearing a pair of Mark's pyjamas. He peeled down her blankets and wrapped fresh wet towels around her ankles. It was something his mother always used to do at home when anyone had a fever. Mark had no idea why, but it always seemed to work for him. Then he pulled the blankets back up and covered her with them, then reached over to the bowl of hot soup that he had set down on the bedside table. She was too weak to help herself so he did it all for her. Small sip followed small sip... and then she vomited again.

***

The next morning Guy sat in the prison governor's office. Waiting. Opposite him, in the governor's chair, a young and cocky prison warder sat and rolled himself another cigarette and blew a wall of smoke between himself and Guy. The ashtray on the desk in front of him, which had once been the property of the Dorchester Hotel according to the words printed in mock gold leaf on its underside, already had half-a-dozen old, self-rolled cigarette ends in it.

A second bored warder sat in a chair which he had pulled right up next to Guy's and stifled a yawn. Guy fidgeted with his frayed shirt cuffs. He shuffled in his seat, a picture of irritation and pure frustration. He let out a long breath as if he'd been holding it in for a lifetime, and started to get up out of his chair. The warder next to him grabbed a handful of Guy's dirty shirt sleeve and yanked him back down. "How much longer?" Guy protested. "We've been here nearly an hour now."

"I'm sorry. Did someone say something?" the warder sitting in the governor's seat said sarcastically to his colleague, who turned to Guy and said "Relax itchy arse. They'll be here when they're here."

Five minutes later Barnes and Adams entered the Governor's office. "Thanks, fellas," Barnes said to the two warders, who were only too happy to finally get up and leave the room. The last warder out of the office took out a thick bunch of keys and locked the office door behind him, then took his place standing guard in the corridor outside. "Okay Schneider, what's on your mind?" Barnes asked Guy matter-of-factly.

Guy didn't even wait for the two MI5 officers to sit down before he started. "I'll trade your five thousand. For a British pass... and immunity for Anna." He looked from one to the other for a reaction. He knew that by making his deal he was making their day. Barnes looked over at his partner and broke into a wry smile. Then he turned back to Guy. "You're too late. Someone else already landed us our big fish."

The balance of power which Guy had hoped would now be in his favour had just shifted. And he knew it was forever.

"We don't need you any more Schneider," said Adams, relishing it. "You're in here for as long as this war lasts."

TWENTY-FIVE

DREAM BABY DREAM

For the next five days Anna slept - and nothing else. Mark, with the patience of Buddha, only moved from the bedside either to help her to the bathroom or to go into the kitchen to get something for them to eat together. Usually, by the time he was back at the bedside she had fallen back to sleep again and her food remained untouched. He tried to get some aspirins into her to attack the fever, either by crushing them into her soup or washing them down whole with a glass of water, but they came back with violence just as soon as they had gone in. He worked from her bedside. Usually sketching, which was something he hadn't done for years. Quite often he fell asleep himself while he was doing it. And so it went on like that for more than seventy two hours, sleeping, drawing and sketching, eating (or not as the case may be) and then sleeping again. As long as she lived, Anna would never be able to tell you what she dreamed of or whether she dreamed at all, or what life was like at any single minute of the time that she lay in Mark's bed. All she did was lie there and waste away.

Everything hurt, her chest and stomach muscles pained her from the constant throwing up, her throat was sore, her head ached from the unremitting pounding and it felt leaden and so heavy that she was hardly able to raise it from the pillow without Mark's help. Her bones ached and she felt so faint, so weak as if she was fading away to nothing. Just slipping away.... Her eyeballs hurt every time she moved them from side-to-side, her back was sore from lying, she felt constantly nauseous and the room spun and faded in and out of focus every time she did manage to open her eyes. Then there were the panic attacks in her few conscious moments - moments when she couldn't draw breath or think clearly and her thoughts were all confused and jumbled, meaningless and frightening - before the feverish nightmares returned and she was drowning again, or she was suffocating, or being chased or beaten, although she would remember nothing about them when she woke, drenched in perspiration.

Then there was the broken heart.

Six long days after she had arrived at Mark's, she woke slowly with the early morning sun streaking through a small gap in the curtains. It was a battle, one she didn't believe she could win, but she managed to force her head up from the pillow long enough to focus her eyes and look over at the chair right next to the bed. She was surprised to see that for once it was empty. She didn't know it yet but she had lost nearly seven pounds in weight, which was a lot for someone who had been slender anyway. She was dizzy and felt faint when she struggled up out of bed for the first time unaided, and slowly crept over to the window. She pulled back the curtains with her slender fingers and the bright sunshine made her squint. She took a blanket off the bed, wrapped it around her, and tottered the few yards into the living room with the awkwardness of a newborn deer just learning to walk. Mark was asleep on the sofa, which he had made up as his bed. She watched him sleep for a moment and then turned to go. She wouldn't disturb him, but her movement had woken him and he called out after her, "morning.''

"Sorry. I didn't mean to wake you."

"It's okay. I'm just pleased you're feeling better."

"A little." She held onto the back of a chair to steady herself.

He smiled at her. "If you hadn't surfaced today I thought it wouldn't be a doctor I'd have to call but an undertaker!" He could see that she had no idea just what an undertaker was, and he didn't know the German word for it. So he tried to demonstrate and drew a cross in the air then made out he was carrying a coffin on his shoulder. "You know...?" Charades really weren't his game, he was still lying down, and she still had absolutely no idea what he meant. She even managed a weak smile at his pathetic effort and he gave up. "They bury you man, they bury you."

"You mean a Totengräber!"

He shook his head and laughed. "He's the one who digs the hole. No, I mean-"

"Mark...?" she interrupted him.

He held her look for a moment.

"Thanks."

"You're welcome."

There was something else on her mind, he could see that the 'something' was awkward for her. She swallowed hard. "Who put me into these?" she asked - 'these' being the green and white-striped pyjamas which she was wearing under the blanket.

But before he could answer her there was a knock on the front door. There was a tense moment while Anna looked anxiously at Mark. He got up, pulled on a shirt, and broke the tension. "Wel, it won't be the undertaker." He gestured for her to stay calm and remain quiet, while he went out and down the stairs to the front door. Anna followed him unsteadily to the living room door, which she held onto to steady herself while she listened to a man's voice from downstairs say.

"I heard you wanted to see me."

"I need an extra ration book. As quick as you can," she heard Mark tell him.

"Maybe tomorrow. Got visitors?"

"Someone from home," Mark lied. "An artist." Then he quickly followed it with "Roland? Make it two."

TWENTY-SIX

MIRROR, MIRROR....

The next morning Anna stood at the bathroom sink wearing one of Mark's shirts, which she had tucked into a pair of his trousers and pulled it all in tightly at the waist by a thick belt. She was washing out the clothes which she had arrived in five days earlier. Her eyes were locked on her reflection in the mirror above the wash basin, trying to find herself in the image. To the outside world, she clearly looked a little better, healthier, but to Anna, she looked far too pale and far too drawn and yes, she really did look like she had lost too much weight in very little time. She stood there hating what she saw reflected back at her when Mark crept up behind her. He looked her over and broke into a smile.

"So how's our patient this morning?"

"There's not a mirror in your place which can tell the truth."

He peered over her shoulder at her reflection. Buried in his oversized clothes, to Mark she managed to look even more attractive; 'cuter' somehow. "Tell me what you see, and I'll tell you what I see," he said to her, the beautiful creature with her clipped and broken wings.

"Anger. Humiliation. Betrayal. Hurt. Fear. Confusion. Loss. You want more?"

"You mean there is more?"

"Oh yes."

She had his sympathy. But he was trying his best to lift her. "Now can I show you what I see?" he asked. Anna said nothing. She only looked ahead, depressed, at her reflection in the mirror - although whatever fire was raging, it was raging deep inside of her. Mark held out his hand for her to take. "Please - trust me." She thought about it. Then she dried her hands on a towel, pulled a stray strand of hair out of her eyes, and let him take her by the hand and lead her off.

Minutes later, up in the atelier, Mark worked away behind his easel with intense concentration and passion, making bold strokes across the canvas with his brush. It was as if all his life - all his work - had been waiting for this one moment. Across the room, from him, Anna sat on a stool. She still looked somewhat depressed. But in the picture of Anna which Mark was painting she looked radiant. As if there was an aura around her. It was bright.

Positive. Confident. And she looked incredibly beautiful, with an enigmatic smile on her face. Mark was painting beauty again.

From her stool, the 'Mona Anna' looked back in the artist's direction and almost smiled.

***

The next morning, Mark came into the living room where Anna was standing ironing her suit - the one she had worn when she arrived at Mark's. She was using the table as an ironing board, with a table cloth spread out on it. "Here. They're yours," he said to her and handed her an old, small egg carton. "I forgot all about it." Full of curiosity, Anna lifted the carton lid. Inside, lying in five of the egg carton's cups were Anna's pearls. Curled up in the sixth was the chain that they had been on. "It snapped when you were sick. I think I managed to pick them all up." Anna stood and stared vaguely at the contents of the carton. She thought she heard someone say "we might be able to repair them" but it was faint and she was already drifting...

She had tried hard not to think about Guy, and about what had happened between them. For one, she didn't know what to think. He had hurt her badly and it was all something way beyond what she could rationalise. The list she had given to Mark before he painted her, it had been about right. Anna felt betrayed. Not just personally; Guy had betrayed something even more precious - he had betrayed what she thought he stood for and believed in.

241

He had chosen to trade in his soul in some pathetic Faustian pact with the devil, who for Anna were now the snide schemers at MI5. So what did that mean? That Guy had indeed been guilty of something? Anna didn't dare think about that. She had believed in him, in his innocence, and she believed he would have his freedom returned to him because of it. That's what the Advisory Committee did, didn't they? They listened, they judged, they decided. What are you afraid of Guy? No, it was easier if Anna didn't think about what she could no longer control or influence any more. Guy had rejected her and what they stood together for. He had released her. Why? "Can you love someone and then not love them just like that?" she asked herself time after time. What did I do? Where was your loyalty Guy?

The old thought returned to her: circumstances don't always change or form character, they often reveal it. But what if I'm wrong, What then? All Anna knew for sure was that she had to survive. For the second time in her life, she had been rejected by someone who she'd shown nothing but love to. She was suddenly forced to face the stark realisation that what she was and what she stood for simply wasn't good enough for someone. When being who she was no longer worked. She had wanted the love of her mother and all she got was blows and spite and pain and loathing. And now it had happened again. She could see it plainly for herself in Guy's eyes. He'd cast her adrift. She was poison to him. Guy had made her ill, and she was hurting. She knew she would be battling on alone.

She had the urge to write to him, but Anna knew that she couldn't. All the mail at Guy's prison was censored, and she couldn't afford to alert the Authorities to the fact that she even existed. She had to simply disappear from the world until the war was either won or lost - and God helps her if it was lost. And in no way would she ever put Mark at risk. She even thought about writing in a sort of code - pretending that she was Guy's aunt Rose (who didn't exist), asking whether his plans to marry were still on once he'd been released from jail because Claire has been asking so he really should write and let her know, just a simple "yes" would suffice - and praying that Guy would understand the code and that the letter was from her. Guy would recognise the handwriting, she knew that. He would also see the hundreds of mistakes she knew she would make - grammatical, spelling, in her choice of vocabulary - and if Guy could recognise that then so would a prison official. I can't drag Claire into this, Anna thought. No, I simply can't do any of this. There's everything to lose and too many people to endanger. Guy will surely get word to me somehow, 'if' that is what he wants. She was lost in those thoughts when she heard a loud banging coming from downstairs. She looked straight at Mark, who was now sitting at the table scanning through the morning paper. He seemed unperturbed by the interruption and calmly got up, left the room and went downstairs to the front door. Anna quickly gathered up her suit, grabbed the steam iron and her egg carton containing the pearls, ran into the bedroom and shut the door.

Mark opened the front door to Roland, who was holding a wrapped parcel, several thick pads of drawing and painting paper, and some small canvases. He also had a small paper carrier bag. Mark beckoned him inside. Up in the living room, Mark took an old tin tea tin out of a drawer, took a small bundle of pound notes which had already been wrapped in a rubber band out of the container, and handed the bundle to Roland.

"Sorry Mark," Roland said, a little sheepishly, "it erm...cost me a 'fiver' more." He could read Mark's dubious look. "Handling charges, you know?"

Mark counted off five more pound notes from the money which was left in the tin and pushed them into Roland's hand. Roland stuffed the money straight into his back pocket. Just then, Anna came back into the room, once more wearing the beige suit with the brown suede collar. She hadn't expected to find anyone there and was surprised. Her immediate reaction was to turn and leave but Mark gestured everything was fine and that she should stay, which she did. Her unease was palpable. Back now to something approaching her best, Roland couldn't keep his eyes off her. Mark looked at the back of the painting block which Roland had acquired for him. The name of the local art college was stamped on it, and on the bottom of the paints too. He eyed Roland suspiciously.

"They erm...they won't be needing them," Roland said, reading Mark's thoughts. "They're all off to war..." and he turned and looked straight at Anna when he added "fighting Germans." Then loaded with sarcasm he added, "This your 'Swiss' visitor then?" He looked her up and down as if he was contemplating buying her at auction, and held out his hand. "Bonjour...' fellow artist. Or should it be Guten Tag ?'" Anna didn't respond to that. She was clearly uncomfortable, but she took his hand and shook it nevertheless. "You'll find a little something in there for you too," Roland said to her. "Right, I'll be off then," he said to Mark. "I'll leave you two to it." And he turned to leave.

"Thanks, Roland," said Mark. "Good man".

As Roland disappeared into the hallway Anna let out a huge sigh of relief. Right then, no company was the best company. She followed Mark up into the atelier, where his clothes-horse mannequin was now wearing a gas mask. Mark took a large knife from the table and used it to slice through the wrapping around the package. Anna stood next to him and watched, eaten up with nerves.

"He knows I'm German," she said.

"Nonsense. How could he?"

"The way he looked at me. He knows."

"The way he looked at you was something else entirely, believe me. Roland's okay. He's an old student of mine. He's now the department Assistant at the college. Old Grant's place. Roland's so sharp..." at that moment

Mark's knife sliced clean through the thick binding around the canvases, "you'll cut yourself on him if you get too close. Not that I'm telling you to do it, mind. The others paint. And talk. Roland makes it possible. He can even get hold of the 'impossible,' which, at times like these, makes him a good person to know." While Mark had been speaking he had been examining the contents of his package - more paints; oils; brushes. Also, there were two ration books. He took them out and threw them across the table to Anna.

"Right, are you an orange kind of girl or a banana kind of girl?" he asked her, picking the fruit out of the paper bag which Roland had given him. "Well, look what we have here!" He held up a bar of chocolate for her to see as if he was holding up a bar of gold or a precious gem. But Anna still wasn't any happier.

***

Five doors up from the Pennington-Coopers' house in Rowlandsgill Gate a bored MI5 agent sat in his car and looked at his watch. Nothing was going on there - nothing had been going on there for the entire five hours that he'd been on watch. He yawned, rubbed at his eyes, then reached forward to the dashboard and started up the car engine.

From behind a downstairs curtain, Claire watched the car pull away. Then she nodded to the fresh-faced young man in a tweed cap who was standing next to her. He reached down and picked up Anna's big old red suitcase

and headed for the door. Half an hour later he was knock-
ing on Mark's door.

***

The following morning the town hall clock in Upper
Bexton had started to run slow. In his daily radio programme "Germany Calling" which he broadcast in
English on Radio Hamburg from Berlin, the fascist propagandist Lord Haw-Haw reported that by eight pm the
clock was a full eleven minutes late. He also described the
long queues outside of Blackett's store in Liverpool for
goods which never arrived, the stormy weather up in
Glasgow and all along the west coast of Scotland, and that
a train on the Newcastle to Kings Cross line had become
derailed near Doncaster. Before the war Lord Haw-Haw
had been head of the British Union's propaganda division
and Mosley's deputy leader until he fled to Germany at
the outbreak of hostilities. In Berlin, he set up his provocative, pro-fascist, anti-British government radio
programme with the sole aim of undermining the fragile
British morale and mocking the war effort. With its up-to-
date knowledge of events back in the UK, such as the
Bexton town hall clock, it left a nervous British public
asking "How on earth could someone in Germany possibly know these things?" A disgusted and livid Major
Walker knew the answer, as he sat in his office and listened to a recording of 'Germany Calling' which the
Ministry of Information had given him. It could only have
come from a network of German spies and agents around

the country. As for the town hall clock in Upper Bexton, Walker knew exactly where that piece of information must have come from. He angrily turned off the tape recorder and picked up his phone. "I want every single damned one of them in" he barked into the receiver. "If they're still out there, they're out there for a reason. British lives are at stake here," he shouted before he slammed down the phone.

TWENTY-SEVEN

PAINTER MAN

Dressed in the fresh clothes which had arrived from Rowlandsgill Gate, Anna circled Mark's atelier and scrutinised the paintings which had been propped up against the walls; each one of dark, gloomy, anti-war imagery. Just two paintings broke the depressing pattern. One was a half-finished Impressionist landscape which had been flung into a corner in disgust some time back and dismissed with a thick streak of black paint across its surface. The other, right next to it, was a portrait of a young woman with long and voluminous red curls, dark feline eyes, and a face which was all sharp angles with full cherry-red lips. A femme fatale of sorts, who possessed both a sense of imminent danger, but also vulnerability. At least that's how Mark had painted her.

What he didn't paint though was what he called her 'Box of Assorted Wiehnachtsguezli Biscuits' smile because every tooth had a different shape and a different colour and a few were invariably broken or cracked or black.

Anna crept up behind Mark and watched fascinated while he worked, laying down a base of more dark colours on one of the fresh canvases which Roland had brought him. "Hello Mister Optimist," she said cheekily.

"You'll never go far wrong in art if you're pissed off at something," he turned and said to her. "If there's a bit of anger in you, you'll be fine in this fucked up world of ours."

Anna looked at him like he was out of his mind. This was a concept totally foreign to her, and expressed in a language she'd last heard from Guy in the prison; one which disgusted her. Art was about beauty - or so she thought. There's plenty of the ugly to see out here in our world anyway she believed. She shook her head and gazed at the canvases scattered around the room.

"This is pure horror."

"What would you prefer me to paint? Naked ladies? Apples and pears in a bowl?"

"Apples and pears in a bowl."

"Which tell me nothing about the world I live in." He shook his head. That certainly wasn't what Mark Hermann was about.

"I've lived through more misery than you'll ever know. I don't need it thrown back in my face."

250

"So which part of your body should I throw it at then?"

"Throw it in the rubbish bin. You can do better than that," she said nodding at the canvas.

"No. I can't. This damned world of ours demands to be described. Only the Gods don't always choose the people who you expect to do it and they don't always do it in a way you want them to. Which can get uncomfortable for some,'' he said and gave her his serious look and then followed it with a wry, mischievous smile. "And I have just as much right to my anger as you have to your pretty pictures of happiness."

"Is that what good art is? Anger?"

"It can have its moments. Which I think should make you a grand master."

"What's that supposed to mean?"

"You came here afraid. You came here hurting. You also came here full of anger.''

"I'm over it."

He shot her a look which read 'really?' Because she was patently over nothing. "Anger and beauty. Love and hate. Tragedy and comedy... they all come from the same dark place Miss Vieti. The same dark place."

He turned back to his work. Slap! More black hit the canvas, even thicker this time.

"And you believe all that?" she said, unsure whether he was kidding her again.

"And you don't?"

"How can you even think that?"

"How can you not? You of all people, with your history? Your people's history. Tell me you're not angry and I'll tell you you're a liar."

This stung. Anna waited for a moment.

"Then I'm a liar. Because what I feel... what I feel... is that whatever horrors and whatever evil have come up against it, love is always greater. Love is greater than anger. Greater than terror. Greater than any tyranny or anything which tries to stand in its way."

As soon as she heard the words spoken out loud Anna wished that she'd never said them. Out in the world for someone else to hear they sounded too naive. Too schoolgirl-innocent. Too 'Marlies' (bless her). but it was nevertheless what she truly felt.

"Noble," Mark said in response. And that was all he would ever say about it. He would secretly admire the sentiment - even envy it - but it wasn't what he believed anymore. He'd seen beauty and love come up against a Nazi jack-boot and he saw who won. It wasn't the Marlieses of this world. Anna would tell him that was only one battle. And a war would always be won by love. Two ways of looking at the same thing, but it would all remain unsaid.

"You're a strange man Mark Hermann."

"That's at least one thing we can agree on." He ignored her for the moment and once again concentrated with some intensity on his work. It was true, there really was a direct line from the deepest, darkest part of him to the picture he was painting. A slab of thick dark brown paint was slapped over the black. Then another.

Anna turned away and looked across the room.

"Who is that?" She was looking at the portrait painting over in the corner, next to the spoiled Impressionist landscape.

"Martine."

Now she was curious.

"And who is, or who was, Martine?"

"I shared the apartment in Paris with two other students. Right next to us was a brothel."

"A what?"

"A bordell. You know what a bordell is?"

Anna nodded. "I'm from Hamburg."

"Martine worked there."

"So she's someone you slept with?"

"I can't remember."

"Yes, you can. You remember all right. You did. You had sex with her and she was the one who taught you all your tricks... Or?"

"She might have taught the two time-wasters who I lived with some tricks... I don't know. They spent every Franc that their fathers sent them in that place."

"But you didn't?" Her voice was full of sarcasm. She was enjoying herself.

"I paid Martine. Yes. I went in there regularly. She'd sit for me. For money. She had a crippled son who needed professional care. In the day she worked in a meat factory and in the evenings she worked in the brothel, and all to pay for the care of her son. There was no other man in her life. Every single thing that Martine did she did for her son. Every decision that she made, she made to keep him as happy and as comfortable as he could possibly be. She would cry every time she talked about him, 'I'm the lucky one' she always used to say. I learned how to paint from a blind man, and I learned dedication and what it meant to love someone unconditionally from a prostitute. How about that? When I left Paris I gave all the paintings that I'd made of her to a small gallery close by - all of them except that one" and he nodded at the corner. "I told them that if any of them ever sold to give the money to Martine."

Anna stood for a moment, looking into the sharp angular features of the compassionate Parisian whore and mother. Would her own mother have done the same sort of thing to ensure her well being? she wondered Just how far would Lena Vieti have gone to secure someone's happiness other than her own?

The faint sounds of the daytime city drifted up through the window. Traffic passed by. Somewhere off in the distance a car horn was blown. Someone down in the street dropped a bottle of milk and the glass shattered. A baby began to cry. A man's voice shouted "hello" and a woman's voice returned it. The local rag-and-bone man was doing his weekly round, "Any old iron?" he called out. Anna heard nothing. She was somewhere else entirely.

Mark's voice sliced into her silent moment. "You know, I don't even know why you came here," he said, still not taking his eyes off either his brush or the canvas.

She turned and faced him with a vague look. "I'm sorry?"

He repeated his question. Anna refocused. "Sanctuary, remember?"

"I mean here, to England."

"I'm an assistant to a Jewish medical Professor. Or 'was'. When he fled from the Nazis three years ago he brought me with him. My father's family are gypsies. If I hadn't come... well, you know as well as anyone how it is right now. So I came. I fell in love, I stayed--" Mark stopped working and turned to face her, and they held each other's look for a deeply poignant moment. "Then everything got taken away," she added. "Paint me a picture of that sometime."

Mark picked a fresh sheet of drawing paper from the table next to him and clipped it to the empty easel which was standing alongside the one he was working on. Then he picked up a thick black pencil. "You do it." He handed her the pencil and invited her to draw something, but she backed away from him with a nervous laugh.

"I can't," she said, meaning both her inability to draw, as well as face up to her past. Mark tried to grab hold of her, but he was too slow and she was gone. He smiled and returned to his work.

***

The MI5 agent who had been watching the Pennington-Coopers' house from his car was in the Major's dingy office with Barnes, Adams and, sitting at his desk, an agitated Walker. The agent shook his head and addressed the Major. "I have no idea Sir. But wherever she is, she's not at the house. Or at her old address in Upper Bexton."

Walker clearly wasn't happy. He scratched his head. He adjusted the patch over his eye.

Adams chipped in, "we've checked the hospital, friends, colleagues... Nothing. I'm afraid the pretty bird seems to have flown."

"Flown what?" demanded Walker.

"Flown high up into the sky,'' Adams said nonchalantly and with some audacity. It was like a taunt; an invitation to a schoolyard scrap. He held on tight to his fedora. He knew he was pushing his luck. It seemed like an age before he gave the Major the golden word; "Sir."

Walker stared at him in astonishment. Barnes jumped in before the Major exploded and it had the chance to get ugly.

"We've handed the Detention Order over to Special Branch to process."

Walker refocused. "Pressure them. You don't run and hide for no reason at all. Find her. And anyone else out there like her."

"Right you are Sir. We'll be straight on it Sir!" Barnes said and quickly grabbed Adams, nodded to the other agent, and the three of them exited the office smartly.

"What the hell was that supposed to be?" Barnes asked as soon as they were walking at pace down the corridor.

"Fun?" said Adams, adjusting his hat.

Barnes broke into a smile. "Yeah... I suppose it was."

***

Later that day Walker almost smiled. The happy occasion was hearing the news that two Germans who had thus far evaded internment had finally been brought in. One had moved in with his sister-in-law in Hampstead and had spent all of his time walking round and around the Heath and the various London parks all day, every day. Until a neighbour spotted him in Regents Park and informed the police. Another, a Jew from Bremerhaven who after the war would go on to become an internationally renowned concert pianist, had gone up to the Lake District to avoid incarceration and had camped out on the fells near Hawkshead. Like Anna, he reasoned that imprisonment of any kind would finish him. He was doing fine up there on his own until he slipped on a mossy rock down at the riverside and broke both his legs and had to be taken into hospital, where his identity was revealed.

***

"We have nothing more for the fire," Anna told Mark that chilly late-summer evening up in his atelier. "We've used up all the wood and coal we have."

"Burn this," Mark said and raked through the pile of paintings in a corner of the room until he found what he was looking for. It was a bizarre image. A shocking im-

257

age. In it, God was sitting behind the counter of a small stall in a once pretty little French market square. He was selling guns and bombs. There was a huge pile of money on the counter in front of Him and a sardonic smile on his face. He had His hair in braids and pinned up over his head, young and innocent Nazi-girl style. It looked like He had a halo of pleated Challah bread planted on the top of his head. With no business that day, He was happy to sit back and paint His fingernails black. On the roof at the front of the stall was a Star of David. It was in flames. A dog had stopped at the side of the stall. It had cocked its leg and, God forbid, was urinating on his Holy Weapons Stand. The rest of the town which the marketplace had once been the centre of had already been wiped off the face of the earth. All that remained was the smoldering rubble and ruins covered in ashes. And God's own 'divine guns and bombs' stall. Anna took the painting from him and looked hard into the image.

Mark watched her study it. "Don't tell me... *your* God is all beauty and goodness and innocence."

"I'm looking at the dog. It happened to me once."

"A dog pissed on you?"

"A Hitler-Jugend did. After he broke two of my ribs."

"Voila!" he said as if it somehow proved his point. He nodded towards the shifty figure in the painting, "Thank the Lord for that."

"I did. I also thanked Him for taking my family away, and for murdering my boyfriend in a police prison. I thanked Him for all the beatings that I got from my mother. I thanked Him for the Professor and for bringing me here to England. I thanked Him for Hitler and Himmler, and Heydrich, and the Nazis, and for the kind old man who lived in the flat downstairs to me in Hamburg who they soaked in petrol and burned alive in the street. I thanked Him for ruining my wedding day. I still thank Him... every day I wake up and I'm still in the world I say 'thanks.' I say 'thanks' for bringing me here to safety. I thank Him for all the love I've known and been shown."

Mark sat in silence and took in what she had said. Then he spoke in a low, sad voice. "I thank Him each day too... for the incurable disease which killed my mother and slowly wasted her away to nothing. The hell on earth that she had to live through and which destroyed everyone else's life around her," his throat began to tighten and his eyes became moist. Then something else took over, "throw it in the fire. Let's watch him burn," he added.

TWENTY-EIGHT

BITTERBLUE

Mark opened the front door, carrying a wicker shopping basket. The fog outside that morning was thick enough to ice a cake. Lying on the mat just inside the door were two envelopes which had been dropped through the letter box. Mark picked them up. In one was an invitation to the opening of an exhibition by an old friend, the French painter Pierre de Trayas, in Earl's Court at the beginning of September. Mark generally didn't like going to those kinds of things with all the back slapping and arse kissing and isn't everything just wonderful and I love your painting sweetie, going on every which way you looked from all the frauds, flakes and fakes. 'I love your painting' more often than not carried the subtext 'what a worthless piece of crap that is.' No, Mark could do without all that nonsense. Let the sellers sell, let the painters paint and let's not all get stuck up our own backsides about it; let's have some honesty. But Mark also knew that the bullshit was part of the territory and was a part of the machinery which sold his paintings and kept food on his table and paint on the end of his brush. So he vowed that on this occasion, he would make the effort to go. Friends are friends, after all, and if they need his support then he'll be there for them. Besides, Pierre de Trayas wasn't only a talented artist, but a good and decent person. Mark knew that the two don't often come along together. You're blessed with the gift, you rarely get blessed with the grace to go with it. Mark dropped the envelope into his basket and set off for the shops, he opened the second envelope while he was walking. It was from his agent Anton and it was a letter saying that he had just sold a painting of Mark's called 'Bitterblue' to someone who claimed to be of Persian royalty.

'Bitterblue' was an abstract painting which he had completed only six weeks earlier, consisting of thick blue lines - vertical and crisscrossed. It was the skyline of a wasted futuristic city days after the apocalypse. Or maybe it was just some random slabs of pretty, blue paint. Mark would let you choose. Attached to the letter was the cheque itself, for three thousand five-hundred pounds. Mark stopped, looked at the cheque, and kissed it. It wasn't the biggest he had ever received, but it was in the top half dozen, and especially welcome at a time when art sales were severely depressed anyway because of the war. And it was for a painting which had meant a lot to him, so the feeling really was a special one. He pushed the cheque into his pocket and changed direction. The shops could wait until later. Mark would be heading to the bank first.

One of the shops where Mark was registered with his ration book was 'J.W. Adams & Sons; General Dealers,' which was on the corner just a street away from where he lived. When he arrived, there was a sign on the shop door saying that they had taken no deliveries that day - "the cargo ship has been sunk" someone had written by hand in red ink - and they had listed underneath that all the goods which weren't going to be on sale that day. Corned beef wasn't on the list, but when Mark asked for a tin of it, white-haired and weathered old Jack Adams himself said that he had sold his last tin the day before and recited for Mark the few things which he still did actually have available in the shop. Mark bought a jar of strawberry jam and moved on to a second shop in Old Brompton Road where he was also registered. The queue of women out-side of 'Pickerings' was long, but that was good news because it meant there was something to get, so Mark stood in line and listened to the local gossip while he waited the forty-five minutes until he could get into the shop itself. He watched as the shop assistant cut carefully around the coupons in his ration book in exchange for a tin of spinach, some oxtail, a few rashers of bacon and the last three sausages in the shop, which looked like they'd been in the world longer than he had. They would probably be better than fried ferret Mark thought. He'd heard a story at Grant's party about someone who kept a pet ferret in a cage in his living room and one week when he couldn't get any meat he had been forced to eat it.

On his way home from the shops, Mark called in at Cleveland House orphanage for boys - just as he did every time he sold a painting - and handed them a cheque for five percent of what he had earned. No one outside the orphanage knew that he did this. And no one inside the orphanage knew why. It was just something he did. Something the world would never know about Mark Hermann.

It was an act born in a Paris whorehouse.

"Are you Andrew McKellar?" a loud voice boomed out behind him as Mark was walking up the steps to his front door on the way back from the shops. He turned and watched a figure emerge out of the thick fog like a zombie. "I'm the new ARP warden for the district," the ghostlike form said. "I'm just updating my lists." It was the local ARP warden's job to know his designated area, and people who lived in it, because when the bombs dropped he would be the one responsible for the head count and the aftermath.

"What happened to old Jack?" Mark asked him.

"He slipped in the bath and broke his hip." This was sad news for Mark because he liked old Jack a lot.

"The McKellars live downstairs," Mark told the new man. "But they're up in Scotland until August."

The warden ran his finger down one of his lists.

"Then you must be Mark Hermann?"

"If that's what your list says, then yes" - and a tick went into the box next to Mark's name on the warden's list.

"And you live here alone?"

"Just the way I like it."

The warden eyed Mark with suspicion.

"The Rogersons next door said there's someone else living here."

"Tell the Rogersons I had a visitor."

"Just for the day?"

"What did the Rogersons say?"

"So what was this visitor's name then?"

"Pennington-Cooper. Grant Pennington-Cooper."

The warder scribbled something down on his list then he looked back up at Mark.

"The Rogersons said it was a woman."

"And Grant's mother," he was growing impatient. "Now can I go in? I have something to celebrate."

"Alone?" asked the warder in a tone somewhere between suspicion and sarcasm.

"Very alone. As I said, just the way I like it. Are you married?"

"What?"

"Because I could arrange an introduction. You and Grant's mother... I see a pretty pair there. Well, what do you say?"

"You hold your lip son."

"I'll do that."

"One last thing," the warden said, "the McKellars are away you said?"

"Until August. They have a business up in Edinburgh. Didn't the neighbours already tell you that?"

The warder ignored Mark and made a quick note on his list. "I'll be back to check on things," he said.

"You do that. And the next time you want to know something about me, you ask me, okay?"

The warder scowled at him and took a small leaflet out of the coarse canvas bag strung over his shoulder. He pushed the leaflet into Mark's hand. "Make sure you read that pal," he said and promptly disappeared back into the mist.

As soon as Mark was walking up the staircase he sensed that something was wrong. For one, there was too much silence. For the past few days, there had always been someone else around the place, leaving their mark in one way or the other. Now there was an unnerving hush in the flat. And more worryingly, there was no Anna. Mark knocked on the bedroom door and went in... to find an empty room. He checked the living room, the kitchen, the atelier, the bathroom - all empty. He shouted out Anna's name. But no one answered, and panic began to set in. He went back to the kitchen to put down his shopping and through the window he caught a glimpse of her through the dense fog, pacing dementedly around the small square of the garden plot down in the courtyard at the back of the house. Something was tearing at her. He threw the basket down onto the table, shot out of the room, and took the back stairs four at a time.

It was everything - her situation; her feelings; what had happened; what might happen; it was Guy; maybe it was even Mark himself now; it was perhaps that the old fight and fire and defiance were back, but she realised there was no one to fight. It was also her morbid fear, of being locked away, it was that which she settled on to explain to Mark. "It's killing me, Mark. Locked up inside all day. Every day. I have to breathe. It's like being in a-" but she stopped short of calling it by another name. She knew that wouldn't be fair; that wouldn't be right.

"You know the situation. You know it's not possible. The neighbours have already seen you around," Mark said and took her by the arm. He tried to guide her back into the house, but she jerked her arm free.

"Let go of me!"

He grabbed her again, but again she pulled away and took a step back from him. They both stood for a tense moment and looked up at the milky white sky as if they were expecting to find an answer to the problem floating somewhere in the fog. Then Anna pleaded, "You have to let me out. Somewhere. Anywhere...?"

"What, to get picked up? Fine... Go! You claim you're free. Well, go. See how far you get. See how prison or the camps suit you. Or see who else will take you." He felt hurt. He felt at that moment that the risks which he had knowingly taken for her, and everything that he had put on the line for her, was being returned with rank ingratitude.

"I'm not free and you know it. I'm not like you. I just... I need air. I need light. I need to..."

"Keep your voice down," he knew how she felt. He even let himself think it over for a second, just how he could manage it, to get them out somewhere. But he shook his head. "As I said, any time you want to go, you go. But don't take me down with you."

She turned and stormed straight past him into the house.

* * *

Across the city, two warders led Guy into his new cell in another wing of the prison. The authorities were finally beginning to cope. As the cell door closed and its locks clunked into place behind him, Guy stood with his meagre belongings under his arm and looked around. It was certainly no world of luxury in there. But it was also a world away from the last hellhole and its crazed, psychopathic occupants. It was cleaner. The walls were painted in a brighter beige colour. The wash basin had even been cleaned that century. There were no cracks in the mirror or cockroaches scuttling across the floor. He wouldn't break his back if he lay down on the bed nor scrape his skin off the bone with the blankets. And he was alone in there. There would be no one to punch or threaten him or disturb his sleep. And that, right then, was heaven for Guy. He would survive.

***

Mark was still angry a good two hours later, but only with himself, when he went up to his atelier and took his frustration out on his work. He felt he had no right to talk to Anna the way he had. It had been too assertive, too inconsiderate, and too dictatorial.

In Mark Hermann's world you don't do things the way Mark Hermann tells you to, but the way you choose to do them. There are no chains around your neck or your ankles. You were, as Mark himself had told Anna, free. Except... Mark knew how high the stakes were for her. She'd told him about her angst and horror at being locked away. And he cared. He didn't want her to be caged any more than she did. So what was he supposed to do? What should he have said? It confused him. He had behaved in a way he hadn't liked. But wasn't that reasonable? He'd suddenly become responsible for someone other than himself. But more than that, he was responsible for whichever fate they would have. He buried himself in his work. There was a wild intensity about him as he scratched and scraped away with a knife and thick oils on an especially hideous, aggressive abstract image in the darkest, most depressing colours. It was his mood right then. It was indeed anger as art. He didn't even hear Anna enter the room. She looked contrite.

"I'm sorry Mark," she said.

Mark turned and faced her. "I'm sorry too. But you know how it is."

And she did. "What I don't know is... just how long I can stand it."

He put down his knife and thought for a moment about what he could do. Then he wiped his hands and motioned for her to follow him.

"The meal's ready," she said. "That's also what I came up to tell you."

"Even better. Come on."

An hour and two bottles of cheap French wine later and the tension had eased considerably as they sat in the two armchairs which they had pulled up to the hearth and stared into the crackling flames of the open fire. They were both now a little worse, or better, for the wine which they had already seen off. It was only the third time in her life that Anna had drunk alcohol. On the dining table behind them were two empty dinner plates, on which had been the meal that Anna had put together from what Mark had shopped for that morning, plus the carrots, potatoes and beans which he had then dug up from the small garden plot which he had constructed himself in the courtyard. 'Dig For Victory' had been the slogan, but that day Mark had dug for anger. He reached over and tried to tap the very last drop from an already empty wine bottle into Anna's glass. "Roland, order for you!" he called out when there were no more drops left. "We're celebrating" he shouted out to his invisible black market man.

"What are we celebrating anyway?" Anna asked.

"Success. I sold a painting."

"To a blind man… an angry blind man no doubt. But congratulations anyway," Anna said with a smile and was immediately angry with herself for asking.

Whilst she was genuinely delighted for him, it also slammed home for her the predicament in which she still found herself - which was total dependence in every way, but especially at that moment, financial dependence - and her smile immediately faded, which saddened Mark, because a small piece of spinach had lodged between her front teeth and for the past two minutes he'd had to stifle a grin every time she opened her mouth wide enough to give it away. He decided to say nothing and to enjoy the comedy of the moment.

"Why are you doing this?" Anna finally asked him.

"Doing what?"

"All of this... helping me?"

"For the same reason, you came here. The alternatives weren't too good."

"And the alternatives were?"

"I don't know about yours, but mine were… I could have thrown you back out onto the street and you would have gone your way and I'd have gone mine. Or I could have turned you in," he smiled at her. "You needed help, and you turned to me for it. I'd like to think that someone would do the same for me."

Anna thought about what he'd said: 'he'd have gone his way and I'd have gone mine.' Just a handful of short words but with a whole world of meaning in them. She was touched; she thought too about how handsome he looked in the firelight. You can purge your mind of that thought right here right now Anna Vieti, she said to herself. What she did say out loud to him was, "what are you grinning at?"

He ignored her question and got up out of his seat. "Besides," he went on as he crossed the room to the cabinet on the opposite wall, "you might also be the most beautiful girl I've ever seen in my life. And I don't just mean up to now. I mean all the bits of my life still to come. Or at least, let's say you're the one with the most beautiful smile." He took a small hand-mirror out of one of the cabinet drawers.

Anna had no idea how to deal with what he had just said to her, about finding her attractive. In the whole time that their fates had been thrown together this was the first time that he had mentioned anything like that. She didn't know how to react. "You don't believe me?" he said and held the mirror up in front of her face. "Go on, smile."

She just looked at him.

"Trust me... smile and you'll see what I see. Believe me, you won't regret it."

271

So Anna looked into the mirror and twisted her face into a sarcastic smile, mocking him, and she saw what he saw. WHACK! It was meant to be a playful slap but the alcohol turned it into a pretty impressive punch on the shoulder.

"How long has that been there?"

"As long as I've been trying not to laugh at you." He sat down, rubbing the top of his arm, proud of his little victory, while she got to work picking the spinach out of her teeth. "Claire should have warned me about you, you know?" he said to her.

"What should she have said?"

"That's my little secret." Then enigmatically he added, "but certainly not my worst."

His allusion was lost on her as she stuck with the 'Claire' theme. "That I'm wild? That I'm dangerous?"

Mark nodded.

"A terrible guest?"

Another nod, this time more vigorous.

"Who drinks all your wine?"

A third nod, while he added, "and who hits her friendly host!"

Then suddenly another mood swing. She became somber; reflective. "And someone who doesn't know when, or how this will all end."

"It will end just as soon as you decide to walk out of that door."

Anna knew that. She drank the very last drop from her glass. "So tell me your secret."

"I just did."

"No. Your very worst. I want to know which 'cadavers' the famous Swiss painter could possibly have hidded..." She knew the word didn't sound right the moment she said it. "Hide, hid, hidden," she said out loud then corrected herself"...'hidden' in his cellar?"

"In English, I think they're skeletons. And they keep them in their closets."

"Well?"

Mark thought hard. Should I or shouldn't I?

"I'm waiting, she reminded him.

"You're not very German, Frau Vieti," he said finally.

"Wonderful secret! And how should a German girl be?"

"Different."

"In Germany that was my problem. Here the problem is that I'm German. So how many German girls can you compare me with?"

"That's my secret!"

Now she was really interested, "so shock me." Her mood had swung again. She was enjoying their little game, but Mark suddenly seemed uncertain. There was something on his mind which it seemed he simply had to get out, yet at the same time appeared reluctant to do so. Anna was now full of mischief. "Ten? Twenty? You keep a harem of German models down in the cellar?"

He became nervous, his composure and his confidence were suddenly dissipating. He was looking as naked and vulnerable as any model he had ever painted, and right then, in the flickering embers of a burned-out day, it was the most beautiful sight Anna had seen in some time.

After a moment of self-reflection, Mark couldn't help himself.

"I have an older sister," he said.

"What does that mean... I have a sister?" She was confused.

"She's German. I'm German."

Anna's empty glass fell out of her hand. She truly was shocked.

"I hold both nationalities. My father comes from Basel. My mother is from the other side of the border. I grew up in a small wine village near Lörrach, on the German side, until I was twelve. Then we moved to Basel. I'm registered here on my Swiss passport. No one knows I'm German. And if they ever did..."

"You'd be the same as me."

Mark nodded his head, sadly, "Wanted. And not so free after all."

Anna looked at him in stunned silence. What he had told her had, at a painter's stroke, turned everything around. Anna suddenly felt like she was floating in an upside-down, inside-out and back-to-front world. And she was also deeply touched and privileged to have been taken so far into his confidence.

They sat in silence and stared into the flickering flames for a long time that night as if they were seeking the answer to a much deeper truth.

TWENTY-NINE

ANNA ESCAPES

Guy started the brand new day in his brand new cell with a brand new routine. "Thirty-nine, forty, forty-one..." he called out breathlessly to himself as he went through a routine of push-ups on the cell floor. He had to stop at forty-five at which point he collapsed onto the floor with trembling arms, but it was a start. His new prison room was lit up by bright morning sunlight which flooded in through the barred cell window. Guy too looked brighter and his eyes once more had some life back in them as he determinedly picked himself up off the cold ground and went through his new drill of sits-ups, squats and thrusts. He thought what was good for Freddie Turnbull must surely be good enough for him.

In Rowlandsgill Gate that morning a police detective, accompanied by young a uniformed officer, knocked on the Pennington-Coopers' front door. A minute later Grant opened it wearing his dressing gown and rubbing the sleep from his eyes. He listened to what the detective said and then shook his head firmly ''no,'' Claire appeared over his shoulder with her hair in curlers and still fastening up her dressing gown. She too shook her head at the detective's question. He then produced a piece of paper and Grant and Claire were reluctantly forced to allow them both to enter.

The Williamsons too had visitors. Two police officers showed their search warrant to Mrs Williamson and followed her into the house.

Later that morning Anna went for a long walk. Round and round the dining table - down the stairs to the front door - back again into the living room where she touched all four walls - then into all the other rooms - then back around the dining table to start all over again. She opened all the windows to the back of the flat, overlooking the small courtyard, and took in gulps of fresh air as she passed each one. She lost count of the number of times she completed the course. Thirty? Forty? Did she manage to top Guy's forty-five? Is this freedom, she asked herself while she walked back up the stairs. And what sort of nonsense concept is that anyway? Who is and who isn't free right now? Guy clearly isn't. But am I? There's a cage around me just as much as there are four walls surrounding Guy… touch the living room wall. Does it depend on who turns the lock and who is the keeper of the keys? I hold nothing, I turn no keys. I'm not free. Who are you kidding Anna?... round the table we go again. This isn't a prison and this isn't captivity. Someone is showing me kindness and generosity and holding out a helping hand, and all at great risk to himself... back into the kitchen. He'll even teach me to paint he says! And there are no locks. No one is holding any keys. I'm free to go he says. To go anywhere, and at anytime I choose. Okay then, I'll go… down the stairs, we go again and touch the electric meter on the wall beside the door. It was driving her crazy. It was, she thought, like looking at the very same thing through opposite ends of a telescope. Through one end it all looked so close and within touching distance. Through the other end, it seemed like it was a million miles away and so out of reach.

And then the big thought hit her. What would I have done without Mark? What would have become of me? What would have become of me if I'd "gone my own way,'' as he put it? How unreal is all this? I'm only on this earth once, and this has been my fate. What is it the English say? 'Out of the frying pan and into the fire?' 'Vom Regen in die Traufe' - aunt Marlies always used to say that one. Why I never escaped to freedom but only to more of the same. Who's kidding who? This isn't the same. No one knows that better than me. I'll accept this fate, whatever it might be. Just please don't lock me up.

Wait, you are locked up. Shut up Anna and walk... back down the stairs again.

Anna had dreamt again that night that she was back in her damned Hamburg hellhole. Her mother was in there with her, biting her all over her body. The moment she bit off Anna's nose and spat it out at her was the moment Anna woke up, convinced that she was covered in her own blood.

Neither Anna nor Mark mentioned the previous night when they had sat down to breakfast, and she was still living her nightmare when she asked him what his plans were - meaning what his plans were for her. "I'm going to work on my painting" was his answer. It was, in fact, his answer to both connotations of her question. The truth was that he'd never really had to think beyond the 'here-and-now' in his entire life and he had no grand plan for their situation any more than she did. He hadn't thought about it and now he'd been asked the question he didn't know what to think. He'd got through the days that they had spent together in the same way that she had - just existing. First through her illness, and then through the days which followed. He hadn't thought beyond anything else. Anna's question was his first confrontation with the problem and his only solution was to shake his head and say "I have no idea. We just have to get you away somehow..."

'Away.' You're on the move again Anna. You came to England and became a gypsy!

***

A friend of Mark's, the French sculptor Serge Chavalerin, called unexpectedly in the afternoon to introduce Mark to his new ballet dancer girlfriend - an impossibly petite but muscular Russian with alabaster skin and perfect teeth, but not a single word of French and not too many more words of English. Anna spent the entire two hours that Serge and his girlfriend were there hidden away in her room not daring to move, with nothing to think about but Mark, and about 'getting away.' When she thought about him she realised that what she had discovered the previous day fitted perfectly, in that everything about him eventually took a twist and nothing was what it at first appeared to be. The person she thought was Swiss turned out to be German. The charismatic but cool, self-centred and single-minded artist with a self-assurance bordering on arrogance turns out to be a warm, kind-hearted and caring creature who wants nothing more than to love and be loved. The artist once obsessed with painting beauty now paints visions of noirish nightmares, pictures of chaos and desolation. It was like a river reversing its course. Just what will the next twist turn out to be? Anna wondered.

At one point, Serge Chavalerin lit up his pipe and the dense smell of the strong French tobacco carried through the entire flat and under the bedroom door and Anna had to fight the compulsion to cough so much that she had to crawl under the bed with her pillow and bury her face in it, and hold on until the urge to cough had passed. Even after the visitors had left she stayed in her room. She opened the window to let in fresh air and the sound of the blackbirds calling to each other from the rooftops drifted in with the breeze, and Anna just sat on the edge of the bed and watched the pretty cloud patterns passing across the sky, letting her mind drift.

That was the pattern for the next three days. She kept out of his way, she let him work, she fought with her feelings – or to understand her feelings. She busied herself tidying up the flat, making meals, changing the beds and washing clothes. When she wasn't doing those things she sat and played Patience with an old pack of French playing cards which had the seven of diamonds missing, and worked her way through Mark's collection of books in the spare room at the rear of the flat. She finished 'Candide' in a day and loved it. Tucked away on the top shelf she found Grant's first book, which he had inscribed, "To the man who, now he has this book, really does have everything. With love, hugs and kisses, Grant" - and tried to fight through it but it usually ended up with her reading the same line over and over again until she fell asleep. At least when she was sleeping she didn't have to think. She only had to fight the war going on in her head, where Guy would chase her down a series of long, pitch-black corridors waving the gruesome knife which always lay on Mark's workbench. And when she woke she thought, 'why did Guy never write to me again? He could have sent it to Grant's. He could have found some way of getting it to me.' Anna didn't know why, but she did know that she was now well out of Guy's life.

***

John Timney was already waiting for Guy in the prison visitor's room when two warders led him in.

After the brief pleasantries and formalities were over the lawyer got down to business. They had a date for Guy's appeal hearing before the Advisory Committee and it was only days away.

"I'm not allowed to represent you before the Committee," Timney reminded him. "Your chance - your only chance - lies in your own defence. In your own 'performance.' 18B isn't internment. It's a policy of 'lock up first, worry about it later.' They've got you in here because of your background... because of what they think is your potential to cause harm. But they'll release you if you can persuade them that you are no threat to them. They may still come up with something else, but we can't deal with what we don't know about. So you play their game. You don't grovel, and you don't simply stand and deliver general denials."

"To hell with them!" Guy protested.

John Timney could see the resistance and opposition written all over Guy's face, but the lawyer was someone who knew that whether the cards are good or bad, they're the cards you've been dealt and you have to play them. "This isn't a trial. What happens to you depends fully on what and how the Committee feels. You have to convince them of your integrity. "You have to--"

Guy looked away.

"Listen to me Guy…"

Guy refocused.

"Get ready for their questions. You need to be sharp, and quick because you won't get long in there. The chairman is a barrister. He will work from his written brief and the reports from MI5 - and he'll ask whatever questions he feels necessary. But, and I believe this, they'll give you a fair chance. It's up to you whether you want to do the same."

Back in his cell, it suddenly hit Guy. Perhaps MI5 really did have absolutely nothing on him at all, and that they had arranged his arrest only so that they could stitch up someone who they suspected of spying – just like the deal which they had offered him. But what good were such thoughts? It was wartime and everyone from the politicians to the generals and the admirals - from the lawmakers to the authorities who implemented them - from those in Parliament to those in the prisons - from the propagandist media to the poets, the prophets and yes, the painters - they were all just making up the rules as they went along.

THIRTY

'SCHICKSAL'

Three days after Serge Chavalerin had called, Anna wasn't able to keep away from Mark any longer. She'd pulled a chair up to the kitchen window and was sitting reading. Next, to her, a beetle had found its way onto the windowsill and fallen on its back and was struggling to right itself. Anna put down her book and was about to help it when Mark came in and grabbed her by the arm… "Wait, wait," she said and quickly righted the poor beetle with her free hand before he led her off and up to his studio.

"You said you wanted to learn… so learn," he said and pushed a thick pencil into her hand and pointed her at a large sheet of paper which he had clipped to an easel for her. The truth was that Anna didn't want to keep away from him any longer - despite what she had been telling herself. So there wasn't too much resistance as he stood behind her and began to guide her hand around the paper, tracing the outline of a church from one of his old paintings.

An hour later she wasn't any better, what was on the paper in front of her in no way resembled what she was trying to draw. They kept breaking out into laughter, which hardly made her efforts any easier. Next to them on the atelier floor lay a few of Anna's previous, discarded attempts at various objects. She could only laugh at her own hopelessness.

"I thought you said you always wanted to be able to do this?" Mark said to her.

Anna stopped drawing. She removed her hand from his. She spun around to face him. She wanted to say something, but she hesitated. She looked deep into his eyes as if she was searching for some sort of courage. Mark held her look. He cherished the moment. He feared it was as fleeting as it was special. That it was only for that one, highly charged moment. They both waited for the other to make the first move. Slowly their faces moved closer. They were that half-second away from a kiss... when Mark pulled away.

"That list of yours - the one with hurt and anger on it - remember?" She didn't answer. She probably didn't even hear his question, because she was lost somewhere in another world now. It was the world behind his eyes. "Is 'free-'" he tried to say, but she put a finger over his lips to silence him. The space between them got smaller and smaller.

"Shh..."

He reached up, took her finger, and kissed it softly. Then, still holding on to her hand, he looked deep into her eyes for an agonising, uncertain moment, waiting for her reaction. He knew they had finally crossed that line; that they were now at that point of no return. Slowly Anna slipped her hand out of his. Then she reached up and wrapped her arms around his neck.

Two hours later, Anna and Mark lay in bed curled up in each other's arms. What had gone before truly had been special. Hot, passionate, uninhibited sex. Maybe even new ground for Anna.

A tiger had been let out of its cage. Mark pulled his arm free from under her. He propped himself up and smiled. He started to run his finger down her face, tracing the contours of her nose, her lips, her chin, her neck - 'drawing' her. He followed the line along her shoulder, as far as the scar tissue at the top of her arm. He ran his finger over the deep indentation. "A present from my mother. She threw a kitchen knife at me" she said and began to guide his finger lower. Then she lifted his hand to her lips and kissed and licked his fingers. He continued to look at her, enchanted. Then she stopped. She stared up at the ceiling.

"What are you thinking?" he asked.

Anna shook her head. She was keeping that thought to herself. She wouldn't tell him that she had grown to love the wrinkles which appeared at the sides of his mouth whenever he smiled, and his penetrating eyes and how they bore right into and through her every time he asked her a question - which made her feel like her answer was the most important thing he could possibly ever hear from anyone. Nor would she confess that she loved his long, painter's fingers - which had just performed their magic on her - and was secretly in awe of his talent but please don't tell him that I said that. Or that she was enchanted by the way he would let her win at cards even when she knew that he held the far better hand, and how always and without exception, he put more food on her plate than he did on his own and claimed they were exactly the same. Or the way, when he said "pissed" in his soft Swiss-French accent it sounded like "peeest" and was more comical than it was offensive. Anna hated to hear people swear, but this... this was somehow less cheap, more childlike and amusing. She had even grown to love the faint clicking noise that he sometimes made with his tongue on the top of his mouth when he was deep in concentration at his canvas. That he had watched over her like a guardian angel the whole time she was ill - which almost moved her to tears whenever she thought about it - Anna knew she would forever feel connected to him. She also wouldn't tell him just how sexy he looked right at that very moment as they looked deep into each other's eyes. It

287

was a charged, erotic, sensual moment. Then Anna put her arms around his neck, pulled him over to her, and it started all over again.

***

For the previous three days, Anna had made an art form out of avoiding Mark but for the following six they were inseparable. They lost themselves in each other. They laughed, lived and loved their lives together - despite the entrapment. On the seventh morning, Anna woke up early and couldn't get back to sleep. She got up quietly, wrapped a large tartan blanket around herself, and wandered into the living room where she picked something from the bookshelf. It was the catalogue from Mark's first exhibition - the one that she had first seen at Claire's. She turned the pages until she found the painting of the lonely girl walking the sands, the one which hung on Grant and Claire's wall. "How can I explain what is happening?" she asked herself as she stood and stared into the image, riding a carousel of emotions. Anna knew she couldn't. It was all way beyond that. She tried to work out whether she was lucky or unlucky, was she lost - or had she been found? All she was able to tell herself back then was that she couldn't have stopped what they had started, even if she had wanted to.

It's "Schicksal," said Mark. Schicksal is the German word for 'fate,' or 'destiny.' Schicksal perfectly defined Anna's story (and those too of Guy and Mark). No one was guilty. No one was to blame. It all came down to 'fate, and the war. She wasn't Anna Karenina and Mark wasn't the dashing young officer who'd ridden in to save her from a safe but stale and suffocating marriage to an old and banal government official. Mark and Guy were much more alike than they were different. Anna hadn't sought out one to compensate for some deficiencies in the other. She didn't simply fall out of love with one. She'd been rejected. Fate played its hand, she'd fallen in love once. Then she fell in love twice. It happens. It happened. And as she said herself, she was free to let it happen. Guy had released her. Mark was what she needed when she needed it the most. It was, just as Mark had said, 'Schicksal.' And you couldn't get out of its way. So why did she feel so bad while feeling so good?

Angel or Devil?

Which was what Mark originally called his painting but then changed it to 'Girl on the Sand' once it was completed. Anna now stared hard at the image in the catalogue. It was a magnificent piece of work, one of truly awesome beauty. She was drawn to it, but in a way which disturbed her. "Hey!" came a voice from behind her. It made her jump. Mark was standing in the doorway, naked. He moved right up to her.

"Who is that?" Anna asked, showing him the picture of the painting.

"Why? Would you like it to be you?"

Anna shook her head. "She's lost."

"Says who?"

"Say I."

"I painted her and believe me this girl's a lot of laughs. In fact, she's heading to a party right now, just here..."

He pointed to a place just out of the frame. "And it's every bit as wild as Grant's."

She reached out and punched him playfully on the shoulder.

"You're making fun of her... so you're making fun of me."

"Ow." He punched her back, softly. "You said it wasn't you."

She hit him again, a little harder.

"You paint just like you make love," she said cheekily. "Unehrfürchtig and inkonsequent." She meant irreverent and inconsequential but didn't know the English words. She was trying to stifle a laugh.

"Thank you."

"How can you paint something like this? This girl is lost. She doesn't need painting. She needs help."

She stretched out her leg and 'kicked' him (although in reality, it was little more than a friendly tap on the shin).

"She does?"

"Yes. If you want to do anything for this girl, help her, don't paint her."

He had never looked at it this way before – this master of perception. Never thought of it like this. It troubled him and excited him at the same time.

"You might be right," he said and kicked her back.

"I know I'm right." She was determined she'd have the last kick.

He looked at her. The wild beautiful gypsy girl with fire in her eyes and her tousled hair all over the place and the cheeky grin. Angel or Devil?

"I think I'm beginning to hate you," he said.

He gave her a long steady stare, which she gave right back to him... then she looked down, "I can see that."

He reached out and grabbed the edge of the blanket which Anna had wrapped herself in and tugged at it, and she began to spin and spin as it unfurled around her. And while he did so he quoted Baudelaire in his native French "Ah, you would like to know why I hate you today. It will no doubt be harder for you to understand than for me to explain it to you; as you are, I believe, the most perfect example of feminine impermeability that one could encounter."

"What are you saying?" Anna asked as she was being spun around, but he ignored her and carried on reciting his favourite poet while he tugged away at the blanket. Even when it was fully off and lying on the carpet he continued to spin her around - until she fell dizzy into his arms. She stretched right up onto her toes and began to kiss his forehead, his nose, his cheek, his lips. Then they fell back onto the sofa and she lost herself in him again.

THIRTY-ONE

ANOTHER VISITOR

The following Sunday Anna and Mark again stayed in bed all morning and played 'twenty questions' - discovering more about each other's pasts and about their secret wishes and desires, the loser would make lunch. There was laughter, but there were also tears. They lay for a while afterwards and took in what they had learned, perhaps even falling a little more in love, and at twelve-thirty they got up. Mark went down to the plot in the back yard to dig up some fresh vegetables, while 'loser' Anna raked through the pantry and cupboards and gathered everything that she could use to make an 'Auflauf' - a casserole of sorts. She found a pair of old dirty socks lying on the floor in the corner of the pantry. They had been there since one freezing cold early-spring morning when Mark had used them as gloves to carry up two heavy sacks of potatoes. He told her to throw the socks into the casserole too, "they'll add to the taste."

Later that day at around four-thirty in the afternoon, while Mark was working and Anna was down in the bedroom with the Sunday paper, Grant's car pulled up in the street outside of Mark's flat. He cut the engine, got out of the car and looked cautiously around him. Then he took the half-dozen steps up to Mark's front door.

A few minutes later he stood up in the atelier watching Mark mix colours for a large new canvas that he had prepared. "This might interest Anna," Grant said and handed Mark an envelope with a crease all the way down the middle. Mark put the envelope down on the workbench and picked up the knife which was lying there and used it to prise the crusted tops off some old tins of paint.

"She's gone back to bed," Mark said while working his way around the paint pot with his knife. "So how are things at home?"

"That was my question. Or rather, our question. Claire has been worried sick about Anna."

"You too Grant. You must be out of your mind with worry too. Or is it something else about her which bothers you?"

Grant ignored his question, "the police came for her again. Walked straight in with a warrant."

"And did they find her?" Grant just shot him a cold look, "then it's good she came here," Mark added. He

293

could sense that Grant was building up to something. Finally...

"You don't do this Mark."

"Don't do what?"

"You know what I mean."

"You're in Hermann's hotel, Grant. It's free. And she's free."

"She's not free. And you know it. Just two months ago she was waiting for someone in her wedding dress."

"You love Claire, right?"

Grant was growing irritated. "Don't start talking riddles, Mark. She was waiting. And someone else is still waiting. In jail!"

"Woah. You've read the wrong book Grant. You read the version where someone shot her right through the heart and then claimed he was the one doing all the dying."

"Whatever you heard, there are two sides to…" Grant told him.

"Pass that red will you?"

"You just don't do it," Grant repeated, this time a little more forcefully.

"I always mix red with it. Or doesn't Professor Cooper approve? Too dark? Too gloomy? Not bright like my old stuff? But you know what, Grant? It's going to be light again from now on. That's what she's brought back into my life. Light. Beauty. Colour. So be grateful for that. And if the truth hurts--" and he spoke the following words with the driest of sarcasm, "then think of her simply as a heavenly gift to Art."

"Oh stop it. I feel a responsibility towards her. Towards them both."

Mark stopped what he was doing. He put the knife down. He moved towards Grant and put his arm on his shoulder and addressed him with a mock sincerity which was almost patronising. "Do you? Well, that's good Grant. That's good. But just be careful you don't take it too far. What's "going on" here is..."

Grant angrily brushed Mark's hand away. "It's not right. What you're both doing is just not right."

"So what would be 'right' then? Lock her up like a criminal for God knows how long? Is that what you think she deserves? That's all she's ever known damn it!"

"Oh shut up Mark. I'm not talking about that, and you know it."

"Then what? What's this all about?"

"There are rules. Mark Hermann might not like the fact or want to play by them but by God, you live in the same world as the rest of us, and you'll have to get along with it like we all have to. And while Guy's in prison, rule one--"

"Rule one's called let's ask Anna. Let's hear what she says," came a voice from behind him.

Grant spun around to see Anna standing in the doorway. For a moment, they just stood and stared at each other, neither knowing what comes next. Anna surprised him by crossing the room, moving right up to him, and kissing him on the cheek.

"Pass that on to Claire, will you?"

Grant was momentarily flustered and uneasy, but he nevertheless managed to fake some sense of normality.

"We heard from Guy," he said to her and nodded to the letter on the workbench. "I thought it might interest you. They've moved him to another wing. They finally got themselves prepared for handling so many."

"Does he mention me?" asked Anna and Grant looked past her at a point on the wall, then around the room.

"He didn't, did he?"

Mark took the chance to slip out of the room, while Anna's question was left hanging in the air unanswered. Slowly, as Anna stared down at the letter and listened to Grant's words, the reality of her situation began to break on her and the confidence and defiance of her entrance drained away.

Suddenly she was back in the prison; in the church; everywhere in fact that she'd ever been with Guy.

"That wasn't Guy you saw in prison Anna," Grant said to her, "that was someone else."

He looked directly into her eyes and slowly shook his head. His displeasure was obvious.

"Do you have any idea what he is going through?"

He had just delivered the exact words to refocus Anna; to reignite her defiance. Her reply was with a real, deep passion.

296

"I know imprisonment better than anyone. That's why I came here. And I was free to do so. Or didn't Guy tell you that part? I was ill because of Guy. I wanted to tear my heart out because of him."

They stood and stared each other down. The tense, charged moment was only broken when Mark re-entered the room. Anna moved next to him in a display of some solidarity. "Mark risked his own freedom to allow me mine."

"Any idea why Grant?" Mark added.

But Grant - angry, disappointed, grossly insulted - just shook his head from side to side: this is so wrong. Then he turned and stormed out, slamming the door behind him. "Have one of your drinks on us Grant," Mark called out after him as Grant raced off down the stairs. He felt like a silly little schoolboy who had just had his legs slapped in front of the class and been ordered to stand in the corner for the rest of the lesson.

'He just doesn't understand,' Anna thought to herself as she heard Grant's car start up down in the street, followed by the sound of tyres screeching as he roared off. 'How could he?' And she concluded that the only people who can fully understand what goes on in a relationship are the people who are in it.

**

That night Anna lay tossing and turning in bed next to Mark. Guy's voice was haunting her. "Two hundred and four. Two hundred and five--"

297

***

An unreal stillness hung over the prison at night-time. But while the others slept, Guy lay on the floor of his moonlit cell and went through his routine once again; "two hundred and six, two hundred and seven, two hundred and eight..." 'Look, God, I'm trying' his inner voice was pleading. I know I've been bad – just give me the chance to redeem myself. He pushed his body to its very limits with a series of strenuous sit-ups - getting faster - and faster - and faster - and...

***

Anna jumped upright in bed. The sweat poured down the side of her head like a waterfall. She was lost in one of those "was it a nightmare or was it reality?" moments. She looked across at Mark next to her, still sleeping, as she fought hard to get control of herself.

***

At the University later that morning, Grant marched along the corridor still in a rage, walking straight past the colleagues who greeted him without saying a word. The meeting with Mark and Anna had impacted greatly on him. Mark had insulted him, but there was more than that. Grant knew that Mark had something which he would never possess, and that was a great and natural and innate talent. Grant envied him so much for it he found that somewhere deep inside of himself he could actually hate Mark. And now he'd taken Anna away from Guy. Or so Grant believed. Was he also jealous of Mark for that too?

Had he secretly desired Anna for himself? Or at least wanted her to want him? Grant didn't even dare to follow that thought any further.

He knocked on a door marked "Dean: Sir Charles de Witt" and walked straight in. The Dean, Grant's boss, was sitting at his desk looking through papers. It was the 'bull' from the party. He motioned for Grant to sit down. He could see directly that Grant was beyond angry.

***

Mark too was still troubled by Grant's visit. He sat motionless, slumped down in a living room armchair. "Are you alright?" Anna asked him.

"Yes," but she could see he clearly wasn't, "just a little sullen," he added, "a little morose."

"I see you and I think I can work out what those two words mean. It's Grant, is it?"

She crossed the room and turned on the radio. More news about further German advances and gains. More land gobbled up, more villages razed, more innocents slaughtered - to the east, to the north, to the south and the west, where they were already at the Channel and eagerly looking even further westwards. Even the Kent coast had come under long-range artillery fire.

"To hell with Grant. He'll grow up one day and get over it. Grant's not our problem."

He nodded to the radio. "We're losing this war, you know that don't you?"

"Define we."

"You know what that will mean to people like you and me."

Anna said nothing to that. She didn't need to.

"So spin the dial," Mark told her. Even he could only take so much depression.

She twisted the tuner and the sounds of Glenn Miller came swinging out of the speaker, "is that better?"

"A little dope for the ears doesn't do anyone any harm… once in a while."

"Where do all those fancy English words come from anyway… sullen… morone?"

"Morose."

"Morose. Where did they all come from?

"I'm a genius."

"You're a fool, '' then an afterthought, "but a pretty fool."

"Thank you."

"And the clever English comes from where?"

"We had an English nanny for five years," he smiled to himself at the memory. "Lillian from Louth, in Lincolnshire. We spoke English with Lilly, French with my father and German with my mother, and at times a crazy mix of everything with everyone. So if there's a fool sitting here - and I'm not going to argue with you there - then that's probably where it comes from."

"Want to dance?" Anna asked, hopeful of cheering him up and followed it with a little twirl.

He shook his head.

"I don't dance."

"Why not? Everyone should dance."

"I don't. I can't."

"Come on. I'll teach you to dance better than you taught me to draw."

"It will be a lot worse. I promise you."

"You're just like…" she started to say, but then stopped herself. She realized that she'd been in this scene with someone else once before.

"I just want to go to bed," Mark said.

"You're tired already?"

"No. I want to go to bed."

"Well, es übertrifft tanzen." And it certainly did beat dancing.

So picture this: Mark's bedroom – not a minute later – two desperate lovers tear at each other's clothes – they fall back onto the bed – Anna takes….

WHUUUUU – the eerie, wailing sound of air raid sirens pierce the still London night. German Heinkel HE 111 bombers are on their way.

If you're Anna, what do you do? Do you break cover? Or stay under the covers? Do you head for the shelters and risk being incarcerated? Or do you take your chances with a German bomb? Which Hermann will define your final moments on Earth? Mark? Or Göring? Will it all end in the arms of the artist, or at the hands of the tyrant?

Anna clung on tight to Mark and buried herself under the sheets with him – while Luftwaffe bombs thundered down on the East End, on Stepney and Hackney, and on a church right in the heart of the City.

But that night, no bombs fell on Fulham, although that would soon change.

THIRTY-TWO

THE ADVISORY COMMITTEE

An armed soldier stood either side of the half a dozen anxious detainees who were sitting in a row in the waiting area at the side of the Advisory Committee room. A third armed guard watched over them from the door. All six detainees whose Appeals were being held that afternoon avoided looking at anything, in particular, most of them simply sat and peered down at their feet as if they'd never seen them before. Guy was among them, sitting at the end of the row. The work that he had put into his body and the work he had put into his mind now showed. He looked much fitter and much healthier. He was clean shaven and neatly groomed.

He was the only detainee who wasn't sitting with his head bowed, and there was a clear sense of purpose in his eyes. John Timney had spent a good hour-long session with him three days before - as was Guy's legal right - drilling him and preparing him as well as he possibly could. But as the lawyer had once said to Anna, "you never know" and that the best laid plans can appear perfect, but only until you come into contact with the enemy. "Just pray that they all get up on the right side of the bed on Thursday," he'd said to Guy with an encouraging smile and a reassuring pat on the shoulder when their session in the prison visitor's room was over.

The six detainees simultaneously looked over at the door when it opened and a brown-suited male clerk showed the detainee whose case had just been heard back into the waiting room. The detainee came in with a cocky, defiant walk and had a dark intensity about him. "Gerhard Schneider" the clerk called out and Guy stood up and followed him into the Committee room.

The room was small and dark, with oak-paneled walls, and three sixty-plus year olds sat behind a long wooden desk. In front of them were two neat piles of files and papers. It was no criminal court and all three Advisory Committee members were dressed as if for business in dark suits and ties. The clerk who brought Guy in took a seat alongside the Committee, ready to take shorthand, and Guy sat down in a chair at the other side of the long table. The Chairman was the oldest of the three, and he sat in the middle. He picked up a sheet of paper from the table and began to read through it aloud. It was the very first time that he, or either of his two colleagues, had seen the files or read the case against any of the day's defendants.

"Schneider. Gerhard. Reason for Order: Acts Prejudicial and Hostile Associations," the Chairman read out from the MI5 report, for his own as well as for his colleagues' benefit.

He was still looking down and scanning the document when he addressed Guy.

"You are German?"

"I'm British, Sir. My mother was born in Bromley in Kent. I didn't renew my German passport when I came here to live three years ago."

The Committee member to the left of the Chairman was the youngest of the three. He still had a full head of black hair above his painfully gaunt face, which was the colour and texture of cement, and a few too many teeth for the size of his mouth.

He reached over for Guy's files and began to flick through them. He removed something from the file then reached over and handed the file to the third Committee member on the other side of the Chairman.

"But you do have dual nationality... you are still German?" the Chairman asked Guy, still with his head down and now scanning the document.

"Technically, yes, Sir," Guy answered.

For the first time, the Chairman lifted his head and peered over his glasses at Guy.

"How well do you know Ulrich von Kondertal?"

Guy looked back at him disoriented. How the hell could they know about that? How could they possibly connect me to him? He tugged at his shirt collar. He tried to compose himself. Don't blow this Guy, he said to himself, don't blow this. He took in a deep breath of the stale Committee Room air and let it out slowly. Then he replied, "The von Kondertals were neighbours. I know the General well enough to hate him and everything he represents. And I don't think I was the only one in our street to feel that way. I went to school with his youngest son. I heard that he killed himself in his first year at University."

The Chairman made a quick note and pressed on. "And this brother of yours? The one in the German Embassy in Lisbon?"

"I haven't seen him for over three years, Sir. And even if I live another three hundred I still won't."

"What did you intend doing with the photographs?" asked the Committee man with the teeth. He had the packet containing Guy's photographs on the table in front of him but was covering the packet with his arm to conceal them from Guy.

Guy looked at him bewildered. "Which photographs?"

The Chairman continued to peer over his glasses at Guy. He studied him and long and hard. Then there was silence, as the three Committee members took some moments to look through the material in front of them. Finally, the Chairman removed his glasses and addressed Guy.

"That's all, thank you. You will be informed in due course about the outcome of your appeal."

Guy stood for a stunned moment; was that it?

"May I say something, Sir?" he asked.

The Chairman looked at his watch. "If it's brief."

Guy cleared his throat. It felt like it was coated in sand. He swallowed hard. The eyes of the three Committee men burned right into him. "My parents sent me to Britain to study. And I returned here and made it my home because... because it felt like my home. People don't normally have that choice, Sir. They're born somewhere and they never get the chance to break away from there. But I did. To somewhere better... somewhere finer. And for three years I knew how lucky I was."

Old 'buck teeth' coughed. He took out the handkerchief which poked out from his breast pocket and wiped a huge dollop of phlegm from the side of his mouth. Guy waited for him to settle before he continued.

"I hate German National Socialism and everything it stands for with a passion only someone who has lived with it and seen it can know. This... Britain... this is where I chose to make my home. Where I'm proud to belong to... despite what happened to me. I was locked up on my wedding day. And yes, she was a German girl... someone who was forced to flee from the Nazis. But I'm not here on trial today for who I fell in love with, am I?"

He stopped. His emotions began to take over. "My bride's dream died in a Bexton church. Mine in a prison cell…" He stopped again. He began to tear up. He blinked hard, rubbed a hand over his face and fought to get control of himself. The eyes of the three Committee men in front of him continue to burn. "I still have no idea why I was locked away. I'm no threat to this country's security. I never have been, or will ever be. If I have done anything wrong… if I'm guilty of doing anything at all to harm Britain's cause, or guilty in any way of supporting its enemy, then put me on trial, produce your evidence, and shoot me. I'd deserve it. But if I'm guilty of where I was born, or who my family is, then I'm a free man. And you must let me be that."

"Let me ask you something, Schneider. Would you be prepared to fight for 'your' country?" the Chairman asked.

"With respect Sir, but I wasn't arrested for opposing the war."

"Is that your answer?"

"My answer…" he stopped. And for an anxious split second his mind raced. How do I answer this? What do they want to hear? His inner voice was screaming 'just let me out of here!' But how? In the end, all he was left with was the truth. "My answer is that I will never, ever oppose what Britain is fighting for."

The Chairman looked at the members on either side of him. They both signalled that they'd heard enough, and the member on the Chairman's right pointed down at his watch.

"Thank you," the Chairman said to Guy, as emotionless and matter-of-factly as if Guy had just delivered him his Sunday paper.

"Sir, one very last question... which photographs do everyone keeps asking me about?"

The Chairman's face gave nothing away. It never would. "Thank you, Mr Schneider" is all he said.

The clerk stood up and led Guy back to the waiting room. Once they saw the Committee room door close behind him the three members began to confer.

"I thought he was going to break down on us like that vicar last week," the member to the right of the Chairman said.

'Buck tooth' held up Guy's files with a dismissive 'so what are they wasting our time with, this time?' look on his face. "What do we have here anyway?" he asked the others in a seemingly unconcerned manner.

"Let me see those photographs again," the Chairman said.

***

Sir Charles de Witt sat in the back office of his local police station. Across the desk, from him, a senior police officer picked up the phone, dialed a number and said to whoever was on the other end of the line, "we have someone here who claims he knows where a German girl is being hidden." Then of what he heard, he said, "right away" and put down the receiver. The 'bull' broke into a broad and vengeful smile.

THIRTY-THREE

SOMEONE'S WATCHING

Standing close to the living room window, Mark was brought into sharp focus through a powerful binoculars' lens. He had set up an easel in the living room and was hard at work, painting with his usual intensity, and continually looking up and across to the other side of the room as he laid down his bold strokes on the canvas with the precision of a surgeon's scalpel. Then the voyeur swung his lens to the right, to the second window in the room. The curtains there had been drawn, but a small gap had been left in order to let in as much light as possible while at the same time trying to conceal something. The gap was enough for the voyeur to make out Anna's face. What was out of direct sight was that she was lying on the sofa, naked and in the reclining position of Manet's 'Olympia' - confident and self-assured. Across the room on Mark's canvas was the evidence indeed of a return to his old style of painting - bright; radiant; optimistic. He stood proud and relaxed behind his easel. There was a faint smile where the frown used to be. On another easel behind him was the half-finished and degraded impressionist landscape painting which Anna had looked at a few weeks earlier, now completed and as powerfully brilliant as any of his earlier works.

The voyeur's gaze lingered on Anna for a while. Then suddenly she got up from the sofa as if she'd been disturbed and aware of someone's presence. She wrapped Mark's dressing gown around her and moved over to the half-curtained window, and ever so carefully, she edged the curtain back a further inch and looked out. It was almost as if she could sense someone was watching her. She looked straight out across the road. And then suddenly something directly down below in the street caught her attention. She spun away from the window in sheer panic.

In the house directly across from Mark's a hand placed the binoculars down onto a window sill. The figure who had been looking through them was about to move away from the window when he saw what Anna had seen down in the street below the window. It was Adams and a uniformed police officer, who were getting out of a police car. Roland - the voyeur - moved so that he was hidden by the side of the curtain as he took in a scene which had just taken an abrupt turn.

"It's the Police...they're outside!" Anna shouted to Mark in a frenzy at the same time as a loud knock came up from the front door.

Mark went over to the window and looked out.

"Get your things together... everything!" He pushed a key into her hand. "Get it all down into the cellar and stay there."

She stood frozen to the spot. Mark looked at her as if she was out of her head. "I can't," she said, trembling. "Isn't there..."

Before she could finish there was another knock on the front door, this time much louder and a lot more urgent. Mark grabbed Anna and shoved her towards the living room door and into action.

"MOVE! And don't miss a thing."

From the house across the street, Roland watched Mark at his front door trying to buy himself time. While up in the flat Anna frantically threw her things into her suitcase.

Down at the front door, Adams and the officer tried to enter but Mark, still trying to buy more time, stood across the doorway and blocked them.

"Do you have a search warrant?" he demanded to know, and Adams produced a piece of paper and waved it at him impatiently.

Up in the flat Anna, still in Mark's dressing gown, moved like lightening down the back staircase carrying her suitcase and her two paintings.

At the front door, Adams and his colleague were all out of patience.

"I want to call my lawyer," Mark insisted.

Adams ignored him and pushed him to one side as he entered the flat.

"Yeah, and I want to open the batting for England mate but it isn't going to happen," he called back over his shoulder as he set off up the stairs with his police colleague.

Down in the cellar, Anna stood and looked into the blackness of the cellar. She was paralysed with fear. All her nightmares had returned to haunt her. She couldn't go in there. She stood for a moment and weighed up her options. And realised she had none. She stepped inside with all her things and quietly closed the door.

Up in the flat, Adams and the policeman poked around the living room. Anna had done an expert job of covering her tracks. Not even Mark noticed the faint lipstick traces on the tea cup which she'd left standing in the middle of the table. Luckily, neither Adams nor his police colleague did either.

They moved into the bedroom, but there was no trace of Anna there either. Until the three of them turned to leave and Mark spotted a stocking which had caught around a bedpost. Quick as a flash he positioned himself between the bedpost and the two officers as they passed him to go out. He was slipping it surreptitiously into his pocket when Adams turned round to face him, "we'll take a look in the cellar."

Mark's heart stopped beating as they set off down the stairs.

"Give me the key," Adams said when they were outside the cellar door, and he held out his hand to Mark, who was just about to say 'I've lost it' when the policeman tried the handle.

"It's open," he said, and Mark stood paralysed as the door slowly swung open and the policeman went in, followed by Adams.

Inside, among all the assorted junk and art stuff, stood a big red suitcase. And behind that, face down was Anna's two paintings. And that was all there was.

They say that when the canons were being fired at the battle of the Somme in 1916, you could feel the earth shake all the way across the Channel in London. Well, the day that MI5 called at Mark's place in Fulham they could probably have heard the booming of Anna's pounding heartbeat all the way back across to northern France as she stood pressed up tight into a corner of the small courtyard at the back of the building, hardly daring to breathe. Her eyes were closed. Her hands were clasped tight in front of her chest. Her teeth almost punctured her bottom lip. She was trembling madly.

Five minutes later, after Mark had closed the front door on an angry, frustrated Adams, he went back up the stairs to find Anna standing at the top of the landing.

"How could they know?" was all she said. Mark had absolutely no idea.

THIRTY-FOUR

THE DEALS

Grant sat alone in his study. He emptied the very last drops from a whisky bottle into his glass, downed it in one and flung the empty bottle down onto the ground. Right at that moment, he hated himself more than he could hate anyone. He was someone who had risen through the ranks at the University thanks to his keen ambition, hard work and application, and an insatiable appetite for his subject. But crucially, he had achieved it by cultivating a very close and special relationship with his boss, the Dean. Now though, Grant regarded himself in exactly the same way that Anna had thought about Guy; that he had betrayed something precious. That he had corrupted himself. That he had abandoned himself. He'd become a monster. He kicked out at the empty bottle lying at his feet and sent it flying across the room. It shattered into pieces on the door frame.

***

In Major Robert Walker's office at MI5, someone else also hated the world. Walker angrily waved a sheet of paper at Barnes. "The bloody Advisory Committee has revoked another twelve orders. Behrens and that photographer Schneider are among them."

"They're going soft Sir," was all Barnes could think of to say.

The Major looked at the Home Office memorandum which he'd been waving about. He thought for a moment. "Get to Schneider before they release him," he ordered Barnes, "we can use him to nail that other traitor at the Foreign Office."

***

Barnes and Adams were once more with Guy in the prison governor's office. Barnes scratched the top of his smooth, hairless head. "They're not going to release you. You know that, don't you?" he said with an edge in his voice.

"I've heard nothing," Guy replied.

"Well, we have," Adams told him. But Guy didn't respond. "You're in here for the duration Schneider. We're giving you one last chance."

"The chance the Committee wouldn't give you," Barnes added. "Don't be a fool."

318

Only more silence from Guy.

"Come on, Schneider. Don't piss us off. We're the good guys," Adams said, and he probably really did believe it.

But the look Guy gave them this time around was cold and resolute.

***

Roland followed Mark up the stairs and into the living room carrying two headless and unplucked pheasants. Anna was sitting reading the newspaper which Mark had brought in earlier that mid-August morning. Roland dropped the pheasants onto the table in front of her. "Here, for the pheasant plucker," he said to her and she stood up and took a step back from the table, leaving the paper open at the report she'd been reading. 'Adlertag,' or Eagle Day had been declared by the Germans and the Luftwaffe had begun their bombardment of RAF airfields and radar installations in preparation for a full invasion. Bombs had been dropped on Southampton, resulting in death and destruction. Bombs had been dropped on Norwich and a railway goods depot had been destroyed. Now two pheasants had been dropped on the table in front of Anna, and what followed was another bombshell.

Roland turned directly round to face Mark.

"I...erm...I found out who she is," the news was like a fist to the guts for Mark.

He just stared at Roland, then over at Anna, then back to Roland, barely able to believe what he'd just heard. He rolled his eyes and looked up at the ceiling. Anna's hand shot up to cover her mouth.

"Who told you?" Mark eventually asked.

Another charged moment passed in which no one said a word. Then, with a sly look in his eye, Roland smiled like a man who had just been proved right.

"You just did," he said. Mark banged his fist on the table, but before he could get even angrier Roland reacted. "Hold on, hold on... Listen, I'm sorry Mark. But it wasn't that hard to work out. I saw the police here. Which means I'm not the only one who suspected something? But I'm the only one who can help you. I know someone who can arrange a passport for her, with the papers to get you both on a ship to America. You'll be okay anyway," he said looking at Mark.

Mark stood in numbed silence. Anna jumped in, "we have to take the chance Mark. We can't go on hiding for God knows how many years. If he-" (she nodded to Roland contemptuously) "could find out..." What she didn't add was that it was driving her crazy – the claustrophobia, the isolation, the imprisonment of a different kind. She'd controlled it as well as she was able to so far, but what happens when it starts to control her? And she knew that point was getting ever closer.

"How quickly?" Mark asked Roland, "and how dependable is this person?"

"It'll cost. A lot. How quick? I don't know yet. Maybe three days?" He gave Mark a 'take it or leave it' kind of look then turned to go, "I'll put the pheasants on the tab," he said as he was going out, "have a pleasant day plucking, you two," he added and headed off down the stairs.

A minute later Anna and Mark were alone in the room. "I don't trust him," Anna said. She looked worried and chewed on her bottom lip while Mark was back to his cool, calm self again.

"You have an alternative?"

Anna didn't. She just stood hating the fact that her fate was in the hands of someone like Roland. But she knew that Mark was right; there simply was no alternative. He tried to make light of her anguish. "Don't worry. Roland's on our side. Come here." Deeply worried, still far from convinced, she was happy to move into his open arms.

***

Guy was led into the Governor's office by one of the warders. The warder turned and left the room. The Governor handed Guy two sheets of typed documents. Guy stood for a moment and looked quickly over them. Then he broke into a smile as wide as the Thames. He was free!

***

Adams and Barnes were together at their desks in their shabby MI5 office. Barnes put down the phone and said over the desk to his colleague "The boss wants us to keep an eye on Schneider once he's out. He might lead us to the girl."

"You want to leave that one to me?" Adams asked him with a smile.

321

***

Guy strolled across the prison exercise yard, where the detainees were enjoying their hour of clean fresh air and 'freedom.' Someone had set up an impromptu cricket match using a long slat of wood for a bat, an old tattered and frayed tennis ball, and some weeks earlier someone had chalked a wicket onto the prison wall but over the summer it had begun to fade badly.

Other inmates just smoked and chatted and did their various deals, while the rest walked, usually in pairs, around and around the compound. One of them was the tall, ginger Geordie, Jackie Brandling, who was doing his rounds with his cellmate. Guy caught up with them and walked alongside.

"I'm being released." he said to Brandling almost in a whisper. "I've heard you can arrange passports. I need one... British." Brandling just kept on walking in silence, looking directly ahead, while Guy waited for an answer which just wouldn't come. Until eventually, he asked, "Am I right?" and Brandling turned, looked Guy up and down, then gave the slightest of nods. "How does it work?" Guy asked him.

"I'll get word to you."

Guy peeled away from Brandling and his mate and headed over to the other side of the yard to watch the cricket match. For the first time in many weeks, he was beginning to feel good about life.

***

There was bright sunshine outside Mark's flat in Fulham. Inside, there was only darkness. The thick curtains had been drawn, and the once spacious and airy room now looked and felt much smaller, gloomier, claustrophobic. Anna sat on the sofa, but she was now a different person from the one who had lain down there, so confident and so secure in herself, for Mark to paint. She was now morose, anxious, sullen. The words she'd learned from Mark, but the feelings were all her very own. The painting had been put back on the easel near the living room door after the police visit and it now looked across at her, ridiculing the radiance and confidence which she had projected only a couple of days before.

Anna and Mark sat in tense silence.

Each moment felt longer than the last. They were both lost in their private thoughts. They knew the noose was tightening.

***

The next morning at ten o'clock, the main prison gates opened slowly and Guy walked out, dressed in his wedding suit. In one hand he was carrying his top hat, on the other hand, was a paper carrier bag. He stood for a moment as the gates closed behind him. He took in a deep breath of air and then let it out slowly and looked around him - at the world just going about its business the way it always did and always would do.

No one was outside to meet him. Because nobody knew.

Guy set off down the road. He knew what he had to do.

***

That same morning a small wooden packing case arrived for Mark containing some specialist oils which he was keen to use. The package had been shipped from the USA. A few weeks earlier, his previous delivery had gone missing – no doubt it had been pilfered by wily dockers in Liverpool, only to eventually find its way into clever 'dealers' hands; dealers such as Roland. Mark carried the case into the living room and had to go up to the atelier to get his old knife with the serrated blade in order to force open the slats which sealed the top of the case. When it opened, he put the knife down on the table and rushed off to catch the bank before it closed, while Anna went for her daily walk in the darkened flat. Up the stairs and down the stairs - round the kitchen, and the bedroom - touch all four walls in the living room, then four times round the table where Mark's knife and a small pile of threepences and sixpences for the electric meter were lying. And repeat.

Two miles away across the city, Claire put down the phone as Grant came into the hallway. She had a huge smile on her face. "It was Guy. He's been released and he's coming round later." Grant met her look with an uncertain expression. It concealed a conscience eaten up by guilt. And he also knew that trouble lay ahead. Claire sensed he was uneasy about something.

324

"What's wrong?"

"Nothing. It's-- it's good news."

Then it hit her, "what do we tell him about Anna?"

Grant shrugged his shoulders. He had no idea. Claire's anxious look now mirrored his.

***

When Mark came back from the bank an hour later, Anna was still walking. She hadn't seen anything new on her trip or met anyone exciting. But she hadn't expected to. Mark put the money which he'd drawn from the bank into the old Ming vase which stood on a shelf in the kitchen and then made them both a cup of tea. It was the very last tea in the flat. And their last milk and sugar.

PART 3

MR. TAYLOR AND HIS PICTURES OF ANNA

Guy stood on the pavement outside his shop in Upper Bexton's High Street and looked up at the sign above the shop window. It depressed him. It now reads "Taylor's Industrial Laundering." The replaced shop windows had all been painted white to prevent anyone from looking inside. Guy shook his head. It had finally come to this, to a total denial of who and what he was.

Later, up in the flat and freshly dressed, he sat at the kitchen table with scores of photographs scattered across the table top. Many of them were pictures of Anna. He raked through them and came to a block of passport-sized portrait pictures of her. He picked up a pair of scissors and began to carefully cut one out, then a second one, identical to the first.

***

"Don't forget to put the money on the electric meter," Mark had reminded Anna before he went out to his evening class which he still taught once a week at the local college. Before the war, he'd had two classes, but one had been cut shortly after the outbreak of hostilities, and the remaining group of fourteen had now dwindled to a group of four; two old ladies, the local pharmacist, whose profession protected him from being called into service, and the pharmacist's handicapped but highly talented niece, who the pharmacist wheeled the one and a half miles to class whatever the weather. Mark's classes were his way of 'keeping in touch' with the rest of humanity.

He would readily tell you that isolation and distance might be prerequisites of a painter's way of working, but also that "isolation is a dangerous thing which can also mean death," which he used to say about those artists like himself whose subject matter was the world around them. Mark went off to teach and stay connected while Anna went off on another one of her walks and stayed in isolation. Up the stairs, down the stairs, back up into the Atelier, where she stopped and looked directly at the portrait of Martine.

"You're a saint Martine," she said out loud to the painting, happy for someone new to speak to and for someone new to listen to her. Then, changing into a deep voice and with a thick French accent - not perfect but not too bad either - she spoke Martine's words back to her.

"And what are you Frau Vieti?"

She switched back into her own normal voice to answer herself: "Not a saint. I know that much." She headed off out of the room and onto the top landing.

"Because you've fallen in love?" she said to herself as Martine. But Anna didn't answer. She waited for 'Martine' to continue. "But it feels good, does it not?" the deep, sexy French voice asked.

Then Anna as Anna: "It feels very good."

She smiled to herself. She was even enjoying the crazy little game that she was playing with herself.

Martine: "It *should* feel good. It *is* good. Love is al-ways good. And Mark Hermann is a good man. He needs someone. And he loves you very much."

Switching back to Anna: "I know. But there was Guy. We loved each other and needed each other too. But--"

"Do you think that was true love that he showed you in the end?" the French woman in her countered.

Anna: "Not in the end, no."

In Martine's voice: "He insulted you. He showed you no respect. He called you a whore."

She was heading down the stairs towards the front door.

"But you're a whore too. A very good whore. A kind and loving whore."

"Oh thank you. You know Anna, we have a saying in French. We--"

"Stop this nonsense!" Anna scolded herself in her normal voice. She was at the foot of the stairs now, down by the electric meter on the wall in the hallway. She dropped in the first coin, Ching. "You really are going insane locked up in—''

She jumped. A loud bang on the front door stopped her in her tracks. Her hand hovered over the electric meter with the second coin. A voice called out, "Mark, it's me... Roland... it's about the pass." She stood for a moment, unsure of how to respond. Then the letter box opened and Roland shouted through it, this time more urgent: "Mark, let me in. It's important. I know you're there."

Anna moved closer to the door.

"Mark's at his evening class," she replied to the closed door in a quiet voice.

Then after a short silence: "I have to see you. It's urgent," Roland said through the letter box.

"Come back later."

"I can't. It can't wait. Let me in and I'll explain."

Reluctantly, she turned the lock and opened the door to him. He was standing there in his Home Guard uniform.

"Off to war?" Anna said cynically. She didn't like Roland and she didn't for one second intend to conceal the fact.

"Home Guard practice. No choice I'm afraid. And talking of choice…" He followed her up to the landing at the

329

top of the stairs where, through the open door of the living room, he could make out Mark's painting of Anna, which was standing on the easel. The curtains in the room had remained drawn, but it still wasn't dark enough to stop him from staring at the tantalizing image of her. He was mesmerised. Anna noticed and closed the door.

"There's a slight problem," Roland told her.

"So how much does 'he' want?" she said with more than a little sarcasm.

"It's not that. It's not 'him.' There'll be a small, well, handling charge.''

"So what do *you* want?" Anna asked, thinking she understood what it was about, but there was nothing from Roland except a long lusting stare and the look of someone who had just discovered that he now held all the power. As he began to move towards her, right up close to her, the penny finally dropped. Anna now understood. There was a manic look in his eyes. She was afraid, but she tried to bluff some notion of confidence. She wasn't very good at it.

"Don't you come one step closer..."

"Or what? You'll kiss me to death? He painted you, and I thought, you know, I could too. And then we could, how can I put it... 'Consummate' our little arrangement? Think it over. Not the offer. You really have no choice in that, do you? Just when we can arrange things." He looked her up and down, almost licking his lips in anticipation. Anna stood there trembling, looking so vulnerable, and now so inviting like that to Roland. He moved even closer, to within an inch of her. There was a positively carnal look on his face. He was just loving the control that he now held over her. "Then again...now we've got the place to ourselves..."

"You knew Mark was out, didn't you?" Anna spat out, terrified. She started to back away, only to come up against the closed living room door. Roland was straight up against her. He towered over her and pinned her back against the door with his body pressed right up against hers. His hands pressed her wrists firmly down by her sides. She wriggled and twisted and fought like a tiger to get her hands free and push him away, but he was too powerful for her. He flung her back and her head cracked against the door frame. She opened her mouth to scream for help but he clapped his hand straight over it, shoving her head back to slam hard again against the wall, whilst the other hand was far too strong for her resistance and it moved up the front of her skirt. Okay, okay, Anna, the voice inside was telling her. Stay calm. You can do this, she reassured herself. You'll be alright. You know what you have to do... It's called survival.

Suddenly, after she'd struggled so hard to push him off, he felt her relax under him. Her resistance weakened, her fight was over. Her body became limp against his force. He eased his pressure against her and took his hand away from her mouth while the other remained exactly where it was between her legs. She let out a low moan.

"Okay, okay..." she gave in to him, using the very words that she'd spoken to herself. "But not here, allow me that much dignity."

Roland released her and broke into a self-righteous grin. She's finally come to her senses. She wants this!

"The couch... in there," she told him. He liked the idea and followed her as she turned away from him, opened the living room door and led him inside. Roland reached out and flicked on the light...

... And saw Anna reach straight down to the table for Mark's vicious, serrated-edged knife which she knew was lying there. She grabbed it, spun round with it, and point-ed it directly at his heart. There was now vengeance in her eyes. "Don't doubt for one second that I won't use this before you use that?" she said, nodding down at his crotch. "Now get out!"

The smile still hadn't left his face as he took a step to-wards her, but she didn't give an inch. She stood her ground and shook the knife at him - although her hand was trembling madly anyway. She now looked like she really did mean it. It could have happened one cold win-ter's night three years earlier in Hamburg but it didn't. And Anna was damned if she was going to let it happen right there, right then, with that piece of worthless, scheming shit. Roland looked down at the knife in her hand. The overhead light glinted off the long silver blade. Then he glanced quickly down at his watch and then back at Anna. "I'll be back" was all he said to her. Then, surprisingly and bizarrely, he raised his right arm and gave the Nazi salute. "Sieg Heil," he said proudly. He turned and walked out with a cocky swagger, angrily shoving Anna's painting off the easel as he passed.

When Anna heard the front door close, she let the knife drop out of her shaking hand and fell back onto the sofa. She covered her face with her hands and began to sob.

***

The main room in the Wheatsheaf pub in north Highbury that Tuesday night was very quiet. The serious action was all taking place in one of the back rooms, which was where Guy was making for, as he followed the old barmaid through the pub and down a dark corridor at the back of the building. She knocked on an unmarked door, motioned Guy inside, then closed the door behind him. The room was lit by a single dim bulb which swung at the end of a long cable hanging down from the ceiling. The whole place stank of cheap booze and the air was heavy with the smoke of cheap cigarettes. Stacked against one wall were several crates of gin and whiskey and a mountain of the very same cheap cigarettes which were being smoked. Next to them, piled one on top of another, was a huge stack of cardboard boxes full of mysterious goods, which reached right up to the ceiling - large tins painted green and cans which had had their labels removed. At a round table in the middle of the room, an illegal card game was in full swing. One of the gamblers

333

took a long drag on his cigarette and excused himself from the game. He led Guy over to the far corner of the room and took an envelope from him. He stood and thumbed over the pound notes and photographs which were inside the envelope. He appeared satisfied. He said something into Guy's ear and as he spoke the cigarette which was pasted to his bottom lip began to dance up and down like a happy sparrow's tail. Finally, he offered Guy his hand to shake. A deal had just been done.

***

In Mark's flat, Anna paced through the rooms. She was defiant. She went to the living room window and eased back the curtain and peeped out. The light was just beginning to fade but she could see enough to know that the street outside was empty. She peeled away from the window and began to pace and fret some more. Mark's knife still lay on the floor, just where she had dropped it. She stared down at it. Why didn't I reach out and put it straight through his evil heart she asked herself and was angry for letting the chance slip away.

SOMEONE'S WATCHING #2

Once again, a very keen interest was being taken in someone through a powerful binocular lens. This time, however, it was the 'voyeur' who was being observed, as Roland made his way down the high street in the fading evening light. He was still on a high after his encounter with Anna. It had excited him, and he couldn't wait for the next episode in their story together. And there would be a next episode, Roland knew that much. He walked with the same cocky swagger that he'd left Mark's place with, and only stopped when he reached the entrance to a butcher's shop. Through the binocular lens, the 'someone' who was watching saw him look cautiously up the street and down the street, and then knock lightly three times on the butcher's shop door. After a moment it opened for him.

Inside, he walked right through the shop and into the storeroom at the back, then past the slabs of meat lying on the bench, the cows slit in half right down the middle and swinging on their hooks, the sad hanging pigs and all the other assorted bloody carcasses, and then up a steep flight of stairs.

The upstairs room was filled with around two dozen men in their uniform black shirts. Some wore thin, black polo-necked pullovers. Around the four walls were fascist posters, fascist flags and the notorious 'flash and circle' symbol of the recently proscribed and banned British Union of Fascists and even a few fancy variations of the swastika. Roland took off his Home Guard jacket to reveal his own black-shirt uniform. He fished into his pocket for his BU armband and slipped it onto his arm. As he took his place among the rest of the fascist disciples, the illicit meeting was already beginning to wind down. You could hear a pin drop as Roland watched with the others the dying seconds of a rousing speech given by a short, portly man with more hair on his top lip than on the top of his head. At the end of his speech, he raised his arm and gave the room the fascist salute. Roland joined the others around him in returning it. "Victory will be ours" they echoed back at their fat little Führer.

Minutes later, Roland was with the others as they filed out of the butcher's shop door in their 'civilian' clothes.

Then a shout went up "Right, move in and get the lot!" a whistle was blown, and a dozen police officers emerged swiftly from the shadows to surround the butcher's shop. Two police vans had blocked the street to the left of the shop, and a third had blocked the street to the right. Roland tried to run - first one way, then the other - but the police had all the angles covered. One officer rugby-tackled him while a second was straight on top of him and pinned him to the ground. Roland tried to slip on a pair of knuckle dusters but they fell from his grip in the struggle. One of the policemen kicked them away and into the gutter while the other managed to slap a pair of handcuffs on him.

***

Over in Rowlandsgill Gate, Claire opened the front door with a wide smile on her face. Guy was standing on the top step.

She put her arms around him, pulled him close, and hugged him tightly.

Grant emerged from behind her. He too wrapped his arms around Guy and embraced him, but his smile masked a truly troubled heart. Claire peered out into the black, night-time street. It appeared empty.

Nobody ventured out willingly into the ghostly, mysterious world of the blackout.

She closed the door and followed Grant and Guy into the living room.

"They were even watching us from across the street," Grant told Guy once they had settled down with a cup of tea.

"And this Swiss guy... is he... can he be trusted?"

Claire and Grant both cast uncertain glances at one another. Grant was about to say something, but Claire gestured surreptitiously for him to leave it. Now wasn't the time.

"I've seen her. She's fine," Grant told him.

"Where can I find her?"

"You can't... They might be watching you too."

Claire quickly intervened.

"It's late. You're staying here tonight... Please, Guy?"

Guy - tired, irritated, and now all out of nerves, shot them both a defiant look. "I'm going. I'm going now. And no one will follow me. Okay?" Before Grant could protest some more Guy added, "We've no time to lose. Now, how do I get there?" He looked over at the large Impressionist painting on the wall and stared at the image of the lost girl walking the sands.

"Here," Grant said and broke the spell. He was holding out Guy's wedding ring. Guy looked sadly down at it. Then he took it from him and dropped it into his pocket. The phone rang in the hallway, Grant got up to go and answer it.

***

Mark had felt that he should call Grant. Although he knew that he and Anna were in the right, he hadn't liked how Grant's visit had panned out and he nevertheless wanted to make peace with a friend. So, after his class was finished he went into the small front office of the local college and made the call. Two minutes later he put down the phone, call over, thanked the evening secretary, then trooped disconsolately out of main college door. It was a call which would be pivotal. He looked like a bomb had just exploded in his head. Mark set off towards the bus stop in a daze.

***

Roland had been taken to the local police station, together with five others from the illicit BU meeting who the police had been able to round up.

The small station only had two holding cells. Five of the fascists had all been crowded together in one cell, because Adams and Barnes had commandeered the other to speak to Roland, who was leaning back against the cell wall with his hands in his pockets, stubborn and bullish. He nonchalantly wafted away the smoke from his cigarette.

"So where do we find her?" Barnes snapped at him, probably for the tenth time that evening and now rapidly running out of patience.

"What's it worth?"

"The price will match the goods," Barnes said.

Roland shook his head defiantly. "Price first. A ticket to Dublin."

"Not a chance!" Barnes told him.

"Then no deal," he took another long draw on his cigarette.

Adams jumped straight in. He also almost jumped straight down Roland's throat. He knocked the cigarette out of Roland's hand and moved up to within an inch of his face.

"You don't bargain with us, Nazi! You're sitting in deep, deep shit. Tell us something nice, and we'll see if it's enough to raise your chair a little. We want an address. Where's the hiding hole?" He took a pair of mean-looking knuckle dusters out of his pocket. "The police found these on you. Mosley's bad boys' weapon of choice I'm told. Fancy yourself as a bit of a hard case, do you? What do you reckon Curly... reckon his bite is as bad as his bark?

"I reckon he's just a poodle who's stuck a pair of dentures up his arse and called himself a bulldog. I reckon we've got enough on him to bang him up for the duration."

Adams got serious. He slipped on the knuckle dusters and brushed the back of his hand across Roland's cheek. It was gentle, almost like a soft and sweet caress. Roland jerked his head back. Then Adams punched the wall hard, just next to Roland's head. A piece of plaster chipped away. "We'll decide how much what you tell us is worth. Now talk."

Roland remained impassive and unimpressed. "Is that how bargaining works? I don't think so," he said, shaking his head, "I have something you want. The question is…

340

how badly do you want it?" He looked from Adams to Barnes and back again. Just as Guy had once done.

Half an hour later, Adam's car raced through the blacked-out city streets. They mounted a kerb when they took a tight corner in Chelsea and they hit something in the road as they got closer to Fulham. A cat maybe? Or a dog? Or even a rare pine martin or a badger? They'd never know. The pin-prick headlights of the Morris 10 weren't strong enough to pick anything out. Besides, they didn't care. They were on a mission.

"Do you reckon the Major will agree to his price?" Adams asked Barnes as he stamped down hard on the pedal and the blue Morris 10 tore across the city.

"Do you reckon he even needs to know?" Barnes replied slyly. Adams smiled. He admired his partner's style. "Tomorrow get everything you can, quick as you can, on the Swiss cheese," Barnes added. "The bastard's already tricked us once. You're looking forward to this, aren't you?" Barnes asked Adams as he sped through the London streets. He meant finally getting his hands on Anna.

"Nah," Adams answered with a smirk. "Never given it a thought."

***

As soon as she heard the front door open, Anna raced down the stairs to meet Mark. She hugged him as if her life depended on it.

Moments later, Mark sat on the sofa in the living room, holding her close and listening to her begin her story. When she got to the part about Roland's 'offer' he pulled away from her.

"WHAT?"

"He raised the price of the passes. And I was it."

He knew immediately what she meant. He jumped straight into action, "get your things together. We have to get out of here. If he tried to bargain that with you, you can bet your life he'll be trying to bargain you with someone else. If he hasn't already."

"What do you mean?"

"I spoke to Grant. He told me that he'd heard that Roland was arrested earlier this evening. At a fascist meeting!"

Anna's initial reaction was one of relief. Roland is out of the way. He's out of my way. I'm safe. Until the gravity of the situation hit her. "But where can we go?" she asked.

Mark - his mind racing - didn't have a clue. He got up from the sofa and began to pace across the room. Then suddenly he stopped. "Anton. You met him at the party. My agent. It's our only hope. He has a small place in the country."

He headed off towards the door. "You pack while I go and call him."

"Don't leave me here alone," Anna pleaded.

THE POLICE ARRIVE

A police car with four uniformed officers pulled up in the street outside Mark's flat. The police officers jumped out and took the short flight of stairs up to the front door.

Two hundred yards away, two large suitcases stood in the shadows behind the telephone box at the end of the street. Mark and Anna were squeezed together inside the box and looked back down the road. In the distance, through the dim light, they could just about make out the faint figures of the policemen as they let themselves into Mark's building. They turned back to the phone and Mark flicked on a small torch to illuminate a number written on a scrap of paper which Anna was holding up for him. From behind them, the telephone-box door flew open and the form of an angry policeman filled the frame of the door. "Put out that light," he barked at them.

"Sorry. I couldn't see," Mark managed to splutter out.

"You know the law. Get it out!" The policeman turned to go. Then he had an afterthought. He leaned right into the telephone box and looked Mark up and down using the narrow beam of his pin-prick torch. "Show me your ID card," he ordered him. In his quiet little uneventful street, Mark knew with absolute certainty just where that policeman would have been heading for at this time of the evening, and why. He knew right then that their game was up. Mark began to fumble around in his inside pocket for the pass which would give him away. Anna just gripped his arm tight and secretly said a prayer. Her very first time out of the house in weeks and she'd been caught immediately. While Mark fumbled and made a big play out of searching for his pass he weighed up their options. Do we come out with our hands in the air? Or do we fight our way out? He still didn't know the answer to the question when a police van sped past them down the street with its bell ringing, reminding the policeman that he had serious business to tend to. "You watch it with that light," he said to Mark before he closed the telephone box door, hopped back onto his bike, and rode off in the direction of Mark's flat.

Ten never-ending minutes, later Mark and Anna emerged out of the shadows and jumped into the back of Anton's car as it pulled up outside the telephone box.

As it was picking up speed again, Anton was forced to swerve to avoid hitting an oncoming car which screeched around the corner at breakneck tempo. From the back seat of Anton's car, Anna twisted round and looked out of the rear window. She thought she recognised the car. It was too dark for her to see that the driver was wearing a fancy fedora.

Anton's car travelled on through the dark streets of London, although the bright full moon which shone in the clear and starry sky that night lit up the blacked-out city more than usual. Suddenly, Anton slowed right down. He narrowed his eyes and squinted through the windscreen at the road up ahead, trying to make out what was happening a good hundred yards away. Up ahead of him, the police and a handful of bored Home Guards had blocked the road at one end of a bridge which spanned a railway junction and they were stopping cars. Anton hadn't reckoned on that.

"Merde! What do we do now? I can't turn. There's a car right behind me."

In the back seat, Anna started to unbutton her blouse. She turned to Mark, next to her. "Give me your jacket," he just looked at her confused, "give me your jacket, damn it!!" she shouted, and without a word, he took it off and handed it to her. Frantically, she rolled it up into a tight ball and pushed it inside her blouse, making sure that it sat just right. Anton's car edged up to the checkpoint and he wound down his window, to the deafening background 'boom, boom, boom' of Anna's racing heartbeat. A Home Guard sergeant leaned in.

"Routine night control. Can I see your papers please, Sir?" Anton took his pass out of his jacket pocket and showed it to the Home Guard. The sergeant thanked him and held his hand out for Mark and Anna's IDs. "Where are you heading for?" he asked Anton. As Mark was handing his passport forward to Anton, and before Anton could answer the Home Guard's question, Anna let out a pained, ear-piercing, scream. The Home Guard looked into the back seat. Straight away he understood the situation. Sincerely concerned, he returned Anton's papers and waved them through. Mark let out a huge, silent sigh of relief and squeezed Anna's hand as Anton started to pull away. But the car stalled and came to a stop. He tried again, but the engine spluttered and once more cut out. Then another try. The same no-go. In the back, Anna screamed even louder. The pain was intolerable. A baby was just about to greet the world. The Home Guard signalled to a colleague who was sitting in an army jeep at the side of the road to pull the jeep over to them. The driver started up the jeep's engine and crawled the ten short yards towards Anton' car.

"Get her to the hospital. And quick. She's having a baby in there," the Home Guard sergeant instructed the driver, and he opened the rear door of Anton's car to help Anna out. Just as he was reaching in, Anton's engine suddenly fired into life. Mark leaned right across Anna, pulled the car door shut and managed a grateful smile and a wave to the guard as Anton sped off into the night. The Home Guard stood at the side of the road with his thumb up and shouted after them, "good luck!"

***

Guy turned a corner and walked up to the dark street towards Mark's flat. He was going through his big reunion speech, rehearsing all the different versions of it. Each one started with "I'm sorry Anna."

What he would say was every bit as important to him as the speech which he made to the Advisory Committee. Thirty yards short of the building he stopped dead when he saw the two police vehicles which were standing outside. Just then, another car appeared out of the gloom and pulled up behind the police van. Walker and an MI5 man got out.

As they were going up the steps to Mark's place, an officer passed them on his way out, carrying an armful of paintings. He put them into the back of the police van.

Huddled together in a doorway two houses up from where Guy stood, two old women in curlers and slippers stood and watched all the action.

Guy approached them.

"Do you know what happened?"

"We have no idea. But if they've come for Mark, he already left," the first old snooper said.

Then her colleague chipped in, "I saw him! And with a girl! And she wasn't from around 'ere'." It had been the highlight of their week for the two old corner shop gossipers.

Guy turned away and headed back up the road in the direction he had come from - physically and emotionally shattered.

Up in the flat, the police sifted through drawers and cupboards. One officer dipped his hand into Mark's Ming 'money vase,' but brought it out empty. A floor higher, Adams, Barnes and Walker were together in the atelier. Walker was his usual angry and frustrated self, livid that the catch had once more managed to slip through the net. He raked aggressively through the pile of Mark's paintings. "Subversive, degenerate junk!" he spat out after he flung each painting to one side. "He actually sells this garbage, does he?" he turned and asked Barnes, incredulous.

"Apparently quite successfully Sir."

Adams was looking at Mark's first painting of Anna. "It's not all bad, though," he quipped. From behind the Major's back, Curly Barnes signalled over to Adams that perhaps now wasn't the best time for his comments.

Walker stared down at the last of Mark's works which he'd tossed onto the floor. It was an unfinished image of a German SS general having oral sex with the barrel of a field canon. Queues of Wehrmacht officers lined up behind him waiting for their turn, and in the background, a large crowd waving flags were cheering them on. Walker still had a scowl on his face, although he had to fight himself not to break into a smile at the image. "What do we know about this Swiss pervert?" he turned to Barnes and asked.

"The department's working on it," he replied.

Then Walker to Adams: "Wherever that Schneider goes, we go. Understand?"

***

Anna and Mark settled into their seats in the empty six-man train compartment. A distant whistle blew and the train pulled away in a thick grey cloud of steam. Mark leaned his head back and closed his tired eyes. A minute after the train left the station, two uniformed soldiers entered the compartment and sat down in two of the free seat opposite. Mark opened his eyes, nodded a 'Hello,' and closed them again. Next, to him, Anna was edgy. Her paranoia was running wild. She looked over nervously at the two soldiers. Mostly at their uniforms. They'd come to lock her up. Worse still, to kill them both! Even though one of them smiled at her and asked: "Going far?" Anna - too petrified to open her mouth - just shook her head. She tugged at Mark's sleeve and gestured to him that they were leaving. She got up and began to struggle to get her heavy case down from the rack. One of the soldiers stood up and started to help her. Anna shook her head vigorously and gestured that she'd manage on her own. She jerked the case down and dragged it out of the compartment with Mark following. The two soldiers just looked on bemused.

INTO THE COUNTRY

Picture this: the rolling hills of the English country-side bathed in the soft, red-orange glow of early morning sunshine. Gorgeous golden fields, baked by the heat of the glorious endless summer, faint, cotton-wool clouds beginning to form on the horizon. All of those things would indeed make a perfect picture, but the day that Anna and Mark travelled to the country wasn't like that at all. The morning sky was slate-gray and a thick mist had wrapped itself around the hills and fields that the train passed through. It was a daytime 'whiteout' - impenetrable enough to match anything in the wartime city at nightfall. Anna sat with her head resting on Mark's shoulder. They were alone in the compartment. She closed her eyes and tried to sleep - but couldn't. Mark, with something heavy on his mind, weighed up the consequences of what he was about to say but knew that it was something he couldn't keep from her.

"Grant told me Guy's been released," he said to her eventually.

Anna's eyes shot open and she sat up straight.

They spent the rest of the journey in silence, staring through the dirty train window into nothing, or at the row of empty seats opposite them in the compartment. They were united at that moment only by uncertainty: Anna didn't know where they were going, and Mark didn't know where they were.

Or was it the other way around? Anna never did manage to work that one out.

***

"Think Grant. Where could they possibly have gone?" Guy asked as he sat with Grant in the living room.

"It's no use," Grant tried to reason with him. "You can't go after her. She's..."

"She's what?"

"She's- she's on the run. You'll lead them straight to her."

"I'll lose them."

"You just...can't."

"I can. I will."

Grant had been struggling, and Guy had no idea why other than a concern for his own safety. Grant settled for skirting around the issue. "If you try to help her evade the authorities you'll both be hunted for as long as this war lasts."

Guy leaned towards Grant and lowered his voice, as if the place was packed to bursting with German spies, and took Grant into his confidence. "I've arranged a passport for her, and tickets. We can get away." Then at Grant's blatant unease: "What's wrong?"

Grant was about to say more but finally gave up. He knew that it was something only Guy could sort out. He looked over at the painting on the wall for a moment... then, "wait a second." He got up and went into the hall-way. He searched in his phone book for a number, then picked up the phone and dialed. "Anton? Grant Cooper here. I'm calling about Mark. Mark Hermann."

***

The dense fog had lifted and was already giving way to a beautiful sunny morning by the time the taxi pulled up outside of a pretty, ivy-covered stone cottage, which was surrounded by trees and open fields. The cottage was detached and at the end of a long driveway which cut through a small orchid. The path to the cottage was car-peted with leaves, some of which were a red-orange colour and had fallen from the first trees in the orchard to take on their early-autumn shades. Mark and Anna got out of the taxi and Mark paid the driver. He swept his foot through a deep pile of crusty, rusty old leaves which had blown up and collected in front of the door before he took out Anton's key, turned the lock, and stepped inside. They carried their cases into the main living room with flagstone flooring and wooden low-ceiling beams. It would all have been impossibly romantic... if they weren't two outlaws on the run.

***

Grant and Guy had a large road map spread out on the table. Guy had his finger hovering vaguely over an area in north Oxfordshire.

"Can I take your car?" he asked Grant hopefully. He could see that Grant wasn't keen.

"The bike's still in storage," Guy tried to reason.

Grant thought about it. Then reluctantly he said, "well, okay. But it will have to wait until tomorrow. I still need it today." Guy nodded his head and was forced to agree. "You can stay here again tonight," Grant added, "And Guy... be careful."

Two hours later, Guy stood in the back room of the Wheatsheaf public house in north Highbury, with the card player who he had paid his money to the night before. They were alone in the room. The card player handed Guy a British passport and two American shipping line tickets. Guy looked them over then pushed them into the inside pocket of his jacket and shook the card player's hand.

***

Adams was sitting at his desk in the MI5 headquarters when a young secretary knocked on the office door and entered. She was pretty enough to be a welcome distraction for Adams, and he took the sheet of paper which she handed him with a flirtatious wink. He glanced down at the note and his mood changed immediately. He grabbed for the phone on the desk and pressed a button. "Major? Adams here. I've just received the report on Markus Hermann. The Swiss artist. You're going to love this Sir!" He listened to the Major for a moment then said: "Right away Sir." He put the phone down and said to himself out loud "Hah! Hermann the bloody German!"

***

'Hermann the German' and Anna sat side-by-side on the stone garden wall at the back of the cottage. In the distance, a mile across the corn fields, they could see the stone bell tower of the old village church. Mark had already been to the village earlier and had come back with two rabbits which he'd bought from a local hunter and a loaf of homemade bread and some cheese and butter which he'd got at the only shop in the village. Unlike the cities in wartime, the rural places had enough supplies of fresh farm produce to go around. Anna had a basket next to her on the stone wall with some fruit which she'd picked from the orchard. It should have felt good for them to finally breathe in the clean, fresh country air. But Anna looked troubled and tormented. "He'll come looking for me. You know that," she said, staring across the fields into nothing.

Mark did know. But he remained his calm, cool self. He wrapped an arm around her, pulled her close, and looked down at her with sympathy and understanding -

and even sadness. "There's nothing deader than a dead love... Isn't that what you say in German?" But he looked as unconvinced as she did at the same time, "was anything so wrong ever said?"

"I don't know," Anna replied softly and sadly.

Once Guy's liberty was what she'd wanted more than anything in the world. Now she was in fear of what it might unleash, for herself as well as for those around her. Faintly, from over the fields, the church bells were striking three.

"What is it you want Anna?"

He'd asked the simplest of questions. But the answer was way too deep and complex for a quick or easy response. "Look!" she said, relieved. A ladybird had landed on the back of her hand. It had saved her from answering.

"Make a wish," Mark said.

"No."

Anna had done that once before and she remembered. She wouldn't be making any more wishes to not come true. She watched the ladybird crawl slowly up to the tip of her finger. Then she set it down carefully on a blade of tall grass which had grown up the side of the stone wall where they sat. "It's for us," she told him. Then after a poignant moment's silence, she turned to look at him. "I could tell you that all I want is a place in the world that I can call home. That no one can take away from me, or chase me from. Someone to love and who loves me. It's not too much... it's not the world, is it? But I know that's

355

not what you asked me," she looked deep into his eyes, "I just want us all to be free Mark."

That night, Anna and Mark lay clinging to each other in Anton's king-sized bed. Sleep was a stranger to them. In the eerie stillness, every bird sound was a gunshot. Every rustle of leaf an invader. Mark stared into the darkness and thought. He was a loner. Having someone around him all the time was only suffocating for him. He could only work when he was on his own. But this... this was different. He wanted Anna around him. All the time. She inspired him, she made him happy. She was all he ever wanted. And the thought of her not being around was like the thought of light or air not being around. The thing was, he thought, for the first time in his entire life he cared for someone so much more than he did for himself. And he realised that right then, despite everything - despite all the running and hiding and all the danger and its consequences - it was the happiest he had ever been in his life. He pulled her closer.

A loud scratching sound came from somewhere in the house. It startled them. It became louder and louder and even more urgent. As they lay petrified and listened to it, the scratching seemed to intensify and become deafening. Mark got up, he slowly crept towards where he thought the noise was coming from. He listened some more. He moved into the living room and picked up a large, metal candlestick holder. Slowly, he went to the front door and jerked it open. A large, ginger cat brushed past him and trotted across the flagstones without a care in the world. As Mark stood and watched it disappear into the kitchen, he vaguely remembered Anton telling them something about the 'cottage cat,' which belonged to one of the farms across the field but was happiest in and around the cottage and the orchards. He closed the front door, put the candlestick holder back onto the table, and headed back to the bedroom.

Another cat was on the prowl that night. In the room where Anna once slept in Rowlandsgill Gate, Guy paced back and forth across the room. He was back in his prison cell. He was a caged tiger. He was waiting for the morning to come. Waiting for his moment.

Mark and Anna made love again that night. But there was passivity, a distant coldness about how Anna did it. She was distracted. She wasn't, in fact, the one making love. Mark recognised it and stopped.

GUY'S MOMENT

At nine-fifteen the next morning, someone was watching from the far end of Rowladsgill Gate when Guy got into Grant's car and pulled off. As he passed the end of the quiet, tree-lined avenue and turned left into the main street, Adams' car started up and pulled out after him.

***

Mark and Anna sat at the kitchen table and ate a breakfast of bread and butter with slices of not quite ripe apple and pear from the orchard. A freshly made pot of tea stood on the stove behind them. Anna looked worn and tired. She looked like she'd been wounded in battle. Mark was contemplative. He sat and played with a salt cellar, twisting it around and around and around on the table in front of him.

"What are you thinking?" Anna asked.

"When I was thirteen I went to my first wedding. It was in Basle. The priest who performed the service made a speech. He put out both hands..." Mark demonstrated, holding out both hands in front of him with his palms up. "Imagine a pile of salt on both hands he said." Mark took the top off the salt cellar and sprinkled a small pile of salt onto one of his palms. "The salt is your partner,' the vicar said. 'Now imagine that with one hand you try to hold on to it..." Mark closed his fist tightly on the hand which was holding the salt and the salt ran straight through his fingers and cascaded onto the table. "You end up squeezing and squeezing... And the more you squeeze, the more it runs. Until it's all gone." He opened his palm and showed her his empty fist. "Only on an open hand..." he said and showed Anna his other, open, flat palm, "...will it stay.' I was only thirteen at the time. But I've never forgotten."

***

Clack, clack, clack... then silence. Grant stopped typing and ripped the paper out of his typewriter. He flung it onto the floor on top of the other pathetic pages of text which he had already discarded. He couldn't stand it anymore. He couldn't stand himself anymore and what he had done. He detested what he had stood for. He had already emptied his tumbler of gin, so he picked up the bottle and drank straight from the bottle instead. Then he slammed the bottle back down on his desk and marched off into the kitchen, where Claire was reorganising a cupboard and had plates and dishes covering the kitchen floor.

"Claire... I've done something really horrid."

She stopped working and turned to face him. "I know."

This stunned him. "You know?"

"I don't know what you have done, but I know something's been bothering you badly. And I know it hasn't been about your writing."

She looked straight into his eyes, "don't tell me Grant if you don't have to."

Grant had to. That was why he had come to her.

Claire listened. Then when he had finished she left the plates and dishes just as they were on the floor, turned away from him, and in her usual languid grace and elegance, she went into another part of the house. Grant didn't even see her in their bed later because she slept that night in the spare room, in the bed which had once been Anna's, and only the previous night had been Guy's. The next morning she was gone. Only for three days, but she knew it was long enough to make Grant think. And regret. And long enough to make him worry - that what he had done was enough to lose her. When she returned all she said was, "I hate you for what you did Grant. But I love you for so much more. I won't forget - not easily - but I promise I'll try and forgive because that's what people do when they love someone. Tomorrow you'll tell de Witt that he's an ass, a bigot and a fool, and you'll take whatever consequences which that might bring. We'll take the consequences. You tell him that this war won't last one single day shorter or one single day longer whether Anna is in a prison or not and if the man isn't a total imbecile he'll know that for himself." Claire set down her small case on the floor. She wasn't finished. "The poor girl's been hunted like an animal everywhere she's ever been, and she's a lot less our enemy or an enemy of the values and principles which we stand for than any Charles 'Ignorant' de Witt. Now get to your study and go to work on that book." She picked up her case to carry upstairs, then she turned back around. It was the calmness and poise about her which was intimidating for Grant. "And there will be no more alcohol in this house for as long as I'm here. I'll bring you up some tea shortly."

***

Guy sped along a narrow country lane flanked by tall birch trees with yellow-orange leaves. He had a map open on the seat next to him, which he glanced at from time to time. He checked his rear-view mirror. A couple of hundred yards behind him, Adams and Barnes were still following. Guy remained cool - there was even a slight grin on his face - as if he was waiting for his big chance.

***

Anna and Mark had gone out into the orchard after breakfast and collected some wood which Anna later used

361

to start up the open log fire. While she busied herself throwing on the logs she thought about the cloud that she had seen earlier that morning which she thought looked exactly like the shape of the United States of America. At least that was what she wanted to see it as. A sign! She hadn't pointed it out to Mark, nor told him about it. She was, in this at least, superstitions enough not to 'jinx' their chances of an escape. There was just too much riding on it to allow such a dumb omen as a cloud formation to ruin things. She decided she'd be keeping that dream cloud for herself.

The marmalade cat strolled over and rubbed itself up against her leg, marking its territory. Anna reached down and stroked it under the chin. Mark picked up the basket which Anna had used to collect the fruit. The basket was now empty.

He moved close to her and put his hand on her stomach, "I forgot to ask. Did we have a boy or a girl?"

Anna loved the question, "which would you prefer?" she asked with a cheeky smile.

"I'll tell you when I get back. I'm going over to the farm. See what I can get us."

Anna didn't like the fact she would be left alone, or that he would be out there again in a world which was only out to get them both.

He noticed her unease. "I have to go. There are things we need. I'll be okay. And you're safe here. He'll look after you," he said and nodded down at the cat.

She felt bad, even guilty, asking her next question. But it was another thing which was troubling her. "Mark...do we have enough money?"

"I've enough. For now. I'll pay Anton in kind for all this anyway. He can take any paintings that he wants from the flat.

"Any?" she asked, with a particular vested interest in at least one particular painting.

Mark went over to his suitcase and opened it. He rummaged under the clothes for something. "Here. I brought this for you," he pulled out the painting of Anna reclining naked and 'Olympia-style' on the sofa. He took it out of the protective cloth sheet which he'd quickly wrapped around it and handed it to her.

"You brought it for me? Or for you?"

He smiled at her, kissed her and turned to leave. Anna grabbed hold of his arm and pulled him back. "There's no hope for us, is there Mark?"

"Of course there's hope. There's always hope."

She pulled him close for a long, passionate, goodbye kiss. It was another 'you and me against the world' kind of kiss.

***

Guy approached a crossroads and a hundred yards short of it, just the other side of a small stone bridge, which crossed a stream; he began to slow right down. At a distance behind him, the blue Morris did the same. Guy cut the car's engine for a moment and looked down at his map, which lay open on the passenger's seat. He put his finger on the name 'Overcliffe.' This was wartime Britain and the road signs had all been removed for security, but Guy recognised that at the crossroads up ahead - which was hidden from him by a curve in the road and a thicket of tall trees - was the turn-off that he should take. He started the engine, pulled back out into the road, put his foot down hard and set his indicator to the left for Adams' benefit. Then he took the curve, disappeared momentarily behind the line of trees, and therefore out of Adams' sight.

At the junction, Guy swung the car hard right around the corner, then pulled off the road onto a path covered by thick woodland. Moments later Adams reached the cross-roads – and turned left.

Inside Grant's car, under the cover of the thick bushes and trees, Guy allowed himself a satisfied smile.

**

The main room in the cottage was bathed in a red-orange light from the fire. The flames flickered and the wood crackled as Anna stared over at Mark's painting of her, propped up against the far wall. She was lost in thought. Just killing time. For what, she didn't know. Then her silent moment was shattered by the sound of car tyres on the dirt and gravel driveway that led up to the cottage. She sat absolutely still and listened, first to a car door close, and then to light footsteps approaching the front door. The moment's silence, which followed, seemed to go on forever. Until someone knocked on the door and she jumped. Another knock - and Anna sat frozen to the spot.

"Anna? Are you there?" It was Guy's voice.

Her face was a cocktail-mix of every possible emotion. She knew what lay ahead of her.

Anna? It's me. Guy." Then in a calming voice, he added, "It's okay. I'm alone."

She got up and crept over to the window and edged back the curtain, and saw Grant's car in the driveway and that Guy really was alone. She took a deep breath and crossed the room to open the front door.

Guy stood on the doorstep with his arms outstretched. Anna took a step back from him and turned to go inside. This surprised Guy. He followed her in, closed the door behind him, and once more moved towards her. Again, she kept a distance. They stood facing each other in a charged silence. Anna looked tense. Guy was about to speak, but Anna quickly beat him to it.

"You're looking well again."

"I am well. And I'm free."

Anna knew or thought she knew, what that meant. That quite possibly a deal had been done.

He sensed her doubt.

"My Appeal was successful," he pleaded, but the old wound had been ripped wide open. She couldn't bear to look at him and turned her face away. "It's the truth, Anna. You have to believe it," he insisted.

She kept her back to him and shook her head.

365

"Listen Anna..." Guy said with the sincerest regret, "I know I let you down, but... that wasn't me in there. You know that. I got out the right way. I did."

She turned to face him. "I'd like to believe you Guy. I'd-" She stopped. He held her look for a moment; a moment in which Anna could see that there was something more urgent on his mind than even the truth.

He put his hand into his pocket and took out Anna's new passport. "One of the people I wrote to you about..." He held out the passport for her to take. "I arranged this. We-"

She didn't move an inch. Guy sensed immediately her coolness.

"What's wrong?"

***

Three miles away, the Blue Morris pulled over onto the grass verge of a high-hedged country lane. Adams banged his hand against his steering wheel in frustration. They were lost.

Barnes gestured to him that maybe they should turn and try the opposite direction. Adams swore to himself then swung the car around.

***

"What is it?" Guy asked.

"Why did you come here, Guy?"

Although Guy couldn't know it, her question, and the way she asked it carried a meaning way beyond its simplicity. And it wasn't, in fact, a question directed at him at all. "To get you away from here," he told her, "they've found you twice. They'll find you again. It's all here." He nodded down at the tickets he was holding. "New York. Or maybe on to Florida...You choose. All that matters is that we're together."

"Oh, Guy...Please don't make me do this."

"Don't worry, everything will be fine," he reassured her, still not understanding. He tried to reason with her. "You remember that last time, in the prison? Is that what you want? Because you wouldn't survive it. I know. And it's that. Or this..." Again he held out the passport and tickets. "Freedom. Well?"

She was unable to bring herself to say anything. Guy watched her twist and turn away from him again. Then behind her, propped up against the wall, his eye caught Mark's painting. It was unmistakably her and its meaning was crystal clear to him. Now he understood. On the spot, without a word, he spun around and was out of the door. Anna watched him go, knowing that a part of her - maybe the very best part of her - was leaving with him. She stood frozen, unable to move an inch as she listened to the car engine start up and Guy pull away down the dirt-track driveway. Then she raced out after him and sprinted frantically to try and catch up with the car.

"Guy!" she called after him. "Guy!"

She stopped him just as he was about to turn onto the main road. He could have driven on and left her, but he didn't. He stopped and let Anna open his driver's side door. She knew Mark would be back any minute. "There's a church in the village." She pointed at it. She was trying to catch her breath. "There, across the field. I'll be waiting. Twenty minutes. Please, Guy. Please?"

Without a word he pulled the door shut and Anna stood and watched him drive off. She trooped back sadly to the cottage. The cat was waiting for her on the doorstep.

SIX

GOING TO THE CHAPEL

The path up to the church cut through a small graveyard with its tilted, chipped and weather-beaten headstones from the past two centuries. The silence and the stillness gave the whole scene an eerie, otherworldly feel. Just short of the thick, wooden church door something caught Guy's attention. He stopped. Next to the path was a grave from the year 1798. In it lay a Joshua Schneider, born 1709. Buried with him was his wife 'Em--'. Time, and close to a century and a half of wind and driving rain had worn the left-hand side of the stone away to nothing so it could have been Emily or it could have been Emma. But Guy knew that at least two Schneider's had once lived in that pretty little country parish. He continued on into the small church and down the aisle towards the solitary figure in a headscarf sitting at the end of the second pew on the left. Anna had her back towards him and didn't hear him until he was right up beside her. She pulled back her headscarf and made room for him to sit down next her. They both stared directly ahead in the direction of the altar. "Thanks for coming," she said in a low, scarcely audible voice and without turning. "I had to see you again." It was a tense, highly-charged moment - a deeply emotional moment for both of them. They were back together where it all should have started, in church. When Anna finally turned to look at him, it was as if those intervening months had just melted away, like she was seeing him again for the very first time. Her eyes burned into him. Then she asked a question which right then was so very important for her. "Was that the truth... about your Appeal?"

Guy turned and stared at her, barely able to comprehend the question. It was as if she'd just spoken to him in Chinese. As he held her look, and slowly nodded his head 'yes,' she realised. She turned her face away from him again.

"Why Anna? I didn't deserve that. Even if I let you down. I never betrayed you."

"No one betrayed anyone Guy. But if I've hurt you... right now - seeing you here again like this - I've truly never, ever been so sorry about anything in my entire life." Was there regret in her voice? Or just a deep and sincere sadness? Was she now filled with doubts, or with certainty? "Remember... remember a lifetime ago?" she said to him. "That day we climbed the sand dunes, and you took my picture, and we made a wish?" She reached down into her pocket and pulled out her four-leaf clover. "I wished that moment could last forever. I wished then that I would always feel as free as I felt that day, but the world changed. And that changed everything. For me, for you, for us. You hurt me like no one could ever hurt me, but that's not the reason I--", She stopped. She was unable to go on.

"I died every day in there without you," Guy said in a voice which was barely a whisper.

Anna felt like she was falling like she was tumbling into the abyss and there was no ground there to break her fall. She broke into a cold sweat. She felt weightless like she didn't exist. Finally, she managed to let out, "It was always you and me Guy. But it was just-"

Then silence. She was fighting hard for words which wouldn't come. She looked across the church at a painting of Jesus, high up on the wall, his arms outstretched, his hands held out in front of him, his palms up.

***

Mark walked briskly along the country lane which led to the turn off to the cottage, carrying his basket of provisions and a red rose for Anna.

Two hundred yards behind him the blue Morris cruised down a lane which Barnes and Adams were sure they had already been down twice before. They were hopelessly lost, and running desperately low on petrol. Barnes tapped two cigarettes out of his packet. He lit one up for himself, then the other for his partner. Just as he was handing it to Adams he spotted a figure on the road up ahead. "Let's ask him where the hell we are."

Adams started up the engine and drove the short distance along the road towards the man carrying a basket. He pulled up alongside him and Barnes wound down his window. "Excuse me,'' he called out. "Can you-"

"Well, well!" Adams exclaimed as Mark turned around to face them.

***

Anna was still looking over at the image of Jesus, arms outstretched, palms up. "It was just... I fell in love with..." The moment she spoke those words to him she felt sick as if she'd taken a jack-boot to the stomach. "I'm sorry Guy."

"No one could ever love you as I loved you," Guy said, and Anna's eyes told him that he was right, and he was wrong at the same time. She looked down at her four-leaf clover. "I wish... I wish I could change it all. But I can't."

Guy knew then that he was no longer talking to the girl he was once to marry. "Why did you want to see me again?"

She searched for the right thing to say. "I don't know," she said. And it was the truth. It was all way too complex for an easy answer. Then she fell silent. She felt again like

372

she was floating. "I came to tell you that I'll never stop loving you Guy. You'll always be a part of me." Then she leaned over and kissed him on the cheek, dried a tear, and got up to move past him. He caught her arm and stopped her. Anna surprised herself by letting him. She sat back down.

Guy looked over at the painting of Jesus.

"God this is so hard!" he whispered to himself and took out Anna's new passport and the two shipping line tickets. "All you ever wanted was to be free Anna. Here..." He pushed the pass and the tickets into her hand, "you are now. And free to choose." He looked deep into her eyes. "We're all just passing through Anna. We're all just on a journey. And I wanted my journey through life to be with you. An hour from now I'll still be here. Here in the church. I'll be waiting... if that's what you want. But whatever you choose - whoever you choose - get on that ship Anna. You have no choice in that." Then he released her. "Go."

She got up, pushed the four-leaf clover into the pages of her new passport, and moved off up the aisle.

Guy sat staring at the altar as he listened to her footsteps become fainter and fainter, and then finally the big wooden door closed behind her.

***

Anna headed back towards the cottage in a dazed half walk-half run. She looked down at the British passport in her hand. It belonged to 'Anna Schneider'.

373

Finally her passport to freedom? She was as torn and tormented and confused as she had ever been in all her twenty-six years. Her tears and the anguished look on her face said everything about the impact that the reunion with Guy had on her. She heard his voice imploring her to "get on that ship Anna," and he had gifted her freedom and a choice just as he hoped his gesture had gifted himself a sense of redemption. Her mind was running wild. What do I do with that choice? Then she realized that it was no choice at all, but purgatory. Like a lifetime in hell. She would have to hurt someone badly so that someone else could experience happiness. Her freedom meant someone's heart would have to be crippled, and probably forever. And worse, it could even be the very person who had given her that freedom. Or would it be the one who had saved her? What choice is that? The choice of who I love the most? Does it finally come down to something as juvenile as that? Okay, so who would that be? All Anna knew at that moment was that she had an hour, and she had to get back to the cottage and to Mark. And what then? Toss a coin? Her mind was going round in crazy circles and through her tears, she even managed to laugh at the absurdity of it all, so that she was laughing and crying at the same time. She quickened her pace.

In the cottage up ahead, Adams and Barnes sat on the sofa in the living room, relaxed and waiting. Adams, cool as you like, took a long drag from his cigarette and blew pretty smoke rings up into the air.

At the back of the cottage, out of sight and hidden by a thicket of bushes, a police car from the local station was now parked alongside Adams' blue Morris.

Anna had broken into a run by the time she turned into the long gravel driveway which led to the cottage. She was surprised when she got to the front porch to see that the cat was standing outside scratching at the door and meowing loudly and there was no one there to let it in. She reached out, opened the door and quickly followed the cat inside. And for a moment everything went into slow motion and fell uncannily silent. The passport fell out of her hand and the four-leaf clover twisted and glided slowly down through the air. It seemed to take an age for it to fall - until it hit the ground with a reverberating, amplified thud.

Anna was already inside the cottage by then and looking across to the other side of the room. "Nein! Mark!! NEIN!!!" she screamed.

Mark was handcuffed to a local policeman and held back by Barnes and a second officer. His shirt sleeve had been torn off and the shirt was ripped at the collar. Blood was running down the side of his face from a cut at the corner of his eye. Before Anna could react, two other policemen had emerged swiftly from either side of the front door and grabbed her. She screamed and kicked and fought to get over to Mark but she was held back and thrown into an armchair by the two policemen. One of them pinned her down from behind while the officer in front of her brought his knee up across her chest with his full weight behind it and had his hand over her throat. "Shut it!" he yelled at her when she tried to scream again, and he dug his fingers into the skin around her neck and squeezed tight, choking her.

Adams stepped straight in, "hey, take it easy."

The officer ignored him. He slapped Anna hard across the face and squeezed at her throat. "QUIET I SAID!"

Adams grabbed hold of the cop and pulled him off her. "Back off!! What the fuck are you?" he shouted at him, disgusted. This wasn't at all how he'd envisaged his 're-union' with Anna turning out.

By then the policeman holding Anna from behind had already handcuffed her wrist to his.

It was chaos in the cottage as Mark, fighting like a demon to break free, was prevented from getting to Anna by Barnes and the two other officers, who had him pinned down on the sofa. One of the policemen drew his truncheon and hit him hard on the shoulder with it.

Anna looked up through her tears to see him get dragged away and out of the cottage. At the door, he tried to stop and shout something over to her. But in vain, he was hauled out and was gone.

***

Guy sat in the church and looked at his watch. Just over forty-five minutes had passed. He got up and walked slowly up to the altar, then from there to the back of the church where he again looked outside at the empty

376

churchyard and the quiet road which led up to it, then he turned back into the church and looked at his watch once more. A whole three more minutes had gone by. He stared across again at the painting of Jesus with his arms outstretched. He seemed to be smiling and Guy prayed that it was for him. He prayed with all of his heart that within a quarter of an hour someone would walk through that church door and sail off to America with him. With every second of every minute which passed, he feared it just wasn't going to happen like that. She'd fallen in love she said. He'd hurt her like no one could ever hurt her. Maybe that's what was going on in the painting on the wall. Jesus was mocking him. 'Loser' he was saying with a smirk. You fucked it up. He was showing him, 'look what you've been left with after all your troubles my son, two empty hands.'

Guy looked at his watch and another minute had passed.

***

The cat trotted out first, followed by Mark, who was dragged off around the side of the cottage to the waiting police car where he was pushed inside before the car drove off. Moments later, Anna was led out handcuffed to the policeman. Barnes was alongside her. She looked broken and broken-hearted and now anything but free. She was bundled into the back of Adams' car. Adams himself was the very last one to leave the cottage. He looked sad. He felt dirty. He locked the door behind him, then he noticed something black lying by his feet on the doorstep. He bent down and picked it up. It was a British passport. He was about to call out to the others when he opened it at Anna's picture. He stared down at her image, smiled a sad smile, then he pushed the pass into his pocket. No one ever needed to find out about it.

***

An hour and fifty-five minutes had passed since Anna left the church. Guy waited for her for a further ten minutes, and then he finally accepted defeat. She'd made her choice and Jesus was exactly on the money; Guy was a loser. He'd screwed it up. Anna would spend the rest of her happy life with someone else. That was what Guy believed as he walked back up the aisle. He thought of all the things he'd said that he shouldn't have said. And all the things he didn't say that he should have said. It was a lonely, defeated walk. Etched into his face was the look of someone who had been confronted with one of those defining moments, just as Anna had been in her very last visit to the prison, which was the depressing confirmation that what and who you are is simply no longer good enough for someone. The knowledge that he'd have to carry that weight of failure forever. When he was at the door, he stopped and looked back over his shoulder one last time at Jesus on the wall. 'Well, how about it? Surely my gesture was good enough for some kind of absolution at least?' But Jesus said nothing. He didn't even give him a silent thumb up. His open, welcoming arms now had a rock in each hand. Guy turned his back on him, giving him a target, and walked out of the door.

At the same time that Guy was leaving the church, Adams and Barnes returned to the cottage. Barnes waited in the car while Adams let himself in, picked up Mark's painting of Anna, and drove back to London with it.

**

In a golden wheat field somewhere, Guy wandered aimlessly. In his head was the image of Anna walking up a roped gangway with polished brass rails and onto a fine ocean liner hand-in-hand with a handsome Swiss artist. His world began to spin. How would he ever live with that vision? He didn't know, but he knew that he would somehow have to. He tried to console himself with the thought that at he'd at least done the honorable thing, he had acted nobly and gallantly. He'd wounded her once, but now he had healed her. But it didn't make the pain any easier to bear.

The sun was beginning to go down. Close to him at the end of the field, some crows were pecking at the harvested sheaves of wheat. As Guy got closer they took off. He watched them fly over him. Then they soared, up and up, Guy wished he could be one of them. Echoing around in his head was the word which Mark had once used with Anna, 'Schicksal.' Guy understood it better than anyone now. It was the war which had sealed his fate. The war which had determined his destiny. It was at the beating heart of everything which had happened to him, the horrors of war had brought Anna to him, now it had stolen her away from him. Fascism - totalitarianism - the evil of National Socialism - he despised it even more now than he had despised it before.

Then he stopped walking. Something welled up inside of him. His chest swelled as he took in deep breaths of air. Suddenly it seemed like a charge was flowing right through him. He turned and walked purposefully over to Grant's car, which was parked at the side of the field.

PART 5

I FOUGHT THE LAW...

His call over, John Timney put down the phone and looked across his desk at Guy. "Markus Hermann has been deported to Canada. As for Miss Vieti..." and he made a gesture with his hands which said something along the lines of 'there's absolutely nothing we can do.' Then he leaned on his arm and addressed Guy with a mix of sincerity and sorrow.

"You know, when the history of this war is one day written, they'll write that the course of this infernal war wasn't altered one single bit by locking people like Miss Vieti away; people more anti-Nazi than anyone born here could ever be. But when national security is threatened, the freedom of the individual is..." He leaned back, shrugged his shoulders and threw his arms up in the air; helpless, frustrated, even outraged.

"… is hopeless?" Guy offered, trying to finish the solicitor's sentence for him. That was what Guy used to feel too, hopelessness. Once. Now though he stood up, offered his hand for John Timney to shake, and said resolutely, "there's always hope."

After he had left John Timney's office in London he crossed the city to get back to Upper Bexton. But he did something else first. Something he simply had to do. He enlisted in the British Army. Not as a soldier to kill ordinary Germans in the field, but to work as an army photographer. He'd determined that he would make his contribution that way.

A week later he went to his local barracks and was kitted out for action.

***

A small army truck drove along a wet and windswept seafront road on the Isle of Man. At a row of cordoned off, former seafront guest houses which had now become part of the island's internment camps, the truck turned and cut inland. It had only travelled two or three more streets before it stopped at a high, barbed wire, double perimeter fence which had been erected at the end of a row of terraced Georgian houses. Anna was among a group of a dozen women who climbed down from the back of the truck and into the driving rain. An armed guard emerged from the sentry box at the fence and opened the narrow gate to let the new intake of wartime prisoners file through. A soldier who had travelled with the internees got out with them and turned up his collar against the worsening weather as he stood and watched Anna, choking back tears, carry her case up the path towards the third house in the row. This would be her new home. When she saw it for the very first time, Anna thought it even looked a little bit like Claire and Grant's fine home in Rowlandsgill Gate. It even had a small garden park running right down the middle of the street. When she entered the place for the first time she tried to imagine that she was going inside to see Claire instead. Except there was a barbed wire fence around the street in Douglas, there were soldiers outside the house instead of passers-by, Anna was a prisoner, and she had to share a bed.

Guy will always be a part of me," Anna wrote. "And you too, Mark."

***

A grand steam ship left Southampton harbour and set sail on its journey across the Atlantic. Deep in the belly of the ship, in a tiny windowless storeroom in the hold - which he had to share with five Italian deportees - Mark sat on a straw-filled sack, his bed for the entire voyage. It stank in the cramped and crammed makeshift cabin and was claustrophobic too. Mark had his back against the wall and a small scrap of paper resting on his knee. He looked utterly lost. He looked lonely. He sat and sketched a picture of Anna on the paper with an old, worn-down pencil.

Some days later, Anna - with her long, tousled hair pulled up inside a headscarf - was working alone in the autumn sunshine, on a small plot of fenced off land at the camp. She looked up; Claire was being brought to her by a female camp guard. She'd made the long journey up to the northwest on the same day that two German bombs hit the end of Rowlandsgill Gate and three elderly women lost their lives, a baby lost its mother, and a two-year old boy lost his arm.

The Blitz had begun in earnest and had already reduced great parts of London to rubble.

Claire and Anna greeted each other with a long, emotional hug. Then Claire broke free to hand Anna a newspaper.

In the ship's tiny cabin two hundred miles off the Irish coast, a tear fell onto Mark's finished picture of Anna... Just as an ear-splitting BOOM filled the air and the room was blown into a thousand little pieces.

At the camp allotment, Anna stared disbelievingly at the newspaper headline and the photograph on the front page. It was a photograph of Mark's ship and the headline above it read "Cypress Princess torpedoed by a German submarine". She knew from the harrowed look on Claire's face just what it meant. She turned away and covered her face with her hands. She would cry for a whole lifetime.

***

The next morning, Anna - always the outsider looking in - stood inside the perimeter fence with her face pressed up against the wire. She looked out across to the sea. She felt defeated, just like Mark had done in his tiny cabin on the Cypress Princess. Her heart and her spirit were broken. She banged her hand hard against the fence, and then she gripped it tight, so tight that it began to cut into her skin. But she kept on squeezing, and squeezing...

A trickle of blood flowed; a tear began to fall.

Then the tears really flowed. For those, she'd lost, and for those, she had left behind. For those, she knew she would never see again. And she cried for all those whose precious lives had just been playthings for the politicians and the self-proclaimed 'powerful', with their goddamned blind prejudices and persecutions. "Please make this pain go away" she whispered.

She looked up to the sky.

"Four years. And I never stopped talking to you Guy", she wrote. *"I hoped you would understand..."*

Somewhere northwest of Düsseldorf there is a British army cemetery. In one of the graves lies a 'Gerhard Schneider'. You might have seen some of the pictures that he took of the D-Day landings at Sword Beach and the push across northern France and into Germany. Guy died back in the country where he'd been born but which he hoped he'd left forever, killed by a German sniper near Krefeld. The bullet went clean through Guy's heart. But he probably never felt a thing; his heart had stopped beating four years earlier. He died believing something which was never true. Anna never did have the time to choose. Never had the chance. He died not knowing that it could have been him.

"I hoped you would be watching over me," Anna wrote. *"And you too Mark."*

That night, Anna was asleep in the bed which she had to share with a thirty-year old Austrian girl from Graz. She was at peace. There was a contented smile on her face. She was dreaming.

"And at night, when I dreamed, I dreamed of you."

A mile outside a pretty little Oxfordshire village Anna followed the cat into the cottage to find Mark standing at his easel, painting. His basket of provisions from the farm was on the floor next to him.

"I dreamed you'd be waiting..."

Mark turned and held out his rose for her to take. Anna broke out into a relieved smile. She rushed over to him and covered his face with tender, grateful kisses.

"Other nights... I was lost."

The next evening Anna was back at the camp's perimeter fence, staring out through the darkness at the reflection of the moon on the breaking waves. The pattern of the fence threw shadows across her face which cloaked her expression like a veil. She watched a seagull take off and soar out over the moonlit bay and Anna wished it was her. It looked back down at her alone at the fence - incarcerated; the wild, free gypsy spirit now caged; as lonely as the girl who walked the sands.

"I never loved again, Mark. I never could."

Picture this: an empty, windswept beach. High above it, seagulls soar over the bay's long white sands. In its vastness is a solitary figure walking at the water's edge, her long dark hair blown by the stiff sea breeze.

"Maybe someday, on an empty beach, you'll see a lonely girl walking," Anna wrote. *"It will be me, Guy. It will be me."*

FINALLY DOUGLAS

That's where I met Anna Vieti, fifteen years later - not too far from that beach - in an Isle of Man hospital. She'd decided to stay on the island after the war and found a job there as a ward secretary. She figured she had run all her life from something or some-one, and the island was as far as she would go. And if anyone else wanted to hunt her down... well, they'd find her there, with her two cats. I found her easily enough. I'd taken some time out from my job at the American Art Journal to write my very first book. It was to be about the Swiss painter Mark Hermann. I found out about Anna Vieti and I wrote and asked if she could spare me some of her time.

She gave me her story.

She wanted to try and make some sense of it all, she wanted to understand what had happened and why. I don't think she ever did. We met for three hours on each of the four evenings that I was on the island, and we talked about Mark Hermann. But soon I realised that Anna Vieti's was the story that I wanted to tell. It had to be told. And when she told it there wasn't a trace of anger, bitterness, or sorrow. "Gratitude, that's all I feel" she told me. "I survived. And I found something, however fleeting, which others go through a lifetime without."

In the July of 1940, Mark wrote to his old art lecturer, who had fled to Dublin from Munich at the same time that Mark had got out, "Anna doesn't just occupy space in a room like the rest of us, she lights it up. You feel better for being in her presence... the wild, beautiful, haunted gypsy girl with eyes like two Baudelaire poems." And that's how I felt too fifteen years later. There were a couple of lines around the corners of the eyes which wouldn't have been there in 1940 and the hair was a little shorter, but it was still magnificently black and the eyes still shone like brilliant gypsy diamonds. She certainly had something special. The second time we met, she walked with me along the seafront promenade in Douglas. It was a tranquil, fine September evening and even though the wounds had never healed - and never would - Anna still somehow managed to look radiant. She no longer walked with the ghosts of those she'd left behind. "Do you know how many people like me were murdered? Jews, Romanies, the handicapped...the unwanted?" I shook my head. "Five million? Six? Ten? I know how lucky I was." We walked on along what back home we would call the boardwalk. "Look," she said and pointed at the sandy bay on the other side of the promenade railings. With the deep, azure, late-summer sky and fine sweep of coastline, she had the perfect moment to make her point. "It could have been Auschwitz or Dachau or Belsen or Buchenwald - but I ended up here." Then she smiled that cheeky smile of hers "I don't think the Nazis missed me too much in those places."

After I returned to New York, I went to visit Claire Pennington-Cooper - then called Borini - who was living in Connecticut with her second husband, a retired American-Italian banker whom she married three years after Grant had died.

Some weeks later, Anna did what she had promised me she would do, and wrote down what she hadn't had the time to tell me back in Douglas.

She started it as a letter to Guy, and Mark, but it was really to herself. I told her I'd try and put it into some sort of shape for her.

It took me some time to get around to telling it, what with work commitments, and then the twins arrived, but finally.... well, this is it.

This is Anna Vieti's story. In all its bloody glory, in the end she realized the futility of trying to make any sense of it. "How?" she said. "How can you make sense of the Nazi horrors? Or of war and its consequences? Would it make us stop fighting? No. It will always go on."

Just like Anna's story went on.

She finally ended it with a question. "And what did I learn?" she asked herself. "I learned that no matter how small your chances are, even one in ten million, you have to cling on to hope. You've been given the gift of life... Cherish it. Make the most out of it. And if you've been lucky enough to know love... Hold on to it."

On my last night on the island, I sat alone in my hotel room looking down at a print, which I was holding in my hand. It was Mark Hermann's painting of the lonely girl walking the sand. Then I looked up and out of the window, at the fine, long sweep of the sandy bay. In the distance, I saw a figure walking away from me. I could have sworn it was her. I *wanted* it to be her.

"Make a wish" Anna once said. "Picture It."

THE END.

ACKNOWLEDGEMENTS

Pictures of Anna was written with my eternal and sincere gratitude to: The German National Archives in Koblenz; Alois Hardt; Ms Emma Vogel; my father; Joan Waggott (the 'real Jane Williamson' of the story); Firewoman Purvis; Ronald Hirschfeld, Stephanie Katze, and finally to Sandra David, for her love towards Jutta and her faith in 'Anna'. My grateful thanks and acknowledgement also goes to the outstanding work of A.W. Brian Simpson.

ABOUT THE AUTHOR

Sam Martin is from the north-east of England, and has lived in Germany as well as France and Austria for some years now. Pictures of Anna is his debut novel.
Sam has written two full length feature-film screenplays. The Rights to both were sold to film production companies in Germany and the UK. Filming on one was completed in June 2019. The Rights to the other were acquired by an Academy winning producer and is in the developmental stage.